"That Jones Girl"

By Elisabeth Hamilton Friermood

The Wabash Knows the Secret

Geneva Summer: A Romance of College Camp

Hoosier Heritage

Candle in the Sun

"That Jones Girl"

"That Jones Girl"

Elisabeth Hamilton Friermood

Illustrated by Doris Reynolds

DOUBLEDAY & COMPANY, INC., GARDEN CITY, NEW YORK

Dedicated to the memory
of
DAISY SPRINGER, Librarian

Gentle, soft-spoken, wise; her
belief in the young gave courage
when it was needed most. Remembrance
of her is cherished by all who knew her.
EHF

Contents

"That Jones Girl"

1. *Clanging Bells and Shrieking Whistles*

The band played and the crowds on the sidewalks cheered as the Junior Red Cross girls marched by. Lizzie Lou held her head high, the white muslin scarf on her head rippled out behind in the sharp November wind. It seemed to her that she was not Lizzie Lou Jones but Lillian Gish, a Red Cross nurse in that war moving picture she had seen last week. This was not Main Street in Medford, Indiana, but the Champs Elysées in Paris, and that troop of Boy Scouts up ahead was a troop of Doughboys just arrived in France. Her lips formed a gentle Lillian Gish smile as the crowd on the curb waved flags. She had seen the show through twice, she felt her smile was about right.

From "The Stars and Stripes Forever" the band swung into "Over There." The Junior Red Cross girls began to sing:

"Over there, over there. Send the word, send the word over there, That the Yanks are coming, the Yanks are coming, the drums rum-tumming everywhere . . ."

Lizzie Lou was silent; Lillian Gish would not have sung in a parade, she would have been thinking about the wounded soldiers, the poor French war orphans, and her sweetheart, Robert Harron, in the front-line trenches.

Even though she was a high-school senior, Lizzie Lou loved to pretend she was someone else. When she pretended, she didn't have to be herself, homely, wearing made-over hand-me-downs, and with the name of Lizzie Lou Jones. She could endow herself with Mary Pickford's charm and Irene Castle's grace and move through a dreamworld with ease and assurance.

Aunt Liz, at first, had refused permission for her to march in today's war-effort parade. She didn't approve of parades on Sunday. However, the fact that the ministers themselves were marching won her consent.

Lizzie Lou forgot Lillian Gish as the parade turned at the courthouse square. She could look back down Main Street and see the rest of the parade still coming. What a long line of marchers! She hadn't realized that so many were in it. There must be four or five blocks of them coming back there: the home guard, the Elks' lodge, the Oddfellows, the Knights Templar, the Senior Red Cross, another Boy Scout troop, the K of P, the old soldiers from the Soldiers' Home, and several floats on big trucks. She couldn't see the end, and in front of her were Boy Scouts, more floats, and the policemen and firemen. This must be the biggest parade Medford had ever had.

She hoped it would achieve its purpose, get people to buy more Liberty bonds, give to the Red Cross, and co-operate with Mr. Herbert Hoover on food conservation. After all, what was doing without white bread, using less sugar, and observing meatless days when it meant food for starving Belgium?

"Yoo hoo! Lizzie Lou!" came from the side lines. Lizzie Lou scanned the crowd. There on the front row were her two sisters and brother. Five-year-old Lucy jumped up and down in excitement at seeing her big sister in the parade. Lizzie Lou could see Peggy hold a restraining hand on Lucy's shoulder. How Peggy was growing, only eleven and almost to Uncle Mat's shoulder as he stood behind the children. Dear Uncle Mat, so kind and understanding, nice of him to bring the children to the parade. Father and Aunt Liz must have stayed at home, Aunt Liz to take her usual Sunday-afternoon nap and Father to read, to gaze at Mother's picture and to look out the window with unseeing eyes as he did every Sunday afternoon.

Lizzie Lou waved and smiled at Lucy. Poor little motherless lamb, she had never known Mother, Mother who had died at her birth. Aunt Liz had cared for the child from babyhood and it was Lucy who knew how to find the soft spots in their aunt's nature. Aunt Liz took the rearing of her sister's four children with serious gravity.

Lizzie Lou marched on, the band played and the marchers sang: "It's a Long Way to Tipperary."

It was a long way. They still had to march to the armory on the other side of the river. There would be speeches by the mayor and a visiting senator. But she must get on home and try to finish that short story for English VIII class in the morning. Should she give it a happy ending or would Miss Tamer think an unhappy one more literary? Miss Tamer seemed to admire authors who wrote of life realistically. Maybe she would write two endings, one for herself and one for Miss Tamer.

Lizzie Lou looked at Mary Higgins trudging along beside her, keeping step and singing lustily. Mary grinned as she caught Lizzie Lou's gaze. Sweet Mary. Lizzie Lou knew she was lucky to have Mary for her best friend. They had been friends ever since that first day three years ago when they sat side by side in the high-school auditorium getting instructions concerning their freshman programs. Mary was short, slightly plump, and warmhearted.

The band stopped playing, the parade came to a halt, the Junior Red Cross girls chatted to one another.

"Are you going to stay for the speeches?" Mary asked.

"No. I want to get home and finish my story for Miss Tamer. Have you written yours?" Lizzie Lou asked.

"Finished mine Friday. Guess I won't stay either. We can walk back as far as the streetcar station together. Wish we would start marching again. I'm cold. My feet are freezing."

The parade began to move and the band played again. Lizzie Lou tried to recapture her Lillian Gish role. What a lovely graceful garment that long cape was, the one she wore while driving a Red Cross ambulance out into the night. She wondered if Red Cross nurses really did such daring things in France. Probably not, but it was a wonderful moving picture and so much better to think about than her own dull life.

She didn't have even one relative in the army or navy. Almost everyone at school had an uncle, cousin, or father in France fighting the Kaiser. Neither Father nor Uncle Mat had been drafted and while she was glad they were safe at home instead of in the trenches, still if one of them had enlisted the Jones's front window

15

could have a service star showing through for all the world to know that they were doing their bit.

The United States had been in the war for more than a year now, and the only way she had been able to show her patriotism was rolling bandages for the Red Cross, eating no white bread, observing meatless days, and marching in today's parade.

Would this awful war ever end? A few days before they thought it had, thought an Armistice had been signed. She had read in the Medford paper that many towns had gone wild celebrating, even New York City, but Medford had waited for confirmation of the report and found it false. The town had gone ahead with its plan for today's war-effort parade.

The parade disbanded at the armory and the two girls walked slowly back to town.

"My head's cold," Mary complained. "Mama said she was afraid I'd catch cold wearing this muslin on my head instead of a hat, but it was a good parade. Wish we could have ridden on one of those floats. Didn't Bonnie Mason look gorgeous sitting up there in that nurse's uniform, and did you see those two soldiers lift her down off the truck at the armory?" Mary sighed. "I wonder what it would be like to be Bonnie and have all the boys crazy about you. She is so little and cute. I'm little but people always mention plump instead of cute. I wish I were more like Bonnie or even tall and skinny like you. Maybe I eat too much candy and ice cream. What do you think?"

"I only know that you spend every spare nickel for chocolate ice cream in the cafeteria at noon every day." Lizzie Lou wished Mary had said tall and slender instead of skinny. She tried to feel slender and willowy like some of the moving-picture stars, but, remembering how she looked in the long mirror at home, she knew Mary's remark was apt. And Bonnie Mason—what a cute, pert little thing she was! Sometimes Lizzie Lou had a burning desire to slap Bonnie, slap her hard. Why did she have everything, beautiful clothes, lovely complexion, blond curly hair? When she opened her blue eyes wide, the boys grinned and hung on every word she said. Why couldn't she, Lizzie Lou Jones, be just a little charming? Why couldn't she be at ease with boys and walk with that slow, sauntering slouch as Bonnie did? She had practiced Bonnie's slouch in front of the mirror, but it only made her appear awkward.

The girls parted at the courthouse corner, Mary hurrying toward the warmth of the streetcar station to wait for her car and Lizzie Lou down Walnut Street.

The light was fading fast now and the western sky showed dark streaks above the horizon. She turned her coat collar up as far as it would go and the rough cloth scratched her cheek. This coat was made from one Uncle Mat had grown too stout for and, though she admitted that Aunt Liz had done a good job of tailoring, she wished it were a different color, not this drabby gray, and that it had a soft fur collar.

At home she found Jimmy on the front steps putting on his roller skates. "Are you supposed to skate on Sunday?"

"Aunt Liz said I could skate around the block once before supper." He leaned over his right foot and pulled the strap tight. "You know what? Uncle Mat bought us some paper horns at the drugstore on our way home. Now we'll have 'em ready to make lots of noise when the Armistice gets signed."

"He did? I wonder if he thinks the Armistice will come soon."

"Don't know. But he sure got us nice horns." Jimmy stood up and rolled noisily down the sidewalk.

Lizzie Lou hurried up the steps. Through the front window on the other side of the double house she could see Uncle Mat seated in his favorite rocker reading a newspaper. Inside the Joneses' front hall she hung her coat in the closet and hurried into the living room, closing the door quickly so that the living-room warmth would not escape into the cold hall and up the open stairway. The room was empty and lighted only by the ruddy coals glowing through the isinglass doors of the base-burner.

She stood with her back to the stove trying to get the chill from her body. She reached up under the back of her Red Cross scarf and unpinned it. It was time to help Aunt Liz in the kitchen.

Aunt Liz had a kitchen on her side of the house, but she didn't use it except when Uncle Mat's relatives visited. Ever since Mother had died, five years ago in 1913, Aunt Liz had cooked in their kitchen and the families had eaten together.

Sometimes she wished they could be alone. Perhaps Father would have recovered some of his former interest in life if he had had to take more responsibility for his family. But Aunt Liz managed everything and Father sank deeper and deeper into grief. She got awfully tired of Aunt Liz's managing ways, but lacked the courage to tell her so. Only in daydreams, drawn from the books she read or moving pictures she saw, did she speak and act with assurance and confidence. She felt sure no other girl in high school was as spiritless and scared of things as she was.

She turned and faced the stove feeling her cheeks tingle as the heat waves touched them. How silly, pretending she was Lillian Gish in the parade! That was the sort of thing a twelve-year-old might do, but not a sixteen-year-old, almost seventeen and a senior at that. In some ways she had grown up awfully fast since Mother had died. She had been eleven and had taken care of Peggy and Jimmy, six and two then, while Aunt Liz cared for the new baby, Lucy. Aunt Liz had taught her to cook, sew, wash, iron, sweep, and dust. But being able to do these things didn't help one bit in overcoming her shyness. If she could have one wish granted, she would not wish for riches but for a bushel of self-confidence.

Warmed through by the friendly base-burner she went to the kitchen to help with supper.

It was late when she finished her short story, almost ten-thirty. Peg had washed Lucy and Jimmy and put them to bed. Sometimes Peg was co-operative and helpful, but more often than not she used adroit tricks to avoid household chores. Lizzie Lou thought Peg worked harder evading jobs than she would have if she had done them. Father had retired at nine as usual.

She reread her story, inserting a few commas and semicolons. Folding the sheets of paper lengthwise, she wrote her name, English VIII, and tomorrow's date, November 11, 1918. She tucked the story between the pages of her Virgil and put the book on the table by the hall door. Good thing she had finished translating tomorrow's Latin assignment.

In the kitchen she washed her face, looking in the mirror above the sink. She wondered what kind of soap Bonnie Mason used. If she used the same kind, would her face have that peaches-and-cream bloom that Bonnie's did? She doubted it.

Upstairs, she tucked another blanket over Lucy, sleeping soundly in her small bed, undressed quickly, and crawled into the double bed with Peggy, grateful to get her bare feet off the cold straw matting. Peggy was sprawled catty-cornered across the bed with the blankets tucked around her. Lizzie Lou pulled them loose and pushed Peggy's legs over. No need to worry about waking her, she slept so soundly.

She put her hand under her cheek and closed her eyes. She could see herself marching in that parade, not as Lillian Gish in flowing cape and nurse's uniform, but as she really was, a homely, skinny girl in a made-over coat, a girl who was afraid and shy and tongue-tied around boys.

She erased the depressing image and brought to her mind a scene she had invented several years before, a scene she had used again and again to bolster her ego and which would help her fall asleep happily confident in her own capabilities.

Slowly the picture evolved in her mind. The lights on the stage were soft and as the spotlight touched the black velvet backdrop, she, Lizzie Lou Jones, appeared poised on the tips of her scarlet toe-dancing slippers, dressed in a flaming chiffon costume. She danced with grace and beauty, head held high, lips parted in a smile, eyes big and lustrous. The folds of scarlet chiffon swayed, rippled, and whirled about her graceful body; the audience broke into applause and spoke to one another behind their programs, asking who was this new dancer, this talented dancer who had made up this beautiful and clever dance. She came out again and again to acknowledge their applause, bowing low over the footlights. She reached down to receive a big bouquet but fell asleep before the flowers reached her hands. This imagined scene never failed to relax her and send her off to sleep with a smile of self-confidence on her lips.

She wakened with a start! Lucy was shaking her shoulder, a loud penetrating, persistent noise filled the room.

"Lizzie Lou! Lizzie Lou! Wake up! It's the Armistice! I want to go! I want to see the Armistice!"

Lizzie Lou pulled the little girl in beside her. "It's just the fire whistle, honey, you shouldn't get out of bed, you'll catch cold." The whistle blew on, one long blast after another. She could hear someone up in Aunt Liz's side of the house. The light in the hall flashed on and Jimmy opened the door.

"Lizzie Lou, it's the Armistice! Come on, get dressed. Father says we can go downtown to see it!"

Lizzie Lou sat up. The church bell of the United Brethren Church on the next street began to toll. Lucy hopped out of bed and jumped up and down. Lizzie Lou turned on the light, Peggy slept on.

"Get your clothes, Lucy. I'll put your stockings on as soon as you get into your underwear." She turned and shook Peggy. "Wake up, Peg! It's the Armistice! Jimmy, is Father going too?"

"Yes, he's getting dressed." Jimmy ran back to the room he shared with Father.

Lizzie Lou sat on the bed and pulled Lucy's black stockings up and fastened them.

"There now, you can do the rest. I'll tie your shoes when you get them laced. Peg, are you going with us?"

Peggy turned over and opened her eyes. Another church bell added to the outside noises.

Jimmy skipped ahead as the Wallaces and the Joneses started toward the downtown section of Medford. There were lights in almost every house and hastily dressed neighbors emerged and joined those hurrying along the sidewalk.

Peggy, thoroughly wakened by the sharp night air, squeezed her older sister's arm. "Oh, isn't it exciting? I didn't think it would be like this, did you?"

Lizzie Lou didn't answer. She was trying to hear what Father was saying to Aunt Liz up ahead. "But Liz, it's important that the children see this celebration. This is history, something they'll re-

member all their lives and tell to their grandchildren. It won't
hurt them to miss a little sleep."

It was strange to hear Father overrule Aunt Liz's objections.
Usually he acquiesced to her decisions where his children were
concerned.

Tell it to her grandchildren! She would probably never have
any, would never marry. If she retold tonight's adventures, it would
have to be to nieces and nephews. The din of whistles and bells
dispersed her morose thoughts.

They approached the courthouse square and Aunt Liz stopped
them. "Now there's a big crowd already and likely to get bigger.
Mat, you keep hold of Jimmy's hand every minute and, Warren,
you keep Lucy with you. Peggy, you stay close to Lizzie Lou. I'll
try to keep us all together, but you never know when we may
be separated." Aunt Liz raised her voice above the racket; Lizzie
Lou detected excitement in her tone. "If we do get separated we'll

all meet there on the corner by Hemple's drugstore. I think an hour is long enough for us to stay down. Jimmy, stop blowing that horn a minute."

"Aw, Liz, let him blow it. What's one little horn in all this?" Uncle Mat remonstrated. A truck drove by, the back crowded with people beating dishpans, washboards, boilers, and stovepipes. The screeching of factory whistles now added to the bedlam. Peggy blew her horn and pulled Lizzie Lou toward the center of town.

The street around the courthouse square was teeming with Medford citizens, shouting, screaming, yelling in wild hilarity. They blew horns, beat drums, beat pans, waved flags. The signing of the Armistice had thrown them into a delirium of joy.

Lizzie Lou and Peggy, clinging to one another, were swept along the sidewalk in the tightly packed crowd. Lizzie Lou's throat began to hurt and then she realized that she had been yelling with the others, "The war is over, the war is over!"

Now the crowd was so dense that she had trouble hanging onto Peggy. Peggy dropped her horn but there wasn't room to pick it up. A little farther down the street the big plate glass window in Saxon's department store was shattered to bits by the pressure of the celebrating throng. In the street Lizzie Lou could see automobiles creeping through the crowds, the drivers intentionally causing the engines to backfire to add to the general uproar.

Peggy tugged at her arm and pointed. Coming around the corner was a group of high-school boys pulling an old fire wagon, one that used to be drawn by horses in the days before Medford's fire department had become mechanized.

Lizzie Lou looked at the boy up on the seat clanging the bell. It was Bill Monroe, president of the senior class and center on the basketball team! Look at him wave that flag! It seemed strange for him to be yelling in such a frenzy, he was so calm and composed when he presided at class meetings, so coolheaded and unruffled on the basketball floor.

Pat Brandon was beside him beating a drum. Pat was in her geometry class and spoke to her occasionally but only to ask questions about assignments. But Lizzie Lou had never spoken to Bill Monroe, he didn't even know she was there in Medford High.

The boys pulled the fire wagon into the jumble around the courthouse. Small boys began climbing aboard and the crowd pushed a soldier and a sailor up on the front seat beside Bill and Pat. A tall man tried to organize a parade to follow the wagon, but the crowd would not co-operate; his shouts were lost in frenzied screams and shrieks of uninhibited glee.

"The war is over!" "Hurrah for General Pershing!" "Hurrah for Marshal Foch!" "Hang the Kaiser!"

From a tree on the courthouse lawn, the crowd was doing just that, hanging the Kaiser in effigy, while on the other side of the square they burned a straw dummy, labeled "Kaiser Bill," on a huge bonfire.

By this time the Medford newspaper had out an extra and newsboys tried to make themselves heard. "Read all about it! Extra! Extra! Armistice signed! The war is over!"

People bought the papers quickly, not to read, but to tear into shreds and toss up in the air in ecstatic jubilation.

Lizzie Lou knew Father was right, she would never forget this night. The relief of it, all that horror in Europe at an end; no more suffering in the trenches, no more shell-shocked soldiers like Mrs. Hutton's son, no more of that awful mustard gas she had read about, no more lives lost at sea, no more drafting of men; it was the beginning of new times, a new era, one of hope and peace. The world had been made safe for democracy just as President Wilson had said. The war to end war was over.

2. "A Great Idea"

When she crawled out of bed at seven Lizzie Lou felt as droopy as a piece of wilted lettuce. The family had returned home about 5 A.M. and everyone had gone back to bed. Peggy and Lucy had fallen asleep at once, but Lizzie Lou's mind had been so full of the wild celebration that sleep had been a long time coming.

She pulled her clothes on quietly, brushed her hair hurriedly, pinned the side puffs over her ears, and jabbed hairpins into the knot she twisted up in the back. She would hurry down and, if Father hadn't left for work, she would ask him if Peggy and Jimmy couldn't miss school today, they were so tired.

Father was running water on his breakfast dishes in the sink as she came into the kitchen.

"Father, I meant to get up earlier and get your breakfast. Where is Aunt Liz?"

Warren Jones dried his hands on a towel and smiled slightly. "You know, Lizzie Lou, I believe your aunt has overslept. First time I have ever known her to do such a thing. Mat has had his breakfast and gone to work. He said Liz was sleeping like a baby when he slipped out. I guess the Armistice was too much for Liz."

"Do you think I should let the children sleep? They are so tired."

"Yes. Sleep will do them good. Besides I doubt if there will be any school today. I imagine there will be celebrating downtown all day. Are you going to school?"

"Oh, of course. I wouldn't want to take a chance on not going. I don't want to spoil my attendance record."

Father paused at the dining-room door. "No, I suppose not." He watched her tie an apron about her waist. "Just think, your mother knew nothing at all of this awful war in Europe. How all the misery and sadness would have grieved her. I'm glad she missed that, but I kept wishing that she were with us this morning to join in all that celebrating. She liked crowds and gaiety."

Lizzie Lou thought of her mother while she made herself a cup of cocoa and cooked an egg. Mother had been pretty, small, and with blond curly hair. Peggy was going to be just like her. Now she herself took after Father, tall, dark brown hair, dark skin, and brown eyes. These features made Father look distinguished, but she knew what they did to her. Her eyes were not bad, but there were usually dark circles under them from reading too much. As for her mouth—if only nature hadn't been so generous. When she remembered she kept her lips closed tight and pursed a little to make the mouth look smaller.

After her breakfast, she washed and dried the dishes. As she hung the dish towel on the rod by the sink, she heard the door below open, the door which opened from Aunt Liz's cellar into theirs. Aunt Liz came up the steps.

"Good morning, Aunt Liz."

"Good morning, Lizzie Lou. I'm glad to see you are up and on the job. I declare, I don't know what was the matter with me, I couldn't seem to wake up. Are Peggy and Jimmy ready for school?" Aunt Liz pulled the coffeepot to the front of the stove

"They are still asleep. Father said not to waken them, that there probably wouldn't be any school today anyway."

Aunt Liz got the coffee can from the pantry and measured two heaping spoonfuls into the coffeepot. "Well, I would think Medford had done enough celebrating. Seems to me we ought to get back to normal today. The children should be in school. I'm going to get at the washing right away. Don't know when I've had such a late start."

"If there isn't any school, maybe I'll be home in time to help. It's ten minutes to eight. I'm going."

Aunt Liz looked at her. "I don't see why you don't wear that brown dress I made over for you oftener. You wear this middy suit every day. That skirt is beginning to get shiny. The material in the brown dress is lovely. Mat's sister payed a good price for it when it was new."

Lizzie Lou hurried out of the kitchen mumbling something

about not having time to change now. She hated that brown made-over thing. It was an awful color and made her skin look as brown as the dress itself and she knew she looked like a bean pole in it. This navy blue serge middy suit was the only thing she had that gave her a feeling of being like the other girls. Nobody, but nobody wore dresses like that awful brown thing. The few days she had worn it she had felt miserable.

This middy suit helped her figure a little, she thought. The real sailor tie added a jauntiness to this suit that she knew was lacking in her other two winter dresses, the made-over brown one and the too short green one. When Mary's sailor uncle was home on leave last summer, he had shown the girls how to fold a big square neckerchief into a neatly rolled strip and how to tie a real sailor knot. Lizzie Lou and Mary felt a little superior to those girls who let the back corners of their ties hang below their middy collars. They just hadn't had a sailor to show them the proper way.

She closed the front door softly. Across the street Mrs. Cameron was getting her milk from the front porch. Lizzie Lou waved.

There weren't many people on the streets. Lizzie Lou wondered if some were still downtown celebrating. Surely not. The furious tempo of last night's jubilee could not be maintained this long. She turned up Franklin Street toward Medford High School; only a few straggled toward the building.

She ran up the steps and inside. Glancing up the broad marble staircase at the clock she saw that it was twenty minutes after eight. There were a few seniors gathered outside Mr. Kingston's closed office door. Lizzie Lou's heart gave a strong beat as she recognized Bill Monroe's tall figure. He glanced up as she walked past on her way to her locker.

"Say, you're a senior, aren't you?" he called to her. She nodded and approached the group. "We're going to ask Mr. Kingston to let the whole student body march downtown this morning. I'm sorry, but I don't know your name."

Lizzie Lou looked up into his clear blue eyes. If only she could have said, "I'm Geraldine Fansler," or, "I'm Marguerite Lansdale," or, "I'm Delitha Blackmore," but Lizzie Lou Jones—ugh! She squeezed her Latin book tight in her arm and answered, "Yes I'm a senior, Lizzie Lou Jones."

He didn't laugh but smiled in a friendly fashion. "Oh sure, I ought to know everyone's name in the class," he apologized, "but I don't. We've been wondering if good old Kingston will let the band march down with us, that is if enough of them show up to make a band. If we had more time we could round up some trucks and make some floats but it would take too long. You got any ideas, Lizzie Lou?"

The others in the group looked at her. There was Pat Brandon, Frieda Hempstead, Mark Johnson, Miriam Hardin, Dale Gordon, John Kelly, Tim Hamilton, and Janet French. She felt her face flush. Oh, why couldn't she come up with some brilliant suggestion? Across the hall a door was open to the auditorium; her eyes chanced on the big flags hanging from each side balcony, the American flag on one side, the Medford High service flag with its many blue stars and a few tragic gold ones on the other.

"We might carry our two flags from the auditorium," she offered hesitantly, and then wished she hadn't spoken, it seemed such a silly idea.

"Say, let's do it, Bill." Miriam walked to the door and looked in at the flags. "We could carry them out flat and then our parade would stretch out longer."

Bill and the others followed her. "It's a great idea. Now if Pop Kingston will just co-operate——"

Lizzie Lou stood still a moment watching the group at the auditorium door. They had forgotten her. Should she join them or go to her locker? Students were coming up the stairs in larger numbers now and the halls were buzzing with conversation. Mr. Kingston came and unlocked his office door. Lizzie Lou walked slowly upstairs to her locker, took the key from her pocketbook, and opened the door. "A great idea" Bill had called it. Would he remember her or would he think it had been Miriam's idea? But how could he forget an awful name like Lizzie Lou Jones? Wouldn't he remember it as one did a ludicrous joke or a silly song?

How she disliked her name. When she had entered high school

as a freshman, she had asked Aunt Liz if it wouldn't be all right for her to sign her name Elizabeth Louise. Aunt Liz had said, "Of course not. That would be a lie. Your name is Lizzie Lou, written right there in the family Bible as plain as a nose on your face. The idea!"

So she had signed all the numerous registration cards with her plain ugly name. She would never forget the way Miss Boswell had frowned while calling the roll in algebra class that first day. "Now here's someone who didn't remember that you're not to sign registration cards with nicknames," she had said disapprovingly. "Lizzie Lou Jones."

Lizzie Lou had blushed so that she felt the color of a ripe tomato. "But Lizzie Lou is my real name," she had offered miserably.

What had Father and Mother been thinking of when they burdened her with such a name? She took her geometry and French grammar from the locker and locked the door. When she got downstairs, Miss Clark was standing at the door of her home room. "You're to go to the auditorium, Lizzie Lou," she said. "I think we are going to be dismissed for the day. Quite a few absent anyway."

Lizzie Lou looked in at the vacant desks. Mary must have stayed home, she hadn't seen her in the halls.

The auditorium had many empty seats. Velda Patterson joined Lizzie Lou at the door. "Hi, Lizzie Lou. Were you downtown last night?"

Lizzie Lou nodded. "Did you ever see anything like it. I was awfully thrilled, weren't you?"

"I'll say. My brother is in camp, you know," Velda added proudly. "He would have gone across in a few weeks, probably. My mother was about the happiest woman in town when those whistles started to blow. Come on, let's sit down there in the middle section."

The eight thirty-five bell rang and the buzz of conversation ceased as Mr. Kingston came out on the stage. Lizzie Lou tried to stifle a yawn. She glanced across the aisle and caught Miss Tamer yawning too. The English teacher smiled and shrugged her shoulders. Evidently she too had been celebrating.

Mr. Kingston cleared his throat. "Students, you will stand while

Miss Melby leads us in 'The Star-Spangled Banner' on this glorious Armistice Day."

Miss Melby came out of the wings and stood beside the principal. She was a little wizened woman; always reminded Lizzie Lou of a wrinkled and withered leaf. Now she placed her pitch pipe to her puckered lips and gave a short note, got the key, raised her expressive hands, and the students of Medford High lifted their voices together in the familiar words,

"Oh say, can you see . . ."

They had reached "and the rockets' red glare . . ." when there was a commotion in the balcony. Lizzie Lou looked up. Several boys on each side were untying the many cords which fastened the two flags to the railing. Bill Monroe was among them. So—they were going to use her "great idea" and carry the flags. Bill reached over to untie the center of the service flag and looked down. Was he looking at her? It certainly seemed so. Hastily she turned her gaze to the stage and Miss Melby.

". . . that our flag was still there.
Oh say, does that star-spangled banner . . ."

She sang to the beat of her heart as well as to the rhythm the music teacher beat out with her fine old hands.

The band gathered at the corner and the students lined up to follow by classes. Lizzie Lou joined some senior girls in the street right behind the huge American flag held out flat by several girls. She wished Mary were here. She wasn't sleepy now, the sharp wind made her wide awake; the sharp wind and the fact that Bill was lining the seniors in rows behind the flag, moving here and there to see that there were four in each line. Andy Faris, president of the junior class, was running up and down the sidewalk calling out, "Any more juniors? Juniors right up here." The junior class was carrying the service flag.

Dale Gordon stood on the sidewalk and pointed to the front of the American flag. "Hey, Bill!" he shouted. "Need another girl there to carry the corner. Where's Bonnie?"

Lizzie Lou watched him look back through the crowd. Always Bonnie, always Bonnie Mason, whenever the fellows thought of girls, she was the one they thought of first. How Lizzie Lou disliked her, so beautiful, so sure of herself. It wouldn't do them any good this morning for beautiful Bonnie had not shown up. Lizzie Lou jabbed her hands down hard in the pockets of her rough tweed coat and turned her head away. Bill mustn't catch her looking at him. A gust of wind got beneath the brim of her gray beaver hat and tried to dislodge it. Hastily she withdrew her hands from her pockets and saved it. That would have been a pretty sight, her hat sailing down the street and she running to retrieve it.

"Hey! Hey you—Lizzie Lou!"

Someone was calling her, it sounded like—— He *was* yelling at her! It was Bill!

"Hey, Lizzie Lou, come on up here in front and carry a corner of the flag, will you?"

She withdrew her hands from her hat and walked toward the front of the flag. How did it happen that he had called her? Probably because no one could ever forget her silly name. She took hold of the corner he indicated and tried to think of something to say but couldn't. Instead she looked down at her gray knitted gloves.

Bill looked back down the line. "O.K., gang. I think we are ready to start." The members of the band raised their instruments, the drummer gave a roll, Ted Masterson lowered his baton, and "The Stars and Stripes Forever" floated out on the November air. Down Franklin Street marched the students of Medford High, by classes, the four officers of each class marching in front of that group.

Lizzie Lou was glad they were moving. She never knew what to say to a boy. If she could have thanked him or have smiled up at him and made her eyes big and round like Bonnie did, but instead she had looked down at her gloves. Probably better that she had, since she was sure her face was bright red with blushing excitement.

How good it would be to know what to do, what to say at special, crucial moments and not be so shy and embarrassed. Once, outside geometry class, she had seen Pat Brandon waiting for Bonnie, sauntering slowly toward him. As she approached, Bonnie snapped her fingers several times, hummed a few bars of "Pretty Baby," did a couple of dance steps, and grinned up at him impishly. How did a girl get enough self-confidence to be as free and easy as all that? Maybe if she knew how to dance well, or if Aunt Liz would let her have a date or, most important of all, if some boy asked her for one. But none of the boys seemed to know she was around at all, that is until this morning when Bill Monroe had remembered her name.

She watched him marching with the other three senior officers just ahead. His shoulders were broad and he wore his cap at just the right jaunty angle. He would have looked handsome in a soldier's uniform, but he wouldn't have to wear one now, the war was over and the United States could get back to peaceful living again.

She looked at Frieda Hempstead, next to her, carrying the flag. She could have stepped right out of a fashion magazine. They hadn't marched many blocks on the brick-paved streets of Medford, however, until Frieda turned a wry face to Lizzie Lou.

"My feet are killing me, are yours?"

"No, but they are getting cold. We stood still too long back there at school."

The band stopped playing. Frieda looked ahead. "Hey, Bill! How far do we march?"

Bill looked back over his shoulder. "Down to the courthouse square. You're not tired already, are you?"

"My feet hurt."

"No wonder in those heels. You ought to wear sensible shoes like Lizzie Lou's." He sent a smile in her direction.

Lizzie Lou's heart skipped a beat, she pulled her shoulders straighter, and stepped along smartly in her dark brown, sensible shoes. He had noticed her shoes, these low-heeled, laced shoes that Aunt Liz had chosen for her because she thought they would wear well.

"I suppose I shouldn't have worn these high-heeled ones," Frieda remarked to Lizzie Lou, "but how did I know we were going to march? You were smart to wear your walking shoes."

Walking shoes! Small choice she had; they were the only ones she possessed.

It was amazing to hear the racket still going on downtown. The streets were jammed with yelling, shouting, horn-blowing citizens trying to give vent to their joy. Lizzie Lou wondered if these were the people who hadn't come downtown in the night. Otherwise how could they keep up such antics? If they were some of the night revelers they must have gone home and had a few hours' sleep, they seemed so vigorous and lively.

The high-school students were soon swallowed up in the crowd around the square. The girls folded up the flag and Bill took charge of it. Lizzie Lou found herself pushed by the crowd close beside Frieda and Bill. She heard Bill say, "How about going over to Hemple's drugstore for hot chocolate, Frieda?"

"Love to, Bill, I'm freezing," Frieda answered.

"Fine. Let's see if we can squeeze through here." His eyes met Lizzie Lou's. "Say, you come along too," he offered generously.

Lizzie Lou's hands clenched into fists inside her pockets. He was asking her to Hemple's, the drugstore so popular with the high-school crowd! Should she go? Aunt Liz wouldn't be expecting her for another hour. Her eyes traveled to the gray fur collar pulled close to Frieda's pretty face. Oh, she couldn't, she just couldn't, she wouldn't be able to think of a thing to say to these two.

"Oh, thank you, but I have to get on home. Have to help my aunt Liz with the washing," she mumbled.

She left the crowd behind. The tumult and frenzy of the Armistice seemed of another world, her mind was so taken up with self-recriminations. Why did she have to say that about helping with the washing? Probably Frieda's and Bill's mothers sent their dirty clothes to the laundry or had a laundress come in. What would they think of her? Why couldn't she have gone along and been so clever and witty that Bill wouldn't have noticed Frieda at all?

What a pity that real life didn't happen sometimes as it did in the pictures! She wished she could talk with someone about the way she felt, about her shyness, about how hard it was to talk to boys, about her growing fear that she would never marry. How could you ever get married if you never had a date? She would be seventeen next month and no boy had ever called at her home and taken her anywhere.

If Mother had lived things would have been different she was certain. She could go home now and tell Mother about Bill, about how scared she got sometimes. Had Mother ever been scared? How did a girl get to be grown-up? Not just in body, goodness knows she was tall enough for a grownup, but grown-up in her mind so that she could relax and speak easily to others, especially to boys.

Father was so quiet and withdrawn, she would never be able to ask him anything. How do you suppose Father and Mother met?

At the corner near home she could see Aunt Liz in the back yard hanging up the sheets. Lizzie Lou walked a little faster.

What a day this had been. It seemed years and years since she had walked in the war-effort parade with Mary yesterday.

3. *"Throw It, You Silly"*

Next day at school Lizzie Lou kept looking for Bill Monroe in the halls. Once she thought she saw him going into the chemistry lab but she wasn't sure. She wished he were in some of her classes. But even if he had been she probably wouldn't have the courage to speak to him.

Mary walked beside her from class to class except for third period when Lizzie Lou went to French and Mary to study hall. Mary chattered so about Armistice Day Lizzie Lou was a little relieved when they had to separate, she had so much to think about. She couldn't bring herself to speak of Bill Monroe to Mary. It seemed so absurd that she, who had never had a date at all, should be thinking about a popular boy like Bill Monroe. French seemed very dull.

At lunch she sat beside Mary in the noisy cafeteria and opened her lunch sack. She wasn't hungry, the hard-boiled egg didn't interest her. She nibbled on a bread and butter sandwich. Mary watched her.

"What's the matter? Don't you feel well? Have too much Armistice?"

"Maybe."

"Say, Papa and I are going to the basketball game Friday night. Do you suppose your aunt Liz would let you come with us?"

Lizzie Lou's face brightened then became downcast. "I doubt it. Aunt Liz can't see any sense to people running around to basketball games after supper. We play Kokomo, don't we?"

"Uh-huh. Papa says Kokomo thinks it will be a pushover for them. But we may surprise them. Why don't you ask your father if you can go instead of your aunt?"

"Ask Father? Oh, I wouldn't do that, I don't like to bother him. He isn't interested in basketball as your father is."

Mary finished her sandwich. "Sometimes, Lizzie Lou, you seem to be afraid of your father."

"Oh no, Mary, really I'm not. It's just—well—he hasn't been himself since Mother died. Aunt Liz says he's still grieving for her and that we mustn't disturb his grief."

"But it's been five years since she died."

"I know." Lizzie Lou wished Mary would stop talking about Father. She often wished that she could be free and easy with him as Mary seemed to be with her father. Was she afraid of him? How could she be? He was never cross or angry, only sad and detached. Lizzie Lou wondered if Mother would have wanted him to go on mourning her forever. Five years! Why, it was an age! Father's preoccupation was very irritating at times.

"Oh, look! There's the team coming along the cafeteria line!" Mary sputtered, her mouth full of apple.

Lizzie Lou looked over the heads of the students to the steam tables at the end of the big room. The members of Medford High's basketball team were pushing their trays along, seemingly unconscious of the many glances coming their way. How handsome they looked in their blue and gold varsity sweaters! They had just come from an extra workout in the gym, getting ready for Friday's game.

There was Bill reaching up to take a plate of food. He was tall, the tallest one on the team. No wonder he was a good center. She had seen him play in two games early last spring, games played after school instead of at night. Aunt Liz had let her attend those games. Do you suppose she would let her go Friday? Oh, she just had to. He might look her way and see her there in the bleachers. If he did she would nod and smile, an encouraging sort of smile, one that would show him what confidence she had in his playing ability.

What a silly idea! He wouldn't look at her and if he did she wouldn't have the courage to nod at him. But why worry about it? She wouldn't be able to be there anyway. She looked down at the table miserably.

Their trays filled, the basketball boys left the cashier at the end of the line and filed down the aisle between the tables amid calls to them from both sides.

"How'd practice go, Andy?"

"All ready for Kokomo, Tim?"

"How's it look for Friday, Bill?"

Lizzie Lou looked up just as Bill grinned at Fred Ritter seated at the table beyond. Bill caught her eye as he turned his head and gave her a look of recognition. His lips formed words which she thought were, "Hi, Lizzie Lou," but she couldn't be sure, the cafeteria was so noisy. She turned to Mary.

"I *will* ask my father tonight if I may go to the game with you Friday." She *had* to see him play.

That evening at the supper table Lizzie Lou wondered if it would be a good idea to speak to Father at the table about the game or wait until Aunt Liz and Uncle Mat went home.

"I want some more potatoes, please," Lucy stated, tapping her plate with her fork.

Aunt Liz passed the dish, saying sharply, "Stop that racket, child, Armistice Day is over."

"Aunt Liz, since the war is over, why can't we have meat again on Tuesdays?" Peggy asked. "And maybe butter too," she added as she spread margarine on a slice of whole-wheat bread.

"The war may be over, but there are still hungry folks in Europe and until Mr. Hoover gives the word, Tuesdays will be meatless in this house. As for butter, well it's a rare family that can afford to pay sixty cents a pound. It will have to come down a lot before we'll have it again. I'm sure margarine won't hurt you a little longer. And you are the one who always wants to color it."

Peggy pushed her fork around over her fried potatoes and found a crispy brown piece. "Yes. It is fun to stir it and see the yellow mix through the white."

Lizzie Lou looked at Father at the end of the table, eating slowly, the habitual detached look on his face. No matter what they had to eat he seemed to get no enjoyment from it. Now Uncle Mat, plump, round-faced, and rosy, well, his food really meant something to him. Aunt Liz said she thought he minded "Hooverizing" more than anyone else in the family, since she was able to make so few pies and cakes with the limited amount of sugar and flour.

However, Aunt Liz obeyed Mr. Herbert Hoover's every edict on food conservation, because, as she said, "We've got to help him feed starving Belgium." Little Lucy had heard, "Now eat that crust on your bread, Lucy, or Mr. Hoover won't like it," so often that she called Mr. Hoover "Crusty" Hoover. Aunt Liz didn't chastize her for the name, thinking it might help her remember to clean up her plate and not waste food. Lizzie Lou was sure that no one took Mr. Hoover's slogan, "Food will win the war," more seriously than did Aunt Liz.

She watched Father stir his coffee and sip it slowly. Was this the time to ask him? She put down her fork and cleared her throat.

"Father."

Warren Jones set down his cup and looked at her as one recalled from far away. Aunt Liz frowned. She had told the children repeatedly not to bother their father.

"Father, you know Mary Higgins." He nodded. "Well, her father is going to take her to the basketball game at the school gym on Friday night and they want me to go too. May I?"

"Why I suppose so, if they will walk home with you."

Aunt Liz pushed her plate away. "Warren, that's after supper, you know. Are you sure you want her to be out at night?"

Lizzie Lou held her breath, her eyes on Father's face.

"I'm sure Mr. Higgins will take good care of the girls, Liz. And after all, Lizzie Lou is sixteen."

"Almost seventeen," Peggy threw in.

"Oh, thank you, Father. Thank you very much." Lizzie Lou felt little prickles of excitement. It had been so easy. She should have gone to Father about things long ago. Maybe he was interested in her after all. Aunt Liz could be wrong.

Aunt Liz pulled her lips into a thin line, gave her eldest niece a frown, and shrugged her shoulders. "Jimmy, it is your turn to help clear the table. Be careful."

"Yes, ma'am." The boy put his plate on Peggy's and carried them out.

"You sit still, Aunt Liz, I'll bring in the dessert." Lizzie Lou took Lucy's dishes and her own. In the kitchen, spooning the cherries out of the glass jar into small dishes, she hummed, "Belgian Rose, my beautiful Belgian Rose . . ." Oh, she did love Father. Perhaps if she tried to talk to him more often he would be as he was when she was a child.

In bed that night Lizzie Lou wondered if she would see Bill Monroe in the cafeteria tomorrow. There might be a pep session in the auditorium and he would be on the stage with the team. And Friday night she would be right there watching him play.

So much basketball and Bill Monroe filled her mind, that her oft-recurring picture of herself as a scarlet-costumed dancer was forgotten entirely. Now she became a well-dressed young woman seated in the bleachers watching an exciting basketball game. She smiled encouragingly at one of the centers as he looked up at her before he jumped for the tip-off. A pleasant way to go to sleep, imagining that Bill Monroe really cared that she was there, cheering the team.

The gym was filled on Friday night, filled with noisy, cheering spectators. Kokomo had sent a sizable cheering section of its own with two cheerleaders who kept Kokomo rooters roaring yells of encouragement.

Mary and Lizzie Lou sat on the front row of the Medford side, Mr. Higgins just behind them.

"That's the mayor, Mr. Tompkins, sitting by Papa," Mary whispered to Lizzie Lou. "The mayor loves basketball."

"It looks as though a lot of grown folks do," Lizzie Lou said, looking at the crowded bleachers. "More adults here than students, I would say."

"Uh-huh. There's some talk of trying to have the games down at the armory so more people can get in. They're still coming in and every seat is taken. Oh, look! Bonnie and Janet!"

Lizzie Lou saw them. Slowly the two girls sauntered in front of the bleachers, looking up casually at the crowd, waving occasionally at an acquaintance. They seemed so sure of themselves. Surely they knew everyone was looking at them. If she, Lizzie Lou, were wearing such beautiful clothes, would she have that self-assurance? Probably not. Some people were born shy and scared, and she supposed she was one of them.

The two girls passed in front of her and Mary. Just beyond, Joe Reed and Frank Anderson gave their places in the front row to the two late-comers and sat on the floor in front of them looking as though fortune had smiled on them indeed. Lizzie Lou wondered how Bonnie had the courage to tap Joe's cheek playfully with her gloved hand as he smiled back at her.

A great shout recalled her as the Kokomo team ran out on the floor, lining up around a basket, each team member taking a turn at a practice shot. Kokomo's cheerleaders worked themselves into a frenzy.

Rah! Rah! Rah!
Sis, boom, bah!
Kokomo High School!
Rah! Rah! Rah!

Medford's team dashed out, led by Pat Brandon, dribbling the ball rapidly. Lizzie Lou found herself screaming with the rest of the Medford crowd, all thoughts of shyness forgotten. Ted Hinkle, the active cheerleader, turned a handspring, picked up his megaphone, and from the students came a deafening roar.

M-E-D-F-O-R-D   M-E-D-F-O-R-D
MEDFORD, MEDFORD, MEDFORD!
Fight, team, fight!

Lizzie Lou watched Bill as he stood waiting his turn to shoot. Hands on hips, his black hair slick and shining, chewing gum slowly, he was calm and unruffled, glancing around occasionally at the other team, watching the movements of the players appraisingly. At his turn he dribbled the ball near the basket, leaped, and with a partial twist of his body dropped the ball through the net; recovering it, he bounced it, recovered again, and made a long shot from the side. The ball slipped through easily. Lizzie Lou swallowed hard. He *was* good!

The referee blew his whistle and each team threw its ball to him. The substitutes retired to the side as the Medford five formed a small circle with their arms thrown about each other's shoulders. Lizzie Lou wondered what they said at moments like this, words of encouragement to one another, suggestions on plays, or warnings about the other team. Another blast from the whistle and the group scattered, Pat Brandon and George Faulkner, forwards, on the side nearest Medford's basket, Andy Faris and Tim Hamilton, guarding Kokomo's forwards at the other basket. Bill Monroe took his place in the middle of the floor. The Kokomo center was even taller than Bill. The referee stood between them, the ball in one hand, whistle in the other.

Ted Hinkle stood facing the Medford rooters and shouted through his megaphone, "Come on, let's give 'em three cheers!" Lizzie Lou and Mary screamed with the others.

Rah! Rah! Rah!
Medford! Medford! Medford!

The whistle blew and the referee tossed the ball up between the two centers. Lizzie Lou held her breath, her eyes on Bill. He stooped low, jumped high, got the tip-off with a hard smack toward Pat. Pat made a lucky catch, pivoted and shot. The ball slipped through, scarcely touching the net. The Medford students screamed, the adult spectators roared, they stood up, they whistled. Medford hadn't beaten Kokomo in seven years and to score in the first minute of play!

Lizzie Lou's throat ached from yelling, but she didn't care; here she could express herself and no one would notice her. No one had inhibitions at a basketball game.

Now Kokomo grew wary and the next tip-off was theirs. Kokomo had the ball. Down toward their goal they went, the ball passing from player to player, the Medford team trying to stop the momentum without success. Lizzie Lou wadded her handkerchief into a hard ball. The thud, thud, thud of twenty rubber-soled shoes pounded in her ears through the noise of the crowd. Oh, Bill, Bill, get there, stop them, stop them! But no one could stop them on that play. The ball slipped through! Score—2 to 2! Kokomo rooters went wild!

Mary grabbed Lizzie Lou's arm. "Oh, golly, golly!"

The teams raced up and down the court so fast, the ball snapping from one to another so often, that it was difficult to keep one's eyes on that rapidly moving sphere. Just when Lizzie Lou was sure that a basket would be made, the ball would roll around the top of the frame at the net and fall outside, fall into the hands of the opposing team and they would go speeding down toward their basket.

"Medford has never had a team like this one," Lizzie Lou heard the mayor shouting to Mr. Higgins. "Why, the biggest part of the time they've got Kokomo on the run. Showing real speed, I tell you, real speed. And it's not just a one- or two-man team, all five are good."

Bill Monroe had the ball under Kokomo's basket. Expertly he dribbled away from a guard and gave a long pass from the corner. Tim Hamilton caught it, dribbled to the center of the floor, and shot a long one.

Lizzie Lou rose to her feet with all the other Medfordites, and the roar which came from their throats, as the ball dropped through, was enough to raise the roof. Medford 4—Kokomo 2. Kokomo called time out.

Coach Dawson threw towels to the Medford team as they sat or sprawled flat on the floor. The boys wiped their perspiring faces and tossed the towels back.

Kokomo rooters gave a "Fight—Team—Fight" yell and Medford a "Yea—Team—Go." Mary turned to her father. "Papa, aren't they wonderful?"

Mr. Higgins' reply was lost in the shouts as the referee blew his whistle. Kokomo scored almost at once, then scored one point on a foul. Kokomo 5—Medford 4!

It was almost at the end of the first half that it happened. A Kokomo player made a long pass from the opposite side, catching the player for whom it was intended off balance. The ball bounced and landed right smack in Lizzie Lou's lap!

"Outside. Medford's ball!" shouted the referee.

Whenever Lizzie Lou thought of the incident, later on, it seemed that time had stopped during that next brief second. As one in a dream she stood up, the ball in her hands, as Bill Monroe ran toward her. And, as in many dreams, one's body refuses to move in time of crisis, just so, Lizzie Lou was unable to let loose of that ball. A figure jumped up at her right! Bonnie Mason!

"Throw it, you silly! Throw it!" and Bonnie snatched the ball from Lizzie Lou's hands and tossed it quickly to Medford's waiting center, Bill Monroe!

Lizzie Lou wished that the floor would open up and swallow her. Her neck grew hot and her face burned and although the crowd, intent on the game, noticed her not at all, their shouts seemed to say to her, "You, Lizzie Lou Jones! You held up the play! For shame!" She sat down, numbly aware of the noise about her. Here had been an opportunity so golden that even her fertile imagination had failed to picture it, and she had muffed it. She cast a sidelong glance across Janet to Bonnie. Bonnie had thrown back the big fur collar on her coat showing the frilly white lace of her blouse. "Throw it, you silly!" Bonnie had shouted at her. How cruel she had been, but she was right, it had been silly to stand there with that ball. Mary nudged her with an elbow.

"Oh boy! Lizzie Lou! What a play! Now we're ahead. Oh, if we could only beat them!"

Lizzie Lou tried to concentrate on the game. Medford 6— Kokomo 5. What would it be like to be out there on the floor before all of these people, trying to get that ball in the basket? She shrank from the thought. Bill probably never felt shy or self-conscious as she did. There he was, alert, wary, quick to take advantage of the slightest opportunity to take that ball down to Medford's basket. Probably no one in the world felt as she did inside. It was disgusting. She must try to quit thinking about Bonnie's remark.

The game went on; the half ended 15 to 14, Medford. The teams left the floor during the intermission and the cheerleaders went to work, vying with one another to give the most unusual yells.

The second half started and Lizzie Lou wondered what Coach Dawson had said to them out there. They seemed to anticipate Kokomo's every move, the visitors got very few chances at the basket. It seemed that there were more than five on the Medford team. Lizzie Lou forgot her own self-reproach and screamed with the others.

Time and again Medford shot, only to have the ball roll around the rim and fall back. The home towners groaned at each failure. Kokomo was being outplayed but the score was still 15 to 14 for Medford. In the heat of play a foul was called on Pat Brandon and Kokomo got a free throw. Made it! Score 15 to 15! Now both rooting sections went wild.

"Get in there, Pat! Sink one!"

"Watch that man, Tim!"

"Shoot, Bill, shoot!"

Bill shot a long one from the side which connected. Lizzie Lou was on her feet with the others.

"Fight, team, fight!"

Seventeen to fifteen. Time out—Kokomo—two substitutes sent in. Kokomo made a basket almost at once; 17 to 17! Medford called time out. The boys sat down. Lizzie Lou watched Bill talking earnestly to them, gesticulating with a clenched fist.

"Not much time left," the mayor said. "If they're going to win they've got to do something."

The whistle blew, the boys leaped to their feet. "Come on, gang, let's go!" Lizzie Lou heard Bill shout.

And go they did! Tip-off to Pat, passed to George, back to Tim, and a long pass to Pat under the basket. Now! In it went and amid the tumultuous sound the boys raced back to their places for the next tossup. The scoreboard showed 19 to 17.

The crowd stood up for the rest of the game. Mary and Lizzie Lou grabbed each other as the teams raced up and down the floor.

"There's nothing as exciting as basketball, absolutely nothing!" Lizzie Lou found herself shouting at Mary.

Near the end Kokomo scored a lucky shot and tied the score. Time was running out, no one scored, the ball traveling from one end of the court to the other without connecting. A Kokomo player knocked Bill down in the speed of the game. Foul on Kokomo.

As Bill approached the free-throw line the noise subsided, so much depended on these two free throws. Bill bounced the ball once, stooped slightly, sprang and threw the ball. Lizzie Lou held her breath as she saw it hit the backboard directly above the basket and fall off. Medford fans groaned and Kokomo cheered. The referee tossed the ball to Bill for the second free throw. Bill frowned, bounced the ball twice, and tossed it. Scarcely touching the net, it slipped through! Bang went the gun! The game was over! Medford had won by a point, Bill's point! Medford 20— Kokomo 19!

The Medford students formed a line and started a snake dance, shouting, "We beat Kokomo! We beat Kokomo!"

The mayor and Mr. Higgins walked behind Lizzie Lou and Mary on the way home. A newspaper reporter joined them.

"Mr. Mayor, I've heard a rumor about using the armory for basketball. Got anything to say about it?"

"Oh, hello there, Stanly. Well, you may say that the school board is meeting with the city council next Tuesday night to discuss the matter. It is my opinion that basketball is a coming thing in Indiana. You may quote me on that. Lots of other high schools in the state have outgrown their school gyms because of the expanding interest in the game by citizens of the communities. Medford's got a fine team. Real wonders, those boys, five real wonders. Beat Kokomo. Real playing that."

"Five wonders," the reporter repeated. "Mr. Mayor, you've named 'em! The Wonder Five! Medford's Wonder Five! Mind if I use that?"

The mayor chuckled at his own brilliance. "Why, that isn't bad, is it? No, of course I don't mind, Stanly. Glad to help you out."

Mary clasped Lizzie Lou's arm tighter. "Hear that, Lizzie Lou? The mayor called the team the Wonder Five. Bet it will be in the paper tomorrow."

There was a light in the Jones's living room, and as Lizzie Lou fumbled in her purse for her key, the door was opened by her father.

"You didn't need to wait up for me, Father."

"Found I couldn't sleep until you were in, Daughter. How was the game?"

"Oh, Father, wonderful! Simply wonderful. We beat Kokomo 20 to 19."

Warren Jones raised his eyebrows. "Beat Kokomo? Well, now that's something that hasn't happened in many a moon. Tell me about it. Here, I'll take your coat."

Was that a new note of interest in his voice? Did she detect any real enthusiasm or was he just trying to be nice? It was hard to tell. She tried to get some of the game's excitement in her account to him.

In the cold bedroom, she undressed quietly and quickly. She pushed Peggy over and crawled in. Her mind was a jumble of basketball players and crowds of spectators. But most vivid of all was the figure of a pert little blond girl shouting, "Throw it, you silly, throw it!"

4. Saturday

"'Medford's Wonder Five Beats Kokomo!'" Uncle Mat read from the sports page next morning. He looked across the table at Lizzie Lou. "Must have been quite a game last night. Big crowd?"

"Oh yes. The gym was packed."

"It says here that the school board is trying to get the armory for basketball games. The mayor seems to be all for it." Uncle Mat folded the paper and gave his attention to the bacon and eggs Aunt Liz set before him.

"Glad you were able to see that game last night, Lizzie Lou," Father put in. "It looks as though it might be the beginning of a growing interest in basketball for the whole town. With a few more wins like last night, they may even pack them in at the armory."

Aunt Liz looked at Father. "Well, I must say, Warren, I'm surprised at your interest in the game."

Lizzie Lou watched Father curiously. He really did seem interested.

"I used to play basketball at the 'Y,'" he said, "before Margaret and I were married."

"Well, it seems pretty silly to me for grown men like the mayor to show such enthusiasm for so childish a game," Aunt Liz stated disapprovingly as she went to the kitchen for the coffeepot.

It was Saturday morning and Lizzie Lou's chores hung over her like a great flock of crows over a cornfield, numerous and black. Peggy did the breakfast dishes and made the beds, while Lizzie Lou, her head covered by a dust cap, her dress by a big apron, tackled the living-room carpet with a heavy broom.

There was one bit of sweetness to this dusty Saturday sweeping. Just before he left for work, Father always handed Lizzie Lou a quarter, a quarter for the moving-picture show in the afternoon, five cents each for Lucy, Jimmy, and Peggy, and ten cents for her own admission. When she and Peggy finished setting the house in order, they would get the newspaper and decide which show to see. Jimmy didn't care much as long as there was a comedy with cops and lots of pie throwing.

As she swept, Lizzie Lou thought of Bonnie; Bonnie, so beautiful and sure of herself. The thought made her mad and the dust flew as she took it out on the carpet. She felt she couldn't look at Bill Monroe again, for he must have heard what Bonnie had said to her. What an awkward, dull-witted person he must think her. She hoped the picture would be good this afternoon, maybe she could lose herself in it and forget what had happened.

She and Peggy had some trouble with Jimmy at lunch. Charlie Chaplin was at the Mecca in *Shoulder Arms* and Jimmy loved Charlie Chaplin. But after they explained that Harold Lloyd and Bebe Daniels were in a Lonesome Luke comedy at the Bijou, where Norma Talmadge and Eugene O'Brien were playing, Jimmy gave in. He liked Harold Lloyd almost as much as Charlie Chaplin. But next time, he told them, they'd have to go to the one he wanted.

Lizzie Lou and Peggy loved Norma Talmadge and, as for Eugene O'Brien, well—the way his hair waved up from his forehead, the way he smiled at his leading lady before he kissed her; he was absolutely wonderful!

All thoughts of herself left Lizzie Lou as she sat in the dark theater, holding Lucy on her lap so that she could read the captions in the child's ear and answer her questions. There was so much in a picture that Lucy didn't understand and her many "Why did she do that?" and "Where is he going now?" remarks were likely to annoy others. Lizzie Lou had learned to anticipate her questions and whisper answers in her ear before they were asked.

Norma Talmadge was beautiful, such expressive dark eyes and so lovely in that black velvet dress. No wonder Eugene O'Brien was falling in love with her. From the piano came that new song, "I'm sorry, dear, so sorry, dear, I'm sorry I made you cry." Was he

really going to leave her? Lizzie Lou felt in her pocket for her handkerchief. Peggy dropped their hats from her lap and Jimmy pulled his feet up under him.

"Wish we had gone to see Charlie Chaplin," he told Lizzie Lou in a loud whisper. "This is silly."

"Sh—keep quiet." She shifted Lucy to the other knee wondering why she seemed heavier. Lucy's head fell against her shoulder; she was asleep. Lizzie Lou put the child's head in the crook of her arm and pulled her legs across her lap. Now if Jimmy would keep quiet she could enjoy the show. She gave him a whispered promise that if he would behave they would stay to see the comedy the second time. Lizzie Lou lived with the lovely Norma through the remaining reels. The surrounding aroma of peanuts and the crunch of their shells underfoot did not distract her from the flickering screen world.

Moving pictures had certainly improved since she was younger. She could remember when she went with Mother, years ago, the film broke many times during every performance. On the screen would flash a sign reading: "There will be a slight intermission while the operator repairs the film." And then you would wait and wait to see the rest of the picture.

In those days picture shows, because they only cost a nickel, even for adults, were called nickelodians. Now they charged as much as twenty cents for adults at evening shows. And for Lillian Gish's new picture, *Hearts of the World,* showing next week, they were charging a dollar and a half for the best seats at night, plus ten per cent war tax. Lizzie Lou hoped it would come back later at regular prices, she hated to miss Lillian Gish in anything.

Lizzie Lou had not seen many shows with real people in them: a few vaudeville acts, once a play in the big brown tent at the summer Chautauqua, and once long ago when she was ten, Mother had taken her to see a stock company at the Medford Opera House, playing *Trail of the Lonesome Pine.* It had been all about mountaineers, "moonshiners," and "revenuers." But even though moving pictures were silent and she often wished she could hear what they were saying, Lizzie Lou loved them best.

Lizzie Lou could retain the magic cloak of a moving picture about herself for as long as two hours after leaving a theater. When she could get away from the rest of the family, she often acted favorite parts before the mirror in the bedroom.

Aunt Liz thought moving pictures and the legitimate theater a waste of time. However, Lizzie Lou had noticed that Aunt Liz held her tongue about her low opinion of the stage and actors in front of Father. She wondered why.

At supper that night Jimmy kept trying to tell Uncle Mat about the comedy. Aunt Liz looked at him sternly.

"I'm sure your uncle can get along without hearing all that tosh about Lonesome Luke. Eat your supper."

"But, Aunt Liz, it was so funny the way he——"

"You can tell me about it later, Jimmy," Uncle Mat said kindly. "After you study your Bible verse for Sunday school," he added as Aunt Liz gave him a disapproving look.

If they could eat their meal alone sometimes, Lizzie Lou

thought, maybe Father would talk more. She had read that interesting conversation at meals was a great aid to digestion and, while Jimmy's talk about Harold Lloyd was not exactly scintillating, still she felt he should be permitted to speak about a subject of his own choosing. Sometimes she wanted to shake Father for his silence and shake Aunt Liz for being so bossy. How surprised the family would be if they could read her thoughts.

If she ever had children she would let them speak freely at the table. She looked down at the sausage on her plate without seeing it. Instead, she saw herself seated at a dining table, smiling at her three handsome children, encouraging them to express their ideas. Beautifully dressed in black velvet and creamy lace, she sat erect, self-assured, a sparkling silver fork poised in the long, tapering fingers of her white hand. From time to time she looked across the lighted candles to the shadowy figure at the head of the table to exchange knowing glances at the cleverness of their children. The shadowy figure wavered in appearance, his hair was first curly like Eugene O'Brien's then black and slick like——

"Lizzie Lou! I've asked you twice. Please slice some more bread."

"Oh—yes, Aunt Liz. Right away!" She got up and took the empty bread plate.

"I declare, the way your mind is off woolgathering most of the time is disgraceful. I just don't know what's going to become of you if you don't quit that daydreaming."

"I'm sorry," she mumbled on her way to the kitchen. She sliced the bread slowly, the slices must be even and not jagged. Yes, she did daydream too much, she supposed, but an imaginary life helped make dull realities more bearable. In fancy she could be and do what she pleased. If only something real and beautiful would happen to her.

At half past eight she sat near the base-burner in the living room, alone with Father. This *Little Minister* was a good book; she would ask Miss Tamer to schedule her for an oral book report on it next week. She must thank Miss Gibson, the librarian, for suggesting it. Miss Gibson had said she had seen Maude Adams play it on the stage in Chicago. Lizzie Lou wished they would make a picture of it. She finished the chapter and yawned. She glanced at Father. He sat staring into space, the evening paper lying un-read on his lap.

"Father," she said softly.

Slowly his eyes lost their unseeing appearance and he looked at her. "Yes, Daughter."

"You haven't read your paper yet."

"Oh, so I haven't." He unfolded the news sheets with a rattling sound and scanned the front page.

Lizzie Lou stuck a finger between the pages of her book to mark her place as she watched him. What did he think about when he stared off like that? About Mother and their life together, she sup-posed. It all seemed so long ago, she could scarcely remember what their family had been like then, with Father and Mother laughing and joking and Aunt Liz staying on her own side of the house more of the time. What a cute little thing Peggy had been, about like Lucy now. Peggy was so pretty.

Why did she have to be the homely one? Once Father had said she looked like his mother. She had never seen Grandmother Jones. Both Father's parents had died before she was born. And now that she thought of it she had never seen any photographs of them either. She wondered why. There was a whole album of Mother's folks. Father had a brother, Will, in California, but they never heard from him. Maybe if Father had some older relatives to take an interest in him he might be different.

Lizzie Lou sighed, opened her book, and read: "By the following Monday it was known at many looms that something sat heavily on the Auld Licht minister's mind. On the previous day he had preached his second sermon of warning to susceptible young men, and his first mention of the word 'woman' had blown even the sleepy heads upright."

This was good! He really was taken with that mischievous Bab-bie in spite of himself.

The room was quiet save for the tick of the clock and the oc-casional rattle of Father's paper. Lizzie Lou lost herself in Gavin Dishart's struggle to disregard the wiles of the bewitching Babbie.

All of a sudden Father gave a loud exclamation. Lizzie Lou

looked up quickly. What was the matter with him? He was staring at the paper and frowning.

"What's wrong, Father?"

Slowly he folded the paper, put it on the table, rose from his chair, and walked to the back of the stove where he adjusted the damper in the stovepipe. By the time he looked at her he had regained his composure.

"Think I shall go to bed, Lizzie Lou," he said, ignoring her question. "The doors are locked and the stove will do till morning. You turn out the lights and don't stay up too late. Remember we should be up by seven in order to get to Sunday school on time."

"Yes, Father." She didn't question him further.

He stood for a moment beside her chair. She looked up at him. There was a new look of pain in his eyes, something different from his usual sadness. He reached out and stroked her hair gently.

"You're a good girl, Lizzie Lou. I don't know what I would do without you. Don't ever leave me."

Lizzie Lou swallowed hard. "I won't, Father, I won't."

He walked across the room, paused a moment at the door leading into the hall, then disappeared quickly. She could hear his slow steps on the stairs as though he was unconscious of the chill in the unheated portion of the house.

She put her book on the table and stared at the red coals in the base-burner. A tiny blue flame played and danced over and between the scarlet embers. What had caused Father to speak like that? Most of the time he seemed to scarcely notice her at all. It must have been something he read in the newspaper. She got the paper from the table, opened it, and scanned the pages.

Here was a picture of some ragged little children, Belgian war orphans; that couldn't have upset him that much, for there had been many such pictures in the last two years. Here was a piece about President Wilson's daughters in the White House. She glanced on the next page. "City Council to Vote on Use of Armory for Basketball."

She stopped in her search for the cause of Father's disturbance and read the article. By January, high-school basketball games might be played at the armory and many more Medford citizens could watch the Wonder Five in action. She thought of Bill Monroe, could see him passing the ball, dodging in and out as he maneuvered to receive the ball under the basket. Would he like playing before larger crowds? One thing she was sure of, she would never sit on the front row of the bleachers again where she might make a fool of herself as she had last night. The pain of last night had dulled somewhat, but she hoped she would not see Bonnie on Monday. If Bonnie laughed at her on Monday she would die, just absolutely die!

She couldn't find a thing in the paper that could have upset Father. She paused at the next page to read what was showing at the moving-picture shows next week. She would like to see Mabel Normand in *Mickey*. Here was an ad for a stage show at the Medford Opera House, Louise Leander in *Till We Meet Again*. Medford was often fortunate enough to get good road shows because it was near Indianapolis, and companies stopped for a one-night stand before a week's showing in the larger capital city. The performance was to be November twenty-eighth, Thanksgiving. She wondered what the play was about. That was the same title as that new popular song. One thing was sure, she wouldn't see it, the seats were all reserved from seventy-five cents to two dollars. What a lot of pictures she could see for the price of one ticket to that stage show.

She folded the paper and laid it on the table, reached up and turned out the chandelier light. Putting up the front window blind she looked outside.

The wind blew the hanging street lamp at the corner back and forth, making moving shadows run up and down the street like filmy spirits advancing then retreating from the lamp's exposing beam.

It was cold by the window, it would be colder in the hall and icy upstairs. If she had her nightgown down here she would undress by the stove. Since she didn't she'd have to be brave and run for it.

Enveloped in the folds of her ample outing-flannel nightgown, she snuggled close to Peggy's warm body. Relaxed at last from the shivering ordeal of undressing, she grew drowsy. Unrelated thoughts chased one another through her retreating consciousness.

Norma Talmadge had lovely eyes . . . Be nice to go to the show by herself sometime, Lucy was so heavy and Jimmy so noisy . . . Aunt Liz would probably make her wear that brown dress on Monday . . . What was it in the paper that startled Father? . . . Would Bill remember how crazy she had been standing there with the ball? . . . Louise Leander in *Till We Meet Again* . . . Beautiful name, Louise Leander . . . What was the Sunday-school lesson? . . . The sermon would probably be about the Armistice . . . She would read some more in *The Little Minister* tomorrow . . . What would Aunt Liz say when . . .

She was asleep.

5. *Real and Beautiful*

Monday morning found Lizzie Lou walking rebelliously to school. Aunt Liz had come over early and insisted that she wear the brown dress, "To get the good out of it."

As if there could be any good in anything so unattractive. What if her middy suit was getting shiny? She felt good in it, felt inconspicuous and like the rest of the girls. But this brown monstrosity made her feel like a long skinny brown caterpillar. No, not a caterpillar, for a caterpillar would turn into a beautiful butterfly and she, Lizzie Lou Jones, would never have anything in common with the airy loveliness of a butterfly.

No, she must not disparage a caterpillar by comparing it to this dress. It must be nice being a caterpillar, easy to bear its ugliness, knowing that beauty would come with time.

Wonder what Aunt Liz would have said if she had stamped her foot and said, "I won't wear it, Aunt Liz. You can say what you like, I *will not* wear it." She hugged the copy of *The Little Minister* closer and gave a quiet laugh of glee. The thought of defying Aunt Liz was very satisfying. She imagined the look of astonishment that would appear on her aunt's face, astonishment that at last the meek one had turned, had dared to question adult authority.

She scarcely noticed the cold wind blowing around the corner as she turned on Franklin Street, scarcely noticed other high-school students on their way to school, so engrossed was she in "sassing" Aunt Liz about her dress. She didn't notice quick steps behind until a figure stepped beside her.

"Hi, Lizzie Lou."

Her brown eyes looked up in startled surprise. Bill Monroe grinned at her.

"I called to you back a way, but you didn't hear me. Must have been thinking about something important."

Her tongue stuck to the roof of her mouth and the words spoken to her so often in childhood dinned in her ears. "What's the matter, Lizzie Lou, has the cat got your tongue? Speak up, Lizzie Lou."

She swallowed and managed a smile. "No, nothing important."

"Glad I saw you before school. We'll have senior meeting this morning. I want to appoint the ring committee and I wondered if you would be on it."

Lizzie Lou felt as though a hand had squeezed her heart, that it had stopped beating, that the blood had ceased to flow in her veins. She grew cold and numb for an instant and then, as though the hand clutching her heart had let go, and the heart, stimulated by the squeezing, had pumped forth furiously, a warm glow surged through her body.

"Why, I don't know." She tried to sound casual, tried not to show her elation. "What would I have to do?"

"Oh, meet with the rest of the committee and me to look over some catalogues from jewelry stores. We'll select several designs to submit for class approval then keep records of orders and sizes wanted. Think you can find time to do it?"

"I think so." She almost added—I'll ask Aunt Liz—but didn't. No matter what Aunt Liz said she was going to do this. He had asked her. Would he mention her humiliating stupidity at last Friday's game? How she hoped he had forgotten.

"Good. I'll let you know when we meet." He pulled his cap down tighter. "A week ago was Armistice Day. Too bad we don't have something cooking today that would let us miss school."

Lizzie Lou nodded. Should she mention basketball or might it make him remember that terrible incident?

"You played a wonderful game last Friday," she said at last. "I never saw such an exciting game."

"Oh, were you there?" He looked pleased at her praise.

Lizzie Lou's courage rose. He hadn't noticed her, so of course he didn't know that she had held up the game. Then she felt slightly deflated that he hadn't recognized her. After all, she had been sitting right on the front row in plain sight. How silly she was! First she was afraid he had seen her, now she was sorry he hadn't.

"Are you going to like playing at the armory if the city council decides to let us have it?"

"I don't know. I suppose it won't be much different, the crowd will just be bigger and I never see the people anyway."

"Why, I don't see how you can help it." Lizzie Lou looked at him.

"Well, the first time I played at a big game and saw all the people, I was scared to death. Threw my game off so that Coach had to take me out. He gave me a good talking-to, said if I wanted to be on the team I'd have to learn to pay no attention to the crowd. I love to play basketball so I've made myself see only the players on the floor. If I keep my mind on the game I never see the bleachers."

"Doesn't the yelling bother you?"

Bill grinned. "Nope. It just sounds like a distant rumbling. After a while I don't even hear it."

They walked up the steps of Medford High and Bill opened the door for her. Lizzie Lou mounted the marble steps inside wondering if this was real, that she could be walking in with Bill Monroe. Talking to him hadn't been hard at all. She spoke to him almost as easily as she did to Mary. He had a nice way about him, polite and considerate.

"What time is senior meeting?" she asked as he walked up beside her.

"Second period."

At the top of the stairs stood a group of girls talking: Miriam, Frieda, Janet, Bonnie. Bonnie saw them first and put a hand on Janet's arm.

"Look what's coming in with Bill Monroe, that Jones girl! The one who was so sappy at the game . . . Hi there, Bill. How's Medford's big tall center this morning?" She left the group and walked toward him, ignoring Lizzie Lou completely. Lizzie Lou wondered if Bill had heard her remark.

"Hi, Bonnie." He glanced at the pretty blond girl, then turned to Lizzie Lou. "Where's your locker?"

"Up by Room 203 on second."

"I'll walk up with you. Mine's just around the corner."

Lizzie Lou had never noticed until this minute that the floor of Medford High's front hall was pure gold and that the walls sparkled with diamonds. What a beautiful place!

Bonnie and the others watched as Bill Monroe walked down the hall with "that Jones girl!"

Lizzie Lou went to senior meeting with Mary as usual, but she felt far away and said little.

"What picture did you see Saturday?" Mary asked.

"Norma Talmadge at the Bijou."

"Any good?"

"Uh-huh."

"What's the matter with you this morning, Lizzie Lou? Are you mad because you had to wear the brown dress again?"

"Brown dress? Oh yes. Why, I had almost forgotten it." She gave a short laugh.

Mary shook her head. "Lizzie Lou, you're crazy this morning, just plumb crazy."

"I know it," Lizzie Lou said happily. "Shall we take our usual seats here in the third row?" she asked as they entered the big science lecture hall, where the seniors met.

When she got home at four o'clock Lizzie Lou went right upstairs, without removing her wraps, to the dresser in her room, opened her drawer, and took out a small booklet, a 1918 calendar diary. There were three blank lines beside each day's date. She had never bothered to write in it before, so little worth noting happened to her.

She turned to November eighteenth, Monday. She looked at it a long time, then reached into the drawer, pushed aside some old hair ribbons left from pigtail days, and brought up a stub of a pencil. Slowly and carefully she wrote on the first line, "That Jones Girl," on the second line, "Ring Committee," and on the third, "Bill." There, that would remind her forever and ever of this day, this beautiful, wonderful day. She didn't mind Bonnie's derision. In fact she rather liked being called, "That Jones Girl." There was a distinction and dignity there that was wholly lacking in the childish name, Lizzie Lou.

She looked in the mirror, took off her beaver hat, and smoothed her hair back. She took up the pencil again and turned to the week before, Monday, the eleventh, and wrote "Peace!"—"Carried flag." That was the day he first spoke to her. What was it Bonnie had said? "That Jones girl. The one who was so sappy at the game!"

Watching herself in the mirror, she gave a little toss to her head and spoke aloud in a haughty tone. "I was, indeed, sappy, Bonnie, my dear. But if Bill didn't know I was a sap, what difference does it make, Miss Smarty?" She picked up her hat with a flourish, twirled around twice on her toes, and ran downstairs. "That Jones girl" was in high spirits.

However, getting supper with Aunt Liz brought her down to earth. Aunt Liz was always out of sorts on Mondays; tired out from doing the big washing, Lizzie Lou supposed as she stood at the sink peeling potatoes.

Aunt Liz stuck a fork in the meat simmering on the stove. "Meat's 'most done. You can put the potatoes in as soon as you get them peeled. Peel about five onions and all those turnips in the basket there behind the door. I'm going out to bring in the rest of the clothes. I declare I don't know where this day has gone, what with——"

The rest of her remarks were lost to Lizzie Lou as the back door closed.

Why did Aunt Liz have to tell her absolutely everything to do? She seemed to think Lizzie Lou didn't know a thing about cooking. Any fool would know enough to fix a boiled dinner, even that sappy Jones girl. She giggled. The sound surprised her. It was kind of good to laugh at herself. Maybe if she could do it more often she might forget how homely and unattractive she was. It was good to laugh. But that Bonnie! She was so sure of herself.

Lizzie Lou kicked viciously at the cupboard under the sink. The outburst relieved her resentment.

She was peeling the onions when Aunt Liz returned carrying the clothesbasket of frozen unwieldy garments, sticking out at the top in all directions. Aunt Liz pushed the door shut with her foot and took the basket to the pantry.

"Maybe these will be thawed by the time supper's over and I can spread 'em out around the stove. This is one of the reasons I despise winter so, takes an age to get the clothes dry."

Lizzie Lou brushed a tear from her cheek with her sleeve and picked up another onion. There was a step in the dining room and Father appeared in the doorway. Aunt Liz, at the pantry door, looked surprised.

"Why, Warren, what are you doing home so early? You're not due for another half an hour yet."

Warren Jones stuck his hands in his pants pockets and smiled slightly. "Don't be upset, Liz. I'll get out of your way in a minute. I left work early today to do an errand." He looked at Lizzie Lou. "Why, Daughter, are you crying?"

Lizzie Lou laughed. "Just peeling onions."

"Lizzie Lou, if I remember correctly you have a birthday coming up on December first."

"Why, Father, I didn't think you would remember. I'll be seventeen." She took the onions and turnips to the stove and put them in the kettle. What had got into Father? It had been so long since he had taken note of anyone's birthday.

"I know, and a girl seventeen deserves something special, so I left the office early and stopped at the opera house."

Aunt Liz gave a little gasp and put her hand over her mouth.

"I'm going to take you to the play coming there on the twenty-eighth. I bought two tickets," Father went on. "I think it high time you saw a good play." He paused and gave Aunt Liz a defiant look, a look Lizzie Lou had never seen on his face before. "And a really capable actress," he added, his dark eyes flashing a message to his astonished sister-in-law.

Lizzie Lou stood at the stove and watched them. It was almost like a scene from a play right here in their kitchen. What was this conflict?

Aunt Liz shook her head slowly. "So you did see that ad in the paper. I was hoping you wouldn't. Do you think it wise, Warren, taking Lizzie Lou?"

"The tickets are bought and Lizzie Lou is going. Let's hear no more about it, Liz." And Father left the kitchen abruptly.

Aunt Liz looked shocked at his vehement tone. "Well of all things, talking to me in that tone!" She turned to Lizzie Lou. "Set the table."

"Yes, Aunt Liz. But what is it? What's wrong about Father taking me to a play?"

"Wrong? What's wrong? Everything's wrong. There, I've said my last word on the subject, so say no more."

Lizzie Lou's mind was a blur of questions as she got the plates from the pantry, questions about this strange discord between Father and Aunt Liz. It had something to do with the play and it must have been the ad in the newspaper that had startled Father, Saturday night. Would he tell her? Just imagine it! She was going to see a really wonderful play with a New York company! Louise Leander in *Till We Meet Again!* What a day this had been!

The rest of the week glowed with the excitement of unusual events. Only last Saturday she had wished for something real and beautiful to happen to her and here it was, so beautiful that it scarcely seemed real. First Bill had walked to school with her on Monday, not seeming to notice her homeliness, her made-over clothes, or her heavy shoes; then he made her a member of the ring committee right there at senior meeting. As if that wasn't enough to satisfy any wish, Father had come home with tickets for a big play.

On Tuesday the ring committee met after school. The five of them went to Miss Tamer's room to look over the jeweler's catalogues. Miss Tamer was faculty advisor for the senior class.

Lizzie Lou sat quietly thumbing through a catalogue while the others remarked about various ring designs they thought attractive. She noticed several she thought pretty. She listened to the others argue about two designs they all liked, then, trembling a little, she asked about the possibility of working out a combination of these two designs. She smiled at Bill as she spoke. She didn't want him to be sorry he had put her on the committee. Miriam Hardin, Medford High's outstanding art student, nodded, took a

63

pencil, and sketched a ring with the letters M.H.S. intertwined in a seal with a 19 on each side.

The design was approved by the class next day and the seniors filled out order blanks for their rings. Lizzie Lou and Miriam stayed after school on Thursday and worked in Miss Tamer's room, arranging the orders alphabetically and making sure that sizes were plainly marked.

Friday, Lizzie Lou stayed to give a report to Miss Tamer on *The Little Minister*. Mary went with her to report on George Eliot's *Adam Bede*. It was Mary who told the English teacher that Lizzie Lou was going to see the play at the opera house on Thanksgiving.

"Why, Lizzie Lou, that's fine. You have a real treat in store. Louise Leander is a fine actress. I was in New York in 1916 and saw her. She was wonderful."

"I suppose you girls heard the news about the armory," Miss Tamer went on. "In January all our games will be played there."

In contrast to the stimulating events at school, things at home were uncomfortable. Aunt Liz was silent and morose, saying as little as possible to Father. Father ignored the unpleasantness and behaved in his usual quiet manner.

Sunday, Aunt Liz had a headache and didn't go to Sunday school or church. Lizzie Lou knew that something was troubling her aunt deeply.

She felt that it was more than Aunt Liz's disapproval of her seeing a play. After all, Aunt Liz didn't object when they went to the pictures every week, a picture show wasn't so awfully different from a play.

Thanksgiving was a dull, gray day, cold and threatening. Uncle Mat came into the Jones's kitchen at seven-thirty, looking troubled.

"Good morning, Uncle Mat." Lizzie Lou smiled at him. "Where's Aunt Liz?"

"Your aunt has another headache and says she is going to stay in bed today, that is if you think you can manage to roast the chickens."

"Another headache, Unce Mat? Oh, I'm sorry. Of course I can

manage the dinner." Her aunt must be terribly agitated, two headaches so close together. "Do you know what's bothering her?
What's wrong between her and Father?"

Uncle Mat turned away and got plates from the cupboard.
"I'll set the table for you," he said, ignoring her question.

So—he did know, but wouldn't tell her.

It was fun, being boss in the kitchen. Peggy was helpful and
Jimmy and Lucy came out to see if there wasn't something they
could stir or mix for their big sister. At half past eleven as she was
kneeling beside the open oven door basting the chickens, she
looked up and saw Father at the door. He smiled down at her.

"How are you getting along, Daughter? Can I help in any way?"

"Do you really want to help, Father?" she asked incredulously.
What had come over him?

"Of course."

"I wonder if you would get the big dinner plates from the good
set on the top shelf in the cupboard and put them up in the warming oven. I could get them, but they are heavy and I wouldn't
want to drop them."

Warren Jones stood on a kitchen chair and took down the plates.

"Get the big platter and deep dishes while you have the chair
over there," she added, peering into a kettle on top of the stove.
"My, with all the help I have dinner will be ready in short order."

Flushed and triumphant, Lizzie Lou sat down to the table
with justifiable pride. The mashed potatoes were hot, the gravy
steaming, the chickens brown, the onions creamy, the cranberries
beautiful, and the celery crisp. She had tried to remember everything. Father said grace, then smiled at her.

"Lizzie Lou, you have done a fine job. Don't you think so, Mat?"

Uncle Mat nodded and sniffed hungrily. "Liz couldn't have
done better."

"Are you sure Aunt Liz doesn't want to eat?" Lizzie Lou asked.

"No, said she didn't want a thing. Jimmy, give me your plate
and I'll put a drumstick on it."

"Me too, Uncle Mat. I want a drumstick," Lucy put in.

"I'm so sorry she's sick. I'll make some tea and toast for her as soon as dinner's over. Maybe she could manage that. Do you want gravy on your potatoes, Lucy?" Lizzie Lou enjoyed watching her family's evident satisfaction in her cooking.

Later, she took tea and toast to the other side of the house. She tapped at Aunt Liz's bedroom door and entered at a muffled response. The shades were drawn and Lizzie Lou could scarcely see her aunt's face on the pillow.

"I thought you might like to try to eat a little, Aunt Liz." She looked down at her aunt. How much younger she looked with her hair loose and spread out on the pillow. Lizzie Lou remembered a picture of her in the album as a young girl, really pretty.

"Oh, I don't think I can eat a bite." Aunt Liz put her hand to her forehead. "My head throbs so. How did you get along with dinner?"

"All right," Lizzie Lou replied modestly. "Food probably wasn't as tasty as yours, but everybody ate heartily."

"Be sure to see that the kitchen gets cleaned up properly."

"Oh, that's all done. Father came out and helped with the dishes."

"He did? What's got into Warren? I suppose it's that——" She stopped. "Just put the plate on the chair and push it closer. I'll see if I can drink a little tea. What are you going to wear tonight to the show?"

Lizzie Lou's spirits sank to her toes. Was Aunt Liz going to make her wear the brown one? She pushed the chair beside the table and set down the plate. "Why, I thought I'd press my middy suit and wear that. This green dress is sort of short."

Aunt Liz peered at the bottom of the dress below the big apron. "Yes, I guess it is. Too bad there's no more hem to let out." She sighed and put her hand over her eyes. "I wish you had a nice Sunday dress to wear, a serge or soft flannel, but with war prices so high, I just wasn't able to manage it this fall, the other children needed so many things. Yes, wear the middy suit, for I know you don't like the brown dress, though I don't know why; it's such good material. Well, she probably won't see you anyway." Aunt Liz raised up on her elbow and reached for the cup.

"Who won't see me?"

"Oh, never mind. Just leave me alone. I'll try to nibble a little toast."

Lizzie Lou shut the door behind her and stood in the hall. What was wrong with Aunt Liz besides a headache? All this concern about a Sunday dress for her, she had never had more than three winter dresses. And that about someone not seeing her; was the pain so bad that it was making Aunt Liz a little addled?

She shrugged at her own bewilderment and went downstairs to press her middy suit. Only a few hours until she and Father would be leaving for the Medford Opera House! Beautiful, wondrous, magnificent thought! The theater, with real live people on the stage! The theater, with Louise Leander!

Lizzie Lou hugged herself in ecstasy!

6. *Louise Leander*

An icy wind blew against their hunched shoulders as they waited for the streetcar at the corner. Lizzie Lou's toes grew numb in spite of her heavy shoes and rubbers. The approaching streetcar was a welcome sight and its jangling bell sounded promise of protection from the cold.

They sat near the center, close to the stove, but even though its iron sides were red hot, Lizzie Lou's feet got colder, there was such a draft on the floor. The conductor came along and took Father's two nickels, pulled twice on the cord to ring up their fares in the register box above the door.

While they waited on the switch for the car coming from town, the conductor shook down the ashes in the stove and put in more coal. Lizzie Lou looked at the other passengers and wondered if any of them were going to the Medford Opera House. Father was silent, looking before him in that unseeing way of his. Lizzie Lou wiggled her fingers in her pockets to try to warm them.

They were half an hour early at the theater, but Lizzie Lou didn't mind. There was so much to see before the curtain went up.

It was warm inside the lobby. She unbuttoned her coat as Father fumbled in his pocket for the tickets. At one side was a large glass showboard filled with photographs of the actors and scenes from the play. Lizzie Lou gazed at the large picture of the star in the center.

"That must be Louise Leander, Father."

Warren Jones stood beside her and looked long and hard at the striking face in the picture. It wasn't exactly a beautiful face, Lizzie Lou decided, the features were a bit too pronounced for that, but there was a certain magnetism, a sensitiveness about the generous mouth, a warmth of understanding and compassion in the large dark eyes that gave the face a beauty she had never seen in the faces of her beloved moving-picture stars.

"Did you ever see such big eyes, Father? So soft and beautiful."

He didn't answer. She looked at him. He seemed to have forgotten her as he stared into the face of the photograph. She touched his arm; he started, turned, and looked at her, a good long look.

"Yes, the eyes are lovely," he answered. "Shall we go in?"

She couldn't believe it when he led the way to the first floor, she had thought they would sit high up in the gallery or at best in the upper balcony, but the first floor! This was a night to remember.

The usher took them to two end seats in the seventh row. Father put his hat in the wire rack under his seat and helped her off with her coat.

She looked around. These must be the two-dollar seats! Father had really splurged; over four dollars when you counted the war tax. Lizzie Lou's frugal mind thought of all the things needed in the family which that four dollars could have bought; shoes for Jimmy and Peggy, a good payment on the grocery bill or coal bill; it would more than pay for her class ring, she had only a dollar toward that, so far. But this was a once-in-a-lifetime thing; she must enjoy it to the utmost to get the good out of Father's generosity.

She would look at the program as soon as she had her fill of this beautiful, wonderful theater. Lighted from above by a large, crystal chandelier, the bronze-painted pillars at each side of the stage shone like real gold, and gilt paint, decorating the three boxes on each side, made the place like a fairy-tale palace.

This was her first good look at a box. You couldn't see them well from the gallery. She wasn't sure she would like to sit there, even though there were comfortable chairs and lots of room. You couldn't get nearly the good view of the stage that you got from right here in the seventh row. These were the best seats in the house.

She looked at the painting on the asbestos curtain. She had been ten when she first saw that curtain with Mother. She had asked so many questions about the picture on it that they had gone to the library next day to find out about it. It was Dance of the Nymphs, painted by Corot.

She could almost hear music as she looked at it, the nymphs danced with such joyous abandon. The blending of the browns, pale greens, and silvery grays was so delicately lovely. She marveled that anyone could paint like that, her own ability in art was so small. She liked the shy nymph seated on the right, the one whose hand was being pulled by another, coaxing her to join in the dance. Lizzie Lou felt a great understanding for that shy one.

Father was reading his program. She looked at hers. The play was in three acts: I, the home of the J. Whittington Craigs of Philadelphia; II, apartment in New York City; III, Red Cross hut somewhere in France. She wondered what it was all about.

People were filling the red plush seats about them. She wished she had another pair of eyes, there was so much to see, ladies in silk dresses, large sparkling combs gleaming in their hair. Lizzie Lou hunched her middy-blouse shoulders back against her tweed coat and tried to be inconspicuous.

The people in the boxes didn't arrive until it was almost time for the show to begin. She wondered if they did that on purpose so that there would be lots of folks to see them arrive in their finery. All the boxes were filled now except the front one on the right. If the people for that one didn't hurry they would miss the beginning, for the members of the orchestra were entering the pit down in front from a tiny door under the stage.

The violinists began tuning their instruments and the pianist arranged sheets of music under a little green-shaded light fastened to the top of the piano. Lizzie Lou looked up at the curtain. What magic world did those nymphs hide? What would the first scene be like? She clasped and unclasped her hands on top of her hat and her throat felt tight with excited anticipation. This not knowing, this glow of expectation, this waiting for a concealed delight was one of the best moments of a stage play she decided. Moving pictures were going on when you went into a picture show and still going when you left, but a play, it was so special, a one-time thing played just for you with real people saying their lines for your particular enjoyment. And here she was about to see one of the best from New York City.

There was a movement in that front box on the right. Lizzie Lou looked up to see the people, a man, woman, and young girl. She looked again. The girl removing her coat was Bonnie Mason, her blond hair beautifully waved, and dressed in a light blue taffeta dress. Her arms gleamed white below short puffed sleeves.

Lizzie Lou fought back the feeling of envy and dislike that rose within her. She mustn't let Bonnie spoil this beautiful moment. After all one could enjoy a play just as well in a middy suit as in a taffeta dress.

The house lights dimmed and the orchestra struck the first note. The footlights came on and it seemed to Lizzie Lou that the nymphs on the curtain came alive in the brilliance and really swayed and danced to the rhythm of the music. Her heart beat faster and as the curtain began to rise slowly she clenched her hands and her mouth was dry.

The curtain up, Lizzie Lou felt as though she herself were right in the middle of the scene. The drawing room was an elegant room, as fine as Lizzie Lou had ever seen in a moving picture, long red velvet drapes at the windows, a grand piano, a green brocaded divan, several carved, high-backed chairs, and the walls looked like oak panels, really a grand place.

The Craigs must be awfully rich, but from the way the two beautifully gowned callers talked, she was sure she wasn't going to like them; they sounded so snobbish. But now they were speaking of Mrs. Craig's cousin, Kitty Kimble, who was visiting the Craigs. That must be the part Louise Leander was taking. So— the Craigs were trying to marry Kitty off to a rich friend of theirs, but it seemed Kitty wasn't interested in him at all.

Mrs. Craig came on the scene. What a beautiful black velvet dress and how deftly she managed that bit of a train sweeping down the back. The guests left and Mr. Craig appeared. He spoke of the war in France and how fortunate it was that Hastings Bradly, Kitty's rich suitor, had been able to avoid joining the army. So—thought Lizzie Lou—a slacker! She had known from the first that she wouldn't like him.

72

Now there was a figure in the archway at the center; Lizzie Lou caught her breath and the audience burst into applause at the entrance of the star, Louise Leander. How beautiful she was! Dressed in a flowing white chiffon dress, she was tall and stately, yet with a winning grace and charm that made everyone immediately feel in sympathy with the character she portrayed. But it was when she spoke that the real magic began for Lizzie Lou. Rich, low, vibrant tones, so full of meaning, so well spoken that every word could be heard to the last row of the gallery. What a voice it was; quick tears rose to Lizzie Lou's eyes, it was so moving. Lizzie Lou was too enraptured to notice that Father was clasping the arms of his seat so tightly that his knuckles were white with the strain.

The Craigs left Kitty alone to receive the rich Hastings Bradly. When he appeared, Lizzie Lou didn't like him any better than she had thought she would. She knew Kitty would refuse to marry him and she did. After he left Kitty removed his roses from a vase and threw them in a wastebasket. One rose she pulled apart, letting the petals fall one by one from her hands. How full of meaning she made that bit of business. And then the maid showed in Danny Drew, her real and only love. The audience burst into applause at the sight of Danny dressed in army uniform.

It was a moving love scene, sad and sweet. He was sailing the next day for France. He went to the piano and played the title song, "Till We Meet Again," singing the words in a baritone voice; then, clasping Kitty tenderly in his arms, he kissed her and was gone.

Kitty stood beside the piano, then sat down and played a few bars of Danny's song. She sang his words of farewell to her, her voice deep-toned, soft, and rich.

The curtain descended slowly.

Lizzie Lou blinked through her tears as the house lights came on. She fumbled for a handkerchief in her middy pocket, wiped her eyes, and blew her nose. Many ladies were doing the same. She looked at Father. He was pale and had closed his eyes. Touching his arm, she whispered, "Oh, Father, isn't she wonderful? The way she can make you feel that it is all real, it—it isn't like acting, it's as though she were really living this story. I didn't know an actress could be so good."

He looked at her, his dark eyes seemed a little misty too. "She is one of the best," he spoke low, then added, "She could always do that to people, make them feel what she felt."

Lizzie Lou frowned slightly, perplexed. "Why, Father, did you ever see her before?"

He nodded. "I'll tell you about it sometime, not now," and though he looked at his program, Lizzie Lou knew he was thinking of something else and only making a pretense of reading.

She settled back, reveling in the memory of the dramatic moments of the first act. She cast only a casual glance at the front box. Taffeta dresses seemed unimportant now and when she looked at the curtain she scarcely noticed Corot's nymphs.

The remaining two acts passed all too quickly. She knew she would never forget the last scene in the Red Cross recreation hut somewhere in France, with Kitty Kimble in a khaki Red Cross worker's uniform, helping entertain the soldier boys. And that beautiful moment, when, seated at the small piano, playing and singing the boys' favorites, she sadly complied with a request and sang "Till We Meet Again." While she sang, a soldier with eyes bandaged entered, holding the arm of another.

He stood still a moment, then stretched out his hands and felt his way haltingly to the piano. It was Danny, reported missing in action these many months. Kitty had been sure he was still alive, in spite of the Craigs' insistence that he was dead and their constant urging of her marriage to their friend. Now she had found him while doing her bit with the Red Cross and though he was blind she was going to marry him. The curtain came down amidst resounding applause.

Lizzie Lou clapped until her hands hurt. The curtain rose and two khaki-clad figures came forward and bowed. It was Kitty and Danny, the latter having removed the bandage from his eyes. He held up his hand for silence.

Louise Leander stepped nearer the footlights. "Thank you, friends, for your reception of our war play. I am sure we are all grateful that no more of our boys must be sacrificed in France.

Won't you show your gratitude and patriotism by subscribing generously to the current Red Cross drive. It needs your support to go over the top. Thank you."

There was more applause as the curtain hid them from view. The orchestra played a medley of war songs, the people stood up, pulled on coats, looked for lost gloves and dropped programs. Father helped Lizzie Lou on with her coat. A lady in the row behind was humming "Roses of Picardy" along with the orchestra. Father and Lizzie Lou stepped out into the crowded aisle. She remembered Bonnie and looked back, but the box was empty.

She sighed with regret that it was over. She wished it were earlier today, that she was preparing dinner, that she didn't know a thing about the play or that she could be coming into the theater this moment instead of going out.

It amazed her that the street outside the opera house was the same; she had difficulty getting back to reality. Snow came down as they stood under the marquee in front. She pulled her collar closer and looked up at Father. There was a look of indecision on his face as he turned north toward the streetcar station. Lizzie Lou felt sharp stings of snowflakes as the north wind blew them against her face.

They were almost to the corner of Jackson Street when Father stopped abruptly. Lizzie Lou looked up at him. The light from the corner street lamp was not enough for her to see his expression.

"What's the matter?"

"We're going back." He pulled her to the other side of the walk.

"Going back? Where?"

"To the theater." He was walking faster now with quick decisive steps. Lizzie Lou stretched her legs to keep up.

"Did you forget your gloves or scarf?"

"No. We are going around backstage."

Lizzie Lou gave a gasp of incredulity. Was Father serious?

"Whatever for?"

"To see if she will see us."

"You can't mean Louise Leander."

"Of course."

They were back in front of the theater now and Father increased his pace. Lizzie Lou slipped in the snow, clasped his arm tighter, and recovered her balance. At the corner they turned down toward the rear of the opera house. This street was dark save for a small red light hanging above the stage door.

"But, Father, do you know her? Miss Leander?"

"Yes, I knew her long ago. She may not want to see me though. Wouldn't blame her if she didn't."

Lizzie Lou felt this must be a dream. What a thrill to be going backstage into the very heart of the make-believe world she had lived in this evening.

Father opened the stage door boldly and they stepped in. Lizzie Lou felt as though someone had stuck a pin in her balloon of illusions. How horrid the theater looked back here, dirty, bleak, and ugly. Dark brick walls reached up as high as she could see, the floor was rough and splintery, furniture from the first act was stacked in a corner, scenery leaned against the far wall. How flimsy and counterfeit it looked at close range. Stagehands were

76

shouting back and forth as they took down the walls of the Red Cross hut. She almost wished she hadn't come, it made her hurt inside to see the world she had built for *Till We Meet Again* fall and crumble.

Father hesitated a moment, then penciled a few lines on a scrap of paper and handed it to a shirt-sleeved man passing by. "Mind giving this to Miss Leander? We're—we're—old friends," he said hesitating slightly.

"Sure, bud." He gave Warren Jones and his daughter an appraising look and disappeared down a stairway.

A brief wait and then Lizzie Lou saw a figure ascend the stairs and pause at the top, hand on the railing. Was that Louise Leander, that woman wearing a brown flannel bathrobe and with a white towel tied over her hair? The figure spotted them and approached slowly. It was only when she held out both hands and spoke, that Lizzie Lou was sure; there was no mistaking that voice. But what was it she was saying to Father?

"Oh, Waddy, Waddy, is it really you?"

Father took her hands, pulled her to him and hugged her, hugged Louise Leander, the actress!

Lizzie Lou's eyes grew wide in astonishment and her eyebrows arched so high that her beaver hat moved up a bit on her forehead. Was Father an old beau of this famous actress, or what?

"Yes, it's really me, Lou," he was saying. They seemed to forget that she was there. Louise Leander took Father's face in her hands and looked into his eyes.

"It's so good to see you, Waddy, so very good. You haven't changed much. I tried to find you once long ago when we showed in Fort Wayne, but you had moved away and I couldn't discover where. I suppose Liz and Margaret never forgave me."

"Margaret died five years ago." Speaking of Mother reminded him of Lizzie Lou. He turned and said, "This is our oldest daughter, Lizzie Lou."

The actress looked at her. How queer she looked at close range in all that make-up.

"Lizzie Lou," she repeated as she took Lizzie Lou's hands and looked into her eyes. "Why, honey, you're the image of your grandmother Jones with the same lovely dark eyes and expressive mouth." She turned back to Warren Jones. "Don't you think she looks like Mama's pictures as a girl?"

Lizzie Lou gasped. "But Miss Leander, how——"

"Not Miss Leander, darling, but your Aunt Lou." She let loose of Lizzie Lou's hand and spoke sadly. "I suppose you have never told her of me, Warren. No, of course not, Liz would not have approved. Does she live here in Medford too?"

"Yes, with us. She has looked after the children since Margaret died."

"Liz always did her duty. I suppose she can never forgive me and still blames me for——"

Father didn't answer, just rolled his hat around in his hands.

"I'm surprised that you were given my name too." She put her hand on Lizzie Lou's shoulder. "That must have been your doing, Warren. Come on down to my dressing room while I take off this make-up."

The little cubbyhole under the stage was not Lizzie Lou's idea of a star's dressing room at all. They sat on a trunk while the actress sat at a makeshift dressing table, a long unpainted shelf with a big mirror above. The talk went on between her and Father. Lizzie Lou, still numb, incredulous, and dazed at the revelation, could only listen and try to piece together the family drama which had taken place before she was born.

She watched the actress rub her face with cold cream. Somehow she hadn't thought a great actress would look like this off stage. She had imagined she would be dressed in a satin robe or bright kimono, but a brown bathrobe! Its color reminded her of that ugly dress of her own. She tried to tell herself that this was her aunt, Father's sister, but the idea was so outlandish, so foreign to everything in her prosaic life that this seemed but an extension of the make-believe world of the performance of *Till We Meet Again*. Sort of like Kitty Kimble finding Danny Drew in France.

As she listened she learned that Father hadn't seen his sister since she ran away from home eighteen years before and that members of the family had said that the deaths of Grandpa and Grandma Jones had been caused by their grief over the disappearance of their nineteen-year-old daughter. That meant that she was thirty-seven now, really old. In the play she had seemed no more than twenty, how did she do it?

Her face was wiped clean of the paint now and Lizzie Lou watched intently as she powdered it lightly and removed the towel from her hair. She turned toward them.

"There," she said. "Kitty is gone and I'm just plain Lou. Now tell me about your family, Warren. You said Lizzie Lou is your oldest?"

Father began telling about them, Peggy, Jimmy, and Lucy. About Mother's death and how Aunt Liz had taken care of them.

"But when did you leave Fort Wayne?"

"Shortly after Mother and Father died."

Lizzie Lou thought the woman in front of the dressing table bore little resemblance to the lovely Kitty Kimble; she looked old and tired as she listened to Father's account of their tragedy. She spoke so low that Lizzie Lou could scarcely hear.

"I suppose there was a scandal there at home when I left to go on the stage, then Papa and Mama passing away so suddenly. Oh, I've had a lot to live with all these years, Warren. But I had to do it. It was the only way. They would never have let me go if I had told them, you know that. Can you understand a little, Waddy?"

There was that funny name she was calling Father again.

"Yes, Lou, I think I can, especially after seeing your performance tonight. Yours is a special gift, a peculiar treasure, given to few. It would have been wrong to keep your talent from the people. Our ideas about the evils of stage life have moderated somewhat. I understand that many theatrical people lead quite normal, moral lives."

Louise Leander gave a soft laugh. "So normal and moral that I'm sure Liz would never believe it. Of course there are actors whose lives do not bear inspection, but as Jerry always says, there are lots of sinners in every profession, but those on the stage get more publicity."

"Jerry?" Father said questioningly.

She looked away and clasped her hands tightly in her lap. "Jerry is my husband, Jerome Logan. He was a reserve officer and went to France last spring." She paused. "I haven't heard from him for more than three months. I—I—well, all I can do is hope and pray and go on as usual. Jerry has been my manager and director for twelve years. It's not easy making this road tour without him. He always kept bothersome and unpleasant details from me. I'm tired and worn out and worried and anxious to get back to New York. But we have six more weeks of booking, a week in Indianapolis, four weeks at the Blackstone in Chicago, and a week of one-night stands. I hope I can hold out."

Father stood up and pulled out his watch. "We must go so you can get some rest. Forevermore, it's ten minutes to twelve. Guess that means we walk home, Lizzie Lou, we've missed the last car. Are you staying at the Indiana Hotel?"

"Yes. I must catch an eight o'clock train in the morning for Indianapolis." She rose and turned to Lizzie Lou. "Now that my face is clean I'm going to kiss you, honey," and she held her niece close and kissed her warmly.

Lizzie Lou looked into her aunt's face and smiled. How nice she smelled, like delicate sachet and the faint sweetness of violets. There were a few wrinkles about her eyes and mouth and her nose was far from perfect, but the dark eyes were just as beautiful as in the photograph. Her teeth were white and even and the feel of her cheek had been soft as satin.

"I wish I could get really acquainted with you, Lizzie Lou. How old are you?"

"Seventeen next Sunday."

"Seventeen. I was seventeen when I was in that first play at high school, remember, Warren?" He nodded. "I had forgotten anyone could be so young. But I expect you feel pretty grown-up."

"Sometimes," Lizzie Lou answered honestly. "I graduate next spring. I'm a senior."

"And then what?"

"Oh, maybe I'll take a six weeks' summer course at business school here in Medford and then work in an office. Aunt Liz thinks I should stay home and keep house so she'll be relieved of some of the responsibility of our family. But I—I don't know . . ." Lizzie Lou finished lamely.

80

Warren Jones looked guilty as his sister turned to him. "I'm afraid I haven't given much thought to Lizzie Lou's future. I've not been myself since Margaret died. Somehow I didn't realize she was so near graduation."

"For shame, Warren. You say Margaret has been gone five years? Isn't it about time you stopped living in the past and live for your children? Could you come down to Indianapolis next week so we could have more time to talk? We have so much to catch up on." She turned to her niece. "You know, Lizzie Lou, your father was the most wonderful brother a girl ever had. I've admired him ever since I can remember. When I learned to talk I couldn't say Warren, could only manage Waddy. Brother Will was too much older than I, eleven years, but Warren was five when I was born and he took me under his wing from the very beginning. Will thought me a nuisance, but Warren always had time and patience for a pesky little sister." She turned back to Father. "Could you come down to Indianapolis this week, Warren, and bring all the children?"

Lizzie Lou tried to add mentally how much money that would be for train fare; whatever it was, it was more than they could afford even if Father could get away from work.

He shook his head. "Impossible, Lou. You see I'm a bookkeeper at the Indiana Truck factory; I have to be on the job. I can't lose time with a family to feed, war prices being what they are."

"Of course. I didn't think. Maybe when I finish this tour I can come back for a visit. Do you suppose Liz would mind? I wouldn't want to cause any more unpleasantness in your family."

"Come whenever you can, Lou. I'll manage Liz."

Lizzie Lou watched Father embrace his sister. How queer for Father to know a great actress so well.

Near the door, Lizzie Lou turned and smiled. "Good-by," she said, hesitated, then added shyly, "Aunt Lou."

7. *Reflected Glory*

It was snowing Monday morning when Lizzie Lou started to school, but she scarcely was aware of the soft flakes fluttering about her. Her mind was a stage with scene after scene taking place in rapid succession; scenes not concocted in her fancy, but realities which had happened to her in the last few days. After all that had occurred since last Wednesday, school seemed remote.

She would never forget that walk home with Father from the theater. It was almost one o'clock when they arrived at their front door. How Father had talked that night, talked about his childhood, about Grandma and Grandpa Jones, and most of all about his little sister and the things they had done together. How they had coasted in winter, dug caves in summer, and waded in the creek; how he had read to her and how she would pretend to read to him, holding the book upside down, repeating the story with dramatic emphasis and rolling her big eyes up at him now and then to see if he were properly impressed with the cleverness of his little sister.

Lizzie Lou would never forget how Father had laughed as he told her about Aunt Lou as a little child. Then his voice sobered as he spoke of her love of poetry. He said when she was ten she would memorize long poems and then beg him to go to the barn to listen to her recite them. "Poetry that never made sense to me before would become clear and beautiful when she spoke the words," Father had said. "It was inevitable that she should go on the stage. She was born with the gift." His words flowed on and on as though they had broken through the dam of secrecy which had held them back all these years.

Lizzie Lou inferred that Aunt Liz had been the guiding force behind their leaving Fort Wayne in 1901. "We were all very upset by the publicity over Lou's disappearance, especially your mother's

83

sister, Liz," Father had gone on. "And when we heard that Lou had gone on the stage, Liz said Fort Wayne was no place to bring up a family because everyone knew about it. So we moved to Medford just before you were born. It was several years before I knew Lou had taken the stage name of Louise Leander. Then from time to time I would get a New York paper and look for her name, occasionally I would find it. Her first big success came in 1907 when she appeared as Roxane in *Cyrano de Bergerac*." Lizzie Lou had made a mental note to get that play at the library next time she went, she had never heard of it.

Aunt Liz had tried to curb her curiosity Friday morning at breakfast. Father had told Lizzie Lou they would say nothing of the play unless Aunt Liz spoke of it. It was as Father rose from the table to go to work that Aunt Liz could stand it no longer.

"Well, aren't you going to say something about the play you two saw last night? When I think of the things I could have done with the money you must have spent for the tickets, Warren, well, it's a sin that's all, a sin," she had grumbled.

Father's face had flushed. "We went backstage and talked to Lou," he had said.

Aunt Liz had looked briefly at Lizzie Lou. "So—you told her— told her about that——" She had stopped, for Father had put his hand on her arm.

"Yes, I told her about her aunt Lou and furthermore, Liz, it may be that Lou will visit us when she finishes this tour. She wants to get acquainted with her nieces and nephew," he had stated firmly.

Lizzie Lou hugged her Latin grammar tighter, took a little running step, and slid on a slick place on the sidewalk. It was good to have Father speak up to Aunt Liz, he had always been so meek before. What would happen if Aunt Lou did visit them? But of course she wouldn't. Lizzie Lou couldn't imagine a great actress like Louise Leander in their plain, ordinary home. She was probably used to living in fine places.

The snow was coming down faster now and she pulled her collar closer to keep the flakes from her neck. Yesterday's seventeenth birthday had seemed insignificant after all that had befallen her on Thanksgiving.

She saw Mary waiting for her at the next corner. They walked slowly as Lizzie Lou began to relate the fantastic events of last Thursday. Lizzie Lou could tell a good tale and, encouraged by her friend's openmouthed attention, she really let herself go on the details of the play, the enthusiastic description of Louise Leander's appearance, her expert acting, and Lizzie Lou's reverent account of her glorious, moving voice. But when she began telling the backstage part of the tale, Mary stopped walking, and looked up into Lizzie Lou's face, incredulous.

"Lizzie Lou, you're kidding me, aren't you? She couldn't really be your aunt!"

"No kidding, honest, Mary. I'm telling you the truth just as it happened. Then she asked us to go down in her dressing room." Lizzie Lou enjoyed Mary's astonishment.

They stood there, oblivious to the snow, oblivious to the passing high-school students, and to the passing time, while Lizzie Lou continued. "And I think she is going to visit us when she finishes touring with this play. Her husband is in France and she is pretty much broken up because she hasn't heard from him for so long."

"My gosh, a real actress in your house! Why it's almost like having Mary Pickford come to town," Mary exclaimed.

"But she is just a picture actress without a voice," Lizzie Lou answered quickly. "My aunt Lou is a real New York actress who speaks on a stage, speaks in the most divine voice I've ever heard," she went on with pride.

Most of the students had passed them now. As they slowly approached Franklin Street, someone came hurrying up behind them.

"Hey, don't you girls know it's late? Better get a move on." It was Bill Monroe.

They looked up and increased their pace. Bill fell in step with them.

"Kind of hard getting back to the old grind after vacation," he remarked.

Mary, walking in the middle, glanced at Lizzie Lou to see if

85

she was going to answer the senior class president, but Lizzie Lou was looking straight ahead, silent as a picture actress, so Mary replied, "Well, it's quite a come down for Lizzie Lou after all the excitement she had during vacation."

"Yes? What happened?"

Mary launched into an account of the performance at the Medford Opera House and of Lizzie Lou's adventure backstage. Lizzie Lou cast a shy look at Bill during Mary's recital. He certainly was interested. Mary's own excitement crept into her voice. By the time they reached the steps she had finished the narration.

"Golly, Lizzie Lou, that's some story!" Bill exclaimed. "You know what? I think you should write that up for the next issue of Medford High *News*. Captioned—Medford Student Visits Aunt Backstage—it would be hot stuff, really hot stuff!"

Lizzie Lou turned and smiled at him. His enthusiasm overcame her shyness. "I'll do it if you think anyone would be interested."

After she had spoken she felt exhilarated. She must try to speak out on impulse more often. Bill was so nice to her and she had to start fighting this shyness if she was ever going to grow up.

The three hurried up the steps and in the front door. The clock inside showed five minutes before the first bell. At the top of the stairs a noisy group chattered back and forth, pausing occasionally to listen to the central figure, Bonnie Mason.

Bill put his cap in his overcoat pocket as they reached the group.

"What's all the excitement?" Bill asked. "You sound like a lot of squawking chickens."

"Bonnie saw that stage play at the opera house last Thursday," Miriam answered, "and she's been telling us about that gorgeous Louise Leander."

Bill turned to Lizzie Lou and winked. "You should ask Lizzie Lou about her; she's her aunt."

Lizzie Lou would never forget the look that appeared on Bonnie's face, a look of disbelief, of irritation, of humiliation and rancor at being shorn of her glory in one fell swoop; for all the girls turned from her and plied Lizzie Lou with questions.

"Yes, it's true," she answered. "And she may visit us when she finishes this tour."

Mary tugged at her sleeve. "Hey, it's late. Come on."

Bill walked with them up to the second floor. "Don't forget that article about your aunt," he reminded Lizzie Lou as he left her at her locker. She stamped the melted snow from her rubbers before she took them off. She unlocked her locker. Who would ever believe that so much could happen to her since she had locked it last Wednesday?

All week the rosy cloud of Aunt Lou's glamour hovered about Lizzie Lou. Girls who never had payed her the slightest notice before would stop her in the halls and ask questions about her actress aunt. She found it exhilarating. Good, faithful Mary told everyone she met about Lizzie Lou's famous relative. Miss Tamer was very much interested and called Lizzie Lou back after class to talk about it.

"Miss Leander is one of the best performers I have ever seen," she told her. "You should be very proud to be her niece."

Lizzie Lou was proud and her pride began to show in various ways. She carried her head higher, stopped ducking it to avoid looking at those about her, in fact she found herself searching the faces of students and teachers and wondering if they knew that she was the niece of a well-known actress. It was intoxicating, all this unaccustomed attention.

She began to put on a few airs, snarled her hair underneath at the sides so that the ear puffs were larger, wore her gray beaver hat pulled down over her right eye at a jaunty angle, wore a red tie with her navy blue middy, a tie she had thought too conspicuous before, and she began carrying powder and a powder puff, so she could apply it to her face in the girls' room during lunch period.

If Aunt Liz had been aware of all this she would have told her that she was riding too high, that pride goeth before a fall, and all those other old adages she was so fond of quoting to take the wind out of one's sails. But Aunt Liz hadn't been herself since Father had announced that Aunt Lou was coming for a visit. She was silent and scarcely noticed the children. Lizzie Lou wondered if perhaps she weren't reliving the past, when she, Uncle Mat,

Mother, Aunt Lou, and Father had been young together in Fort Wayne, before Aunt Lou went on the stage.

On Friday after lunch Mary left Lizzie Lou to attend a meeting of the Latin Club officers. Mary was secretary of the organization. Lizzie Lou went to her locker, collected books for afternoon classes, and sauntered slowly down the hall to the girls' room to put on a little powder.

Inside she put her books on the floor and her pocketbook on the narrow shelf below the wall mirror. Beyond the swinging door she could hear girls washing their hands at the washbasins and yanking paper towels from the containers.

She took a large handkerchief from her purse, unfolded it carefully from about the powder puff, and, looking close into the mirror, applied the puff to her face. She patted each cheek and spread the powder around evenly. There, she thought with satisfaction, it really did hide the sallowness of her skin and helped cover the dark circles under her eyes. She caught up some straggling hairs, tucked them into the ear puffs, and pushed the hairpins more firmly in the back. The voices in the other room grew louder and more distinct as someone turned off the water faucet. Lizzie Lou put the folded handkerchief back in her purse and stooped to gather up her books from the floor.

"Well, I don't believe it. I think she made the whole thing up just to get attention, especially Bill's."

Lizzie Lou straightened and stared at herself in the mirror. That sounded like Bonnie.

"But she wouldn't dare. A lie like that would be sure to catch up with her."

"I don't think she has sense enough to know that. Remember how she stood holding that ball at the game like a ninny? You don't know how impossible this aunt stuff is; you didn't see the play. That goofy Jones girl couldn't possibly be any relation to that wonderful actress. The way she has put on airs since she gave us that aunt routine, looks as though she has kidded herself into believing it. And the powder she puts on! Her face looks like she's made up for the first act. Probably trying to live up to her pretended stage relative."

Tears made two streaks down the white face in the mirror. She grabbed her purse, put it on top of her books, and rushed out the door. Room 224 was empty; she sat at a desk, took a handkerchief from her middy pocket, and began rubbing her face vigorously, swallowing hard to keep the sobs back. That Bonnie! What made her like that? You would think anyone that pretty could be kinder. Lizzie Lou was sure that if it had been the other way around and she had been blessed with good looks she would have been nice to the Lizzie Lou in school. Or would she?

She stuck her handkerchief in her pocket, walked to the window, and looked out at the snow-covered landscape without really seeing it. If she had blond, curly hair, a pert, cute face, a nice name, and pretty clothes, maybe she would be conceited too. Look at what knowing about Aunt Lou had done to her. Bonnie was partially right, she had been putting on airs, trying to make herself think she was a somebody just because she had a talented aunt. After all she had nothing to do with Aunt Lou's successful career, hadn't even known she had an aunt Lou until last week. Why should she try to impress people with a reflected glory? But how she disliked that hateful Bonnie.

She sighed, pulled down her middy at the hips, and picked up her books. Almost time for the bell. She felt depressed, deflated, let down, as flat as a burst bubble. If Bonnie hadn't made all those nasty remarks—oh well, she might have known she couldn't keep on feeling important and on top of the world.

There was the bell; she must get down to 106 for French class. Maybe she would go to the library and get a good book this afternoon. There was nothing like losing yourself in a book to forget your troubles.

When she got home at four she found Aunt Liz in a stew. She said Father had come home at noon in great agitation. He had received a telephone call at the factory from a doctor in an Indianapolis hospital. Aunt Lou had been taken there, very ill of influenza. Father had packed a bag and had taken the afternoon train.

Lizzie Lou felt a pang of fear at that dread word—influenza. Many had died from it all over the country. It had been very bad in Medford last spring, so bad that schools, moving-picture shows, and all other gathering places had been closed for two weeks. Their family had been fortunate enough to escape it thus far.

"I can't see why he had to go down there. He'll expose himself, catch it, and bring it home here to the rest of us. But Warren doesn't have any sense where that sister of his is concerned. It isn't as though she isn't getting good care there in a hospital," Aunt Liz complained.

Lizzie Lou wondered what they would do about the play without Aunt Lou. Would the rest of the company stay there in Indianapolis until she got well? She was glad Father had gone, just in case the other actors had left town. It would seem so pitiful for Aunt Lou to be there in the hospital with no friends or relations to see after her.

Saturday morning the cleaning went on as usual, but the Saturday-afternoon picture show had to be forgone, since Father was not there to give the quarter for admission. Peggy wanted to ask Aunt Liz for it, but Lizzie Lou said they better not; Aunt Liz was in no mood to be asked for anything. She was cleaning her side of the house like a fury, slamming and banging the furniture about, sweeping, beating, shaking rugs like a violent whirlwind.

Instead, Lizzie Lou took the children to the library. Peggy, Jimmy, and Lucy went in the children's room while Lizzie Lou browsed through the adult shelves, taking down books here and there to sample and taste.

It was wonderful that anyone could have all this fun for free; never any admission required, just abide by the rules, get your books back on time, that was all. Lizzie Lou sighed; yesterday's pain was receding. Yes, she had been showing off, she admitted; it was not right to take credit for someone else's accomplishments, even if that someone was your aunt. But Bonnie had said she was goofy, a ninny, and that she had lied. That last hurt most of all. She would like to pull out some of that blond hair! She tried to think of something else. *Cyrano de Bergerac?* She went to the card catalogue. How would you spell it? She looked for all the various ways and found it at last under the one she thought most unlikely. It was by Edmond Rostand, in the 842's. In the stacks she ran her finger along the backs of the books and blew the dust from the tops; it must have been some time since Medford readers had taken any interest in Cyrano.

When she took the book to the charging desk, the librarian, Miss Gibson, raised her eyebrows as she stamped the book card. "Who aroused your interest in this play, Lizzie Lou, your French teacher?" Miss Gibson had known Lizzie Lou for years, had watched and encouraged her various interests.

Lizzie Lou started to tell about Aunt Lou, then thought better of it. No, she would not tell that story again, not even to Miss Gibson. "Just thought I would like to read it. What made you think my French teacher suggested it?"

"It's translated from the French of Edmond Rostand. You will like it, it's very dramatic. You haven't read many plays, have you?"

"No, just the Shakespeare we have studied. But I think I will from now on," Lizzie Lou stated decisively. When Father returned she would find out what other plays Aunt Lou had played in and would try to get them.

"Good. I've always loved reading plays. Be sure to tell me how you like Cyrano. He is one of my favorite characters, so ugly without and yet so beautiful within," the librarian said as she slipped Lizzie Lou's library card in the book pocket.

Lizzie Lou thanked her, took the book, and walked toward the children's room. She felt so comfortable and at ease with Miss Gibson, who had been librarian for years and knew all about everyone in Medford. Each year Lizzie Lou had new teachers to get used to, but Miss Gibson was always the same, a good friend to count on, offering help on tough school assignments, ready to suggest a book for leisure reading, and ready to chat about it when it was returned. If anyone would be interested in Aunt Lou, it would be Miss Gibson. Maybe, later on, she would tell her when no one else was around.

After the supper dishes were washed, Lucy and Jimmy bathed

and put to bed, Lizzie Lou and Peggy pulled chairs near the stove and read. Peggy was reading *Mary Ware in Texas,* one of the many *Little Colonel* books she fancied at the moment. Lizzie Lou remembered when she was in the *Little Colonel* and *Five Little Peppers* stage; if she remembered correctly Peggy would get to the *Texas Bluebonnet* series next and then probably all of Louisa May Alcott. It was fun seeing her own reading pattern repeated by Peg, fun to have these old friends brought into the house again.

It seemed queer not to have Father here with them. She began reading *Cyrano.* Unusual, she thought, having the first scene a theater, with the audience gathering for a performance. She pulled her feet up under her and lost herself in the printed pages.

At nine-thirty she sent Peggy to bed. At ten-thirty she was still reading. It was eleven before she got to bed. What was it Miss Gibson had said about Cyrano? "So ugly without and yet so beautiful within." Yes, he was, and kind of braggy too, but then he was so clever as a poet and so adept with his sword, he had plenty to brag about. It wouldn't be so bad being homely if you were as smart and talented as Cyrano. She wondered what he would have said to Bonnie if she had called him big nose or a ninny.

She pulled the covers up and thought of the way he could have told Bonnie off, but on second thought, would he? Bonnie was as pretty as Roxane and Cyrano was so chivalrous. There seemed to be a different set of rules for beautiful girls. It seemed queer that Roxane was so taken in by that dumbbell, Christian, but, of course, her not finding out was what made the play. If she ever got to talk with Aunt Lou again she would ask her about the costumes she wore as Roxane. They must have been beautiful. Guiltily she remembered that she hadn't read her Sunday-school lesson. Maybe she could look it over in the morning.

She said a prayer for Aunt Lou's recovery and went to sleep to dream that she was playing the part of Roxane but didn't know a line of the part. Cyrano kept getting angrier and angrier as she tried to improvise suitable lines in reply to his. At last he shook his sword under her nose and shouted, "Get off this stage, you goofy little ninny, and let Bonnie be Roxane; she not only knows the lines but also looks the part. Get out!" Lizzie Lou woke up with a start and turned over. What an awful dream!

It was after four o'clock on Sunday afternoon. Lizzie Lou had popped a dishpanful of popcorn and they were munching it in the living room when Father returned. He set down his bag and Aunt Liz turned on the light. There was a strained silence. Uncle Mat looked up at Father. "Well, Warren, what about Lou, how is she?"

Father stood with his back to the base-burner for a few moments and didn't answer. He took the bowl Lizzie Lou handed him and filled it from the dishpan on the table. Lizzie Lou pushed his chair closer to the stove; he sat down and began putting popcorn into his mouth slowly and methodically, his eyes on the glowing fire.

Uncle Mat hunched his chair nearer the table and refilled his bowl. They all waited, even little Lucy seated on the floor with her popcorn bowl on the funny paper in case she spilled any. Aunt Liz cleared her throat expectantly. Still Father said nothing, just went on eating popcorn.

Lizzie Lou broke the silence. "How is she, Father? Is she going to be all right?"

Father took his handkerchief from his pocket and wiped salt from his lips. "Well, she's been a mighty sick girl. You know what this influenza has been. But the doctor says she passed the worst part last Friday. It will take her a long while to recover entirely. The doctor says she should stay in the hospital for a couple more weeks at least."

"But what happened to the play, Father?" Lizzie Lou asked.

"Oh, that always goes on. Lou had an understudy who was able to step right into the part. The company has gone on to Chicago."

"Then she is in Indianapolis all alone. Didn't you hate to leave her, Father?"

Aunt Liz interrupted before Father could reply. "All alone, in a big city hospital? Don't be silly, Lizzie Lou. She's probably surrounded most of the time with doctors and nurses."

"I know, Aunt Liz, but they aren't friends or kinfolks."

Father gave Lizzie Lou a grateful look. "That's just what I

thought, Lizzie Lou. I hated like the dickens to leave her, but I have to be at work tomorrow. Before I left I made arrangements for her to come here when she can get out of the hospital, come here for the weeks and perhaps months of convalescing she will need."

Silence prevailed, broken only by the ticking of the clock on top of the piano. Uncle Mat stopped rocking, his hand poised in mid-air between his popcorn bowl and his mouth. Lizzie Lou stole a glance at Aunt Liz. Peggy reached down and retrieved a grain of popcorn from the floor. Jimmy tiptoed to the table to refill his bowl.

Aunt Liz's teeth clicked as she snapped her mouth shut. She stood up and walked toward the stove.

"You mean Lou Jones is coming here, coming here bringing all those influenza germs with her?"

Father looked up at his sister-in-law. "Now, Liz, you know she won't be contagious by that time and she isn't Lou Jones, she is Mrs. Jerome Logan."

"Well, I don't care what she calls herself, I'm not going to have a New York actress in my house. Lou Jones made her bed and she can just lie in it!"

Lizzie Lou gasped at her aunt's words.

Father rose, set his popcorn bowl on the table, wiped his hands on his handkerchief, and turned to the angry woman.

"I don't expect you to have her in *your* house, Liz. She is going to stay in *our* house. This place is a double, remember? Lou is my sister and we have been separated too long as it is. We have a spare room. It won't crowd us a bit and I want the children to get acquainted with their aunt Lou."

Aunt Liz bristled. "So—after I've raised them, respectable, you want her to come here and undermine my teaching with her stage ways."

Father drew himself up to his full height. Lizzie Lou had never seen him so striking in his bearing, his dark eyes seemed to flash with the sparks of his kindled anger. His voice, however, was controlled.

"Liz, never speak of Lou like that again. She is my sister and I love her. I hope I can make up partially the wrong we've done her all these years."

"The wrong we've done *her?*" Aunt Liz retorted scathingly with a toss of her head. "I guess you are forgetting, Warren, that your mother and father died of broken hearts because of that girl's willfulness."

"Liz! That will be all!"

Lizzie Lou was dumfounded at Father's tone.

Aunt Liz gave him a look of astonishment, then closed her mouth firmly and walked to the door.

"Come, Mathew," she called back. "Let's get back to *our* side of this double."

Uncle Mat looked from one to the other, his usually calm face troubled. "Liz, I'm afraid you've forgotten the Lou we used to know. I don't believe the stage could change her." Aunt Liz didn't answer. Uncle Mat sighed, took another handful of popcorn, and followed her.

Father relaxed and sat down. "I'm sorry, children, sorry that I lost my temper with your aunt. She is a fine woman and has been mighty good to us. I expect I'd better go over and apologize. Lizzie Lou, I imagine we should start making plans for fixing up that spare room for your aunt Lou."

"Yes, Father." Lizzie Lou pulled her own chair near him.

"I almost forgot," Father said. "Aunt Lou sent you this for your birthday. As sick as she was she made me find her pocketbook and get this envelope with your name on it."

Lizzie Lou opened the envelope. It contained a five-dollar bill, the most money Lizzie Lou had ever had at one time. She could finish paying for her class ring and still have some left over for Christmas shopping. That nice Aunt Lou!

8. *The Arrival*

Aunt Liz did the Jones's washing on Monday, but Lizzie Lou found the dried clothes piled on the kitchen table when she got home from school and no sign of Aunt Liz. Little Lucy came home from Aunt Liz's saying that Uncle Mat and Aunt Liz were going to have supper at their house tonight.

So—Aunt Liz was still huffy at Father. Well, she had better start supper herself. She sent Peggy to the grocery for bread, milk, and hamburger and began preparations for the evening meal.

When Father got home and found Lizzie Lou alone in the kitchen, he pried Peggy loose from her *Little Colonel* book and sent her out to help. As soon as he changed his clothes he joined them, put on an apron, and said he would like to mash the potatoes.

Peggy and Lizzie Lou stared at him standing there in his shirt sleeves, a checkered apron tied about his waist.

"Do you really mean it, Father?" Lizzie Lou asked hesitantly.

"Sure I do," and he laughed at their surprise. "I'll have you girls know I'm a good cook. All I need is a free hand in the kitchen." He took the potato masher from a drawer in the kitchen cabinet.

"But you never——" Lizzie Lou paused.

"No, I haven't been in the kitchen much since your mother died. I guess you've forgotten how I used to help her. Your aunt Liz has always said she didn't like a man messing around in the kitchen, so I have steered clear of the place. Now, where is the milk?"

"There in the pantry window sill to keep cool."

What fun it was getting supper with Father. Jimmy and Lucy joined them and begged to help too. At the table they decided the mashed potatoes were the best they had ever eaten. Father grinned at their praise, a shy boyish grin that Lizzie Lou had forgotten. As she watched him she was reminded of a long-ago time when they had gone on picnics at the city park and Father had played with them and swung their laughing mother in a swing. This was a Father little Lucy had never known and she was delighted. She clapped her hands, left her place at the table, crawled onto his lap, and ate her rice pudding seated on his knee. Lizzie Lou wondered what Aunt Liz would have said if she could have seen their unusual behavior. She hoped the sound of their supper-table gaiety didn't reach the other side of the house.

Peggy washed the dishes, Father dried, and Jimmy and Lucy put away. Lizzie Lou set up the ironing board and did part of the ironing.

"I wouldn't ever mind washing dishes if it was always this much fun," Peggy stated as she put the skillet in the dishwater. "It's when you're out here all by yourself that it's so awful."

Father laughed and put a fork he had been drying back in the dishpan. "Looks as though we need to be out here to check up on the quality of your work, Peg. That fork is still dirty."

About ten, Father locked the doors. Lizzie Lou gave a contented sigh and marked her place in *Cyrano*. What a good evening it had been, such a feeling of oneness of spirit in the family. It had revolved about Father, his interest in them, his jokes and good humor. What had happened to him? It wasn't just the absence of Aunt Liz, because she had been away before, when she had visited Uncle Mat's folks in Fort Wayne. Father hadn't been like this then.

He returned to the living room, folded the evening paper, and put it on the table. "Ready to go to bed?" He picked up her book. "Well, how are you coming along with *Cyrano?*"

"Almost finished. Roxane is at the army camp. She has just told Christian that she loves him for his mind and not because he is handsome. She doesn't know that it was ugly Cyrano who wrote those beautiful letters to her for Christian. You know, Father, this play really makes you stop and think. I wonder a little about some of those handsome moving-picture stars, wonder if they are as dumb as Christian. Some of them are just too good-looking to be real."

Father patted her arm. "Daughter, that's one of the smartest things I've heard you say in a long time. I shouldn't wonder if you aren't over the hump of that big hill, growing up. Thinking of *Cyrano* reminds me of the way I used to tease Lou about her nose and skinny legs. Oh, how her eyes would snap and she would say, 'You hush about my looks, Warren Jones. I may be homely outside, but inside I feel very beautiful and when I can make people understand that inside beauty, then I will be a great actress.' And how right she was. Did you ever see anyone as beautiful as she was in that play?"

"But, Father, she could never have been homely—why—why, she's lovely," Lizzie Lou protested.

"Her features are far from perfect, honey. Her nose is a trifle long, her mouth too big, and her cheekbones are too prominent, but when that spirit shines through her beautiful eyes, all else is forgotten." He put his arm around Lizzie Lou's shoulders and gave her a hug. "And you know, I think your eyes are very much like hers; your eyelashes are even longer."

Lizzie Lou put her head on his shoulder for a moment. If she could hold back time, if she could keep this sweet cloak of understanding about them, she would never feel afraid or shy again. With the assurance of Father's love she could face anyone and anything.

"Father, I hate to go to bed, hate to have this evening end. What's happened to you? You're—you're so different."

Warren Jones dropped his arm from her shoulders and looked slightly perplexed. "I don't know, Lizzie Lou. Maybe it was thinking about Lou, being worried about her, recalling our younger days. Yes, I guess that must be it, I quit thinking about myself and how unhappy I have been since your mother left us. And do you know, I haven't been so happy in ages, as I have tonight."

As the days went on Lizzie Lou wondered when the detached, quiet Father would return, but his good spirits continued. Several mornings he was up before she was and had breakfast started when she reached the kitchen. Aunt Liz kept to her own side of the house most of the time. She cared for Lucy during the day, but sent her home as soon as Lizzie Lou returned from school.

At school Lizzie Lou was careful to avoid all mention of her famous aunt. She would give no further cause for remarks about her bragging or trying to take credit for someone else's accomplishments. Mary was quite provoked at her because she refused to talk about Aunt Lou. Bonnie's little circle of followers ignored her again; evidently they thought Bonnie's premise true, that she had made the whole thing up. Lizzie Lou decided she could wait. Eventually they would discover that she had not lied.

Every morning as she walked to school she wondered if she would see Bill Monroe. The sound of footsteps behind her would make her heart beat fast, hoping each time it might be Bill, but it was not. She saw him pass in the halls and at senior meetings, but no words were exchanged.

She couldn't go to the next basketball game, so missed seeing their team beat Anderson. The students talked a lot about the Hartsville game in January, the first game to be played at the armory.

Lizzie Lou didn't waste a minute of her study periods these days, for she had more home responsibilities since Aunt Liz was letting them shift for themselves and there was little time left for studying at home. The senior rings arrived and she did her part in the bookkeeping involved in their distribution and collection of money still due.

One evening Father took them all up to the spare room. "We must get this place ready for your aunt," he said as he turned on the light. "In another week or so she should be able to leave the hospital."

The room had been closed for a long time. Lizzie Lou saw that the curtains were not only dirty but also worn in many places; the straw matting on the floor was threadbare, and the iron bedstead looked like a lonely scarecrow in the cold bleak room. The dresser had a crack in the mirror. She remembered when that had happened, a long time ago; before they had electric lights. Mother had set an oil lamp too close on a cold night and the mirror had cracked.

Father looked discouraged at the sight. "Oh my, I hadn't realized that this room was in such bad condition. I wonder . . ."

Lucy poked her finger through a hole in the curtain and Jimmy rubbed the protruding straw by the bed with his foot. Peggy gave a disgusted curl of her lip as she exclaimed, "Good night! This place looks awful. If I was a elegant actress like Aunt Lou you wouldn't catch me staying in a room like this. I'd go to a nice hotel."

"Well, you aren't 'a elegant actress' as you put it, Miss Smarty," Lizzie Lou retorted. "I'm sure Aunt Lou would rather be here with her folks than in a hotel any day. And I think we can fix this room up so it will be real nice," she stated with a conviction she was far from feeling. What could they do to such a place anyway?

"I'm glad you think so, Lizzie Lou," Father said in a relieved tone. "It does look sort of discouraging. What do you suggest?"

Lizzie Lou examined the curtains. "I'm afraid these won't hold together for another washing."

"I guess we'll have to buy new ones. What about this dresser?" Father ran his finger across the crack in the mirror.

"We can exchange dressers with the one in our room," Lizzie Lou decided. "We should have a rocking chair and maybe a little table or stand and some small rugs to cover the worn spots. And, Father, don't you think we should have some kind of stove in here? Since she has been so sick she won't be able to stand it in such a cold bedroom."

Father rubbed his chin thoughtfully, took a pencil and wrote on the back of an old envelope. "Hmmmm. We'll definitely have to buy new curtains and a small gas heater. That means there will be less money for Santa Claus. How about it, Lucy and Jimmy? Are you willing to have Santa bring fewer presents?"

Jimmy and Lucy had been impressed by Lizzie Lou's account of their famous aunt and the idea of her visiting them had excited them more than Lizzie Lou had guessed.

Lucy ran across the room and took a slide on the slippery matting. "Will Santa bring me maybe just a little present?" she asked as she turned and prepared to slide back.

"Yes, a little present," Father promised.

"But we'll get a big present," Jimmy put in. "We'll get Aunt

Lou. Not many kids will be getting a real live acting lady. Do you suppose she knows William S. Hart or Douglas Fairbanks?"

Father laughed. "She might. You never can tell about Aunt Lou."

Saturday night Lizzie Lou went with Father to buy the gas heater and material for curtains. They also did a little Christmas shopping, a small doll and hair ribbons for Lucy, hair ribbons and a copy of *Hans Brinker* for Peggy, and a game and a bag of marbles for Jimmy.

On Sunday afternoon Mrs. Cameron called. Father pulled up the best rocker and hung Mrs. Cameron's coat in the hall closet.

The lady looked about the room questioningly. "And Mrs. Wallace, is she well?"

"Oh yes," Lizzie Lou replied. "She, Aunt Liz, is on her side of the house today." Father re-entered the room.

"I'm glad to see you, Mrs. Cameron," he said as he sat down.

Lizzie Lou took scissors and a partially cutout paper doll from Lucy and cut around the face and head. Lucy's fingers couldn't manage the little twists and turns about the hair.

"I've been seeing lights in the Wallaces' kitchen at suppertime, this past week, Mr. Jones. I thought you folks all ate together." Mrs. Cameron looked at Father curiously.

Father glanced at Lizzie Lou and cleared his throat. "Yes, we usually do, but—well, Lizzie Lou is trying her hand at being a cook. I think every girl should learn to cook, don't you, Mrs. Cameron?"

"Oh, of course, Mr. Jones." It was plain she still was puzzled. "I'll tell you what really prompted me to come over though," she went on. "It was this article in the Indianapolis *Star*." Mrs. Cameron took a newspaper clipping from her purse. "It's all about that actress who played here at the opera house on Thanksgiving. Says she's in a hospital down there in Indianapolis with influenza. But it says, here at the end, that hospital authorities said she was going to the home of her brother, Warren Jones of Medford, when she was able to leave the hospital. Now there's some mistake isn't there? But how did they get your name in it?" She handed the clipping to Father.

"No, Mrs. Cameron, it is not a mistake," he said, looking at the paper. "Louise Leander is my sister and she is coming here to convalesce from her illness."

"Well, what do you know! A real actress in the neighborhood! My, my! It says that her husband's been missing in France for some time. That was the thing that interested me at first until I saw your name. The poor thing, sick down there in the hospital and worried to death about her husband. I expect Mrs. Wallace is real busy getting ready for her arrival."

"Mrs. Wallace has been quite busy with some chores of her own," Father answered stiffly. "But Lizzie Lou and the children are giving me a hand in preparing a room for Sister Lou."

"We got some curtain material, last night, Mrs. Cameron. I thought I could make them this next week. I wonder how much I should allow for shrinkage." Lizzie Lou didn't want to ask Aunt Liz and this was a good chance to get some advice.

"Let's see your material."

Mrs. Cameron examined it critically. "Now, Lizzie Lou, why don't you let me take this home and make those curtains myself? I'd love to do it."

Thus it was that Mrs. Cameron took the material for Aunt Lou's curtains. Before she left, Lizzie Lou led her to the spare room so she could get the exact measurements of the windows. They had changed the dressers and there was a rocker from Father's room. Father had found a small table in the attic and had painted it white. The gas heater would be delivered Tuesday. But the worn spots in the floor covering and the shabby bedspread stuck out like proverbial sore thumbs, Lizzie Lou thought, as she surveyed the place critically while Mrs. Cameron measured the windows.

The measuring finished, Mrs. Cameron stood at the door tapping the yardstick on the floor and looking around.

"Lizzie Lou, I have a couple of soft rugs stored away that just as well be used in this room. And I wonder if your aunt would like to have my rising-sun quilt for her bed. I've got so many quilts, I'll not live long enough to use them all. I'd like for your aunt to have it. It's yellow and white and would go nice with the curtains, since the material has those tiny yellow flowers on it."

"Oh, Mrs. Cameron, you are so good! I didn't know what we were going to do about those holes in the matting and that old raggedy bedspread. A yellow quilt will be lovely."

By Thursday the room was ready. In the evening they took Father up to show him the curtains Lizzie Lou had put up that afternoon. He lighted the gas heater to see if it worked properly. The copper piece at the back of the tiny stove gave a warm glow to the room. The curtains were crisp and fresh and the tiny yellow flowers looked well with the pale green vines on the wallpaper. Mrs. Cameron's two green rag rugs covered the holes in the straw-colored matting and her rising-sun quilt provided a homelike atmosphere, friendly and inviting, with its warmth of color in the yellow suns flashing across the width of the bed.

"Look, Father," Lizzie Lou pointed out. "Mrs. Cameron had enough curtain material left to make a narrow runner for the dresser and a small doily for the table."

"It looks nice. I think Lou will like it." Father put his hands in his pockets and walked about with satisfaction.

"Like it!" Peggy exclaimed, rubbing her hand over the quilt. "I think she will be crazy about it. I bet even Norma Talmadge would love it."

"Oh, Norma Talmadge—pooh!" Jimmy scoffed. "Who cares what she would like, her and her weepy stuff. Looky, Father—looky, this is Norma Talmadge." Jimmy put a hand to his flat little chest, heaved a big sigh, rolled his eyes wide, and pulled his face into lines of sorrow. The mimicry was surprisingly suggestive of the screen favorite. Peggy stamped her foot at such disparagement of her moving-picture idol.

"Jimmy, it looks as though you have a spark of your aunt Lou in you," Father laughed.

Lizzie Lou gave her brother's shoulders a friendly shake. "You little dickens. That did look like her. I didn't think you paid enough attention to her pictures to know how she looks."

Jimmy looked pleased with himself.

Friday was the last day of school before Christmas vacation.

There was a general assembly in the afternoon. Lizzie Lou leaned back in her seat and crossed her knees, watching the other students come into the auditorium. Next to her, Mary scribbled in a notebook, then pulled the Christmas edition of the Medford High *News* from between her books and scanned its pages.

"How come you didn't write that article about your aunt?"

Lizzie Lou frowned. "Nothing more was said about it after Bill Monroe mentioned it that day. After all, Mary, you don't go around bragging about your relatives all the time."

"I wonder why Bill didn't tell Jim Buell about it. He's the editor and makes the assignments."

Lizzie Lou had wondered too. It must be that Bonnie's disbelief in her story had reached Bill and he also doubted her veracity. The thought that Bill might believe she had lied was painful.

"When does she arrive at your house?"

"On the afternoon train, tomorrow."

The music teacher, with her ever ready pitch pipe, appeared on the stage, and the students responded to her inspiring direction with enthusiastic caroling.

Lizzie Lou began to feel Christmasy for the first time this year.

Preparations for Aunt Lou had left Lizzie Lou little time to get ready for Christmas. She hadn't even found time to make clothes for Lucy's new doll. Aunt Liz was letting them find out what it was like to get along without her helping hands. It was difficult to understand why Aunt Liz was so set against Aunt Lou because she was an actress. Being on the stage seemed wonderful to Lizzie Lou. Aunt Liz was just old-fashioned in her ideas, she decided.

When she got home from school the house was empty. She could see Peggy and Jimmy in the back yard trying to scoop up enough dirty snow to make a snow man. Be nice if some fresh snow came along before Christmas to make things pretty again. She could hear Lucy's voice talking to Aunt Liz on the other side of the house. She hung her wraps in the closet and went upstairs.

In the room she shared with her sisters, she took the small diary from her drawer and thumbed through it. She turned to the page she had read so often that its words were imprinted on her mind,

That Jones Girl—Ring Committee—Bill! She had written those words on November eighteenth. She remembered how excited and thrilled she had been, thinking that things were going to be different for her at school from then on. She had even felt more independent at home, as far as Aunt Liz was concerned.

How silly; as though she could change, just like that, from a homely, shy girl to the attractive, popular type, one that a boy like Bill Monroe would ever pay any attention to. That Jones girl, that Lizzie Lou Jones! What a name! What a failure! She couldn't dance, to speak of, she couldn't talk well. What could she do? She sat on the bed, held the diary in her hand, and stared at the wall.

She could cook, iron, sweep and dust, and sew a little. Aunt Liz had seen to all that, but such accomplishments didn't help a bit with boys; when Lizzie Lou tried to talk to them she couldn't say, "I can bake a good cake," or, "You should see how well I can iron my sisters' petticoats."

She stood up and stomped her foot! It made her angry at herself, angry at fate, angry at her upbringing that she felt so inadequate to meet life!

She looked in the mirror, straightened her shoulders, tossed her head defiantly, and began reciting a scene from *Macbeth*, the one concerned with Lady Macbeth's sleepwalking.

"'. . . Look, how she rubs her hands.'"

Lizzie Lou rubbed her hands together, then looked at them, repeating in dramatic tones.

"'Yet here's a spot. . . . Out, damned spot! out, I say! . . . Hell is murky!—Fie, my lord, fie! a soldier, and afeard? . . . Yet who would have thought the old man to have had so much blood in him. . . . Here's the smell of blood still: all the perfumes of Arabia will not sweeten this little hand. Oh, oh, oh!'"

Lizzie Lou's voice swelled with grief and horror at the foul deed of Lady Macbeth. She looked closer into the mirror and smiled with satisfaction. Delivering that speech made her feel better, probably because of those two hard-hitting strong words, which she spoke with such vehemence. She could say them without reproach; who could complain if she were quoting Shakespeare?

She puzzled over the paradox of her personality; she was able to express depth and feeling when she pretended she was another and yet felt only shy and inhibited when she was herself. Did Aunt Lou feel this wonderful sense of freedom when she was on the stage? Lizzie Lou wondered if she herself could act a part, really, on the stage. That she did not know, but one thing was certain, if she was ever going to amount to anything she must start pretending to be a surer Lizzie Lou. Perhaps if she pretended hard enough she might actually feel more self-assured.

She walked across the hall to the spare room and looked around. Everything was ready for tomorrow's arrival. On the table was Aunt Liz's treasured pottery bowl, tulip yellow in color and glazed to a soft satin finish. She must have put it there for she would not have trusted it to Lucy's little hands. Did that mean she was getting over her anger and that she was going to be nice to Aunt Lou?

Saturday morning, Father had left for work and Lizzie Lou was washing the breakfast dishes when she heard the connecting basement door open and steps on the stairs. Aunt Liz appeared in the kitchen, a covered kettle in her hands.

"Good morning, Aunt Liz." Lizzie Lou greeted her as though nothing had happened.

"Good morning." Aunt Liz looked about the kitchen critically as she set the kettle on the cabinet. "How are you getting along?"

"Pretty well. Of course I can't do things as well as you do, but I've tried." Lizzie Lou took the teakettle of boiling water from the stove and rinsed the dishes in the draining pan.

"I must say things look real clean," her aunt admitted, her eyes scanning the corners for possible dirt. "I bought a plump hen for you yesterday so's you can make chicken broth for—for Lou. Lucy tells me she's coming today. She'll need nourishing food after that influenza. How are you off for eggs? I'll bake a custard if you've got enough. She ought to have lots of eggs and milk to build her up."

Lizzie Lou smiled. "Oh, Aunt Liz, you are good. I wondered what I should fix for her."

"Well, don't think I approve of her coming here, not for one minute. But a body's got to help when there's sickness; it's just my Christian duty." Aunt Liz paused. "Who's going to meet her?"

"Father is getting off early so he can meet the afternoon train."

"If he comes home for lunch, you tell him Mat has arranged to be there too. He thought there might be suitcases to carry to the streetcar."

"Oh, Father says they will take a taxicab."

"A taxicab! Well, all I can say is, Warren is going to have a hard time making ends meet with all this added expense."

"It was nice of you, Aunt Liz, to put your yellow bowl in Aunt Lou's room."

The older woman looked a trifle sheepish. "Well, that table looked awfully bare and I thought it would look nice with that beautiful quilt of Mrs. Cameron's. Mighty kind of Mrs. Cameron to give you that and make the curtains. I'd have made them if you had asked me."

Aunt Liz cooked the chicken, made custard, and baked apples while Lizzie Lou cleaned the house with Peggy's spasmodic help. But early in the afternoon their aunt disappeared to her own quarters and did not reappear. When Lizzie Lou saw the taxi drive up outside, she wondered if Aunt Liz was watching behind the lace curtains of her front window.

Uncle Mat took two suitcases while Father helped Aunt Lou. Lizzie Lou watched at the front door, ready to open it as soon as they were on the porch. Peggy, Lucy, and Jimmy were at the living-room window to catch a first glimpse of their famous aunt. Lizzie Lou saw Mrs. Cameron's front window curtain fluttering, so she knew she was watching the arrival too.

Aunt Lou leaned heavily on Father's arm. How perfectly stunning she looked! Even in the play she hadn't looked this stylish. She wore a long black sealskin coat, a black velvet hat with a small black plume curled down over one side, her shoes were pointed-toed with high French heels. Her face looked pale under that lovely hat.

Lizzie Lou opened the door. Aunt Lou gave her a faint tired smile as she approached.

"Hello, Lizzie Lou. You see here only the remnant of your aunt, the scrap that the flu left of me."

"Oh, Aunt Lou, you look so tired. I expect you should get right to bed." Lizzie Lou opened the door wider. Uncle Mat took the luggage upstairs to the spare room.

"Yes, she's worn out," Father said as he helped his sister off with her coat in the hall. "Lizzie Lou, will you get her to bed at once?"

Peggy, Jimmy, and Lucy stood, round-eyed, in the doorway to the living room, staring at the strange woman. She managed to smile at them. "Hello there, you three young Joneses. You look as though you were seeing a ghost and I probably look like one. Wait till I've rested and we'll get acquainted. My goodness, Warren, how that child looks like her mother." Aunt Lou looked at Peggy's blond curls.

"Come on, Lou. Let me help you upstairs." Father took his sister's arm and ascended the stairs. Lizzie Lou followed.

At Aunt Lou's direction she opened a suitcase and took out a soft dainty nightgown and bed jacket. She helped unlace her aunt's high shoes, noting the black silk stockings. She hung her clothes in the closet, careful to get the black dress and its white lace collar arranged neatly on the hanger.

Aunt Lou let her head sink gratefully on the pillow as Lizzie Lou pulled the covers over her. Father had lit the gas and it was warm and comfortable now.

"What a sweet folksy room." Aunt Lou looked about. "It reminds me of a room I used to have at Grandma's place on the farm, that sloping ceiling and this lovely quilt. Oh, it's so nice to be out of that hospital and so good of you, Lizzie Lou, to have me."

"I'm glad you like it," Lizzie Lou said shyly. "It's not very fancy after what you've been used to."

Aunt Lou smiled and shook her head briefly. "Oh my, honey, if you could only see some of the rooms I've stayed in, in my time. This room is wonderful and this bed heavenly."

"Let me take the pins out of your hair and then I'll leave you to rest." Lizzie Lou removed the pins from the long dark hair and Aunt Lou sank back with a contented sigh.

"Thank you, darling. I feel as though I could sleep. Oh, this luscious bed."

Lizzie Lou tiptoed downstairs. It was hard to believe that she, that shy, homely Jones girl, had helped a real actress into bed. She hadn't minded talking to her at all; and Aunt Lou had called her darling! What a perfectly scrumptious day this was!

9. Christmas

Aunt Lou kept to her bed all day Sunday. In the afternoon Lizzie Lou unpacked the two suitcases and put the clothes away, admiring the beauty and quality of the materials as she did so. Aunt Lou's trunk would be delivered on Monday. What gorgeous things would probably be in that trunk. She hoped she could help unpack it too. Sunday evening when she took supper up to the patient, Aunt Lou said she was feeling so much better that probably she could come downstairs on Monday.

It was a good thing vacation had begun and Lizzie Lou was at home to attend to things, since Aunt Liz showed no sign of appearing. Aunt Lou said nothing of her absence. Wednesday was Christmas and there would be a lot of marketing to do and cooking too if Lizzie Lou was going to have a good dinner on Christmas Day. She must talk it over with Father.

She came down to get breakfast Monday and heard Aunt Liz's water faucet running for a long time. She must be doing the washing in her own kitchen this morning. Lizzie Lou was glad she was, for with all the other things she herself had to take care of there wouldn't be time to manage the laundry too.

As Father left for work he said, "Don't let your aunt Lou stay up too long today. That flu is not to be trifled with, she could easily have a relapse. She's awfully worried about her husband and that doesn't help any. She had me send our address and the number of Mrs. Cameron's phone to her agent in New York, so if any word comes she will know at once."

"What's an agent?"

"Oh, someone who takes care of her business; he sees to getting good parts for her and all that. She said she hadn't needed one until her husband, Jerry Logan, went to France."

It had begun to snow in the night and the flakes were still floating lazily down from gray skies. Jimmy and Lucy went out with their sleds as soon as they finished breakfast, Lucy gleeful at having her brother home to play with her. Peggy went upstairs, with unwilling steps, to make the beds. It was like pulling hens' teeth, Lizzie Lou thought, getting Peg to do housework. She dried the dishes, then sat at the kitchen table to make a grocery list. As soon as she finished she would see what Aunt Lou would like for breakfast.

Aunt Lou herself appeared in the doorway at that moment. She wore that same brown bathrobe she had worn in her dressing room at the theater and a red silk scarf tied about her head. She didn't look much like the famous Louise Leander, Lizzie Lou thought, just like Aunt Lou, sweet and friendly.

"Any coffee left, honey?"

"Oh, Aunt Lou, I was coming up to find out what you wanted for breakfast. You should have stayed in bed. Father said I was to see that you didn't overdo."

"Good old Waddy, always looking after little Lou." She smiled. "But I'd like to have breakfast right here in this kitchen, Lizzie Lou, if I won't be in your way. Oh, it's so good, so good, to be in a home with a family, *my* family!" Her voice filled the kitchen with its warmth. She sat down at the table.

Lizzie Lou poached an egg and, removing a stove lid, toasted bread on a fork over hot coals in the range. Aunt Lou watched her.

"You are a handy girl in the kitchen," she said admiringly. "It's been so long since I've done any cooking, I expect I'd have trouble even boiling an egg." She watched Lizzie Lou butter the toast and deftly scoop the poached egg from the boiling water with a large spoon and place it on the toast.

"That looks good. I'm really hungry. I take my coffee black."

Lizzie Lou nodded as she poured the steaming black liquid. "There now, what else would you like? Shall I toast another slice of bread for you?"

"This is fine. Sit down and talk to me. What's that you're writing?"

"I'm making a grocery list; there is a lot of marketing to do for Christmas dinner, you know."

"Let me see." Aunt Lou took the paper. Lizzie Lou looked at her beautiful hands. How her narrow gold wedding ring gleamed against the soft whiteness of the skin. "I don't see a turkey on here, Lizzie Lou."

"No, Father said get two chickens."

"Well, I hate to contradict Warren, but you get a big turkey. While I'm here the grocery bill is my responsibility. How do you order all these things; use your neighbor's telephone to call the store?"

"Oh no. I go to the grocery myself. The kids go with me to help carry. Aunt Liz says it's better to see what you're getting. I thought Jim could take his sled this morning since it will be a big load."

"I see." Aunt Lou sipped her coffee slowly. "Doesn't Liz ever come over on this side of the house?"

Lizzie Lou felt embarrassed. Somehow she couldn't come right out and say that Aunt Liz disapproved of Aunt Lou's being here. "Sometimes," she said, and then added, "She's washing this morning."

"I suppose she washes for all of you." Lizzie Lou nodded. Aunt Lou put her fork down on her empty plate. "While I'm here, Lizzie Lou, I want you to send everything to the laundry. I know it's extra work having me. There will be more bed linen to launder and I use lots of clean clothes myself. So next week you and I will count all the garments and bedclothes and have them ready when the laundry truck goes by."

Lizzie Lou felt a sense of relief, for Aunt Liz might grumble at doing Aunt Lou's washing.

"How long do you think it will take Liz to get over her annoyance at my being here and come to see me?"

Lizzie Lou blushed. So Aunt Lou did know how Aunt Liz felt. "I don't know," she answered honestly. "But, Aunt Lou, she is awfully good even if she is sort of severe."

Aunt Lou smiled understandingly. "Of course she is, honey. Don't forget I knew her too a long time ago. How I admired her. She was older than I and I used to despair because I knew I'd never be as beautiful as Liz Carpenter or have as many beaux."

Lizzie Lou looked astonished. "Aunt Liz beautiful? And, and—beaux?"

Aunt Lou laughed. "Oh, you youngsters! You think no one else was ever young, don't you? Yes, Liz was one of the best-looking girls in Fort Wayne, she and her younger sister, your mother, Maggie. Liz's hair was so dark and Mag's so golden and their dispositions sort of matched their complexions, Liz with lots of fire and your mother very gentle. We used to call them Tempest and Sunshine. But Liz's temper didn't seem to scare the boys. I remember Mat Wallace had lots of competition."

Lizzie Lou dropped down on a chair on the other side of the table. "It hardly seems possible. Aunt Liz doesn't seem to approve of—of—well of beaux and—and all that."

"She doesn't? Gives you a hard time, does she?" Aunt Lou grinned impishly. "I guess older people have as much difficulty remembering how they felt in their youth as young folks do in realizing that old folks were young and gay at one time. I suppose Liz has never told you that she was a wonderful dancer. She and Mat Wallace always took prizes for their waltzing."

"Aunt Liz dance! Why she—she doesn't even like me to play popular music on the piano, let alone dance. But I have danced a little with some of the girls at their homes," Lizzie Lou confessed.

Aunt Lou looked across the table into her niece's serious face. "You know, honey, I think I'm going to have to jog Liz's memory for her. Perhaps it's not my stage career that offends her so much as it is that I knew her when—knew her when she was young and very gay." She reached up and untied the scarf on her head. "Well, I believe I'll go up and comb my hair and then rest a little. I seem to tire quite easily."

She pulled the scarf off and Lizzie Lou gasped a little, for the front of Louise Leander's hair was done in many tight little round twists.

"Don't I look a sight in kid curlers? Only those who love the real me ever get to see me like this." She stuffed the scarf in the bathrobe pocket and her eyes grew misty. "Jerry used to say, 'No

114

one would ever pay to see you, Lou, if they once saw you in your curlers.' Oh, if I would only hear from him, I'd never complain again." She rose and grasped the back of the chair.

"I'm so sorry, Aunt Lou. Aunt Liz always says no news is good news."

"Yes, I suppose so. But it's hard to believe that when it's your own husband who is missing." She turned at the door and asked, "Are the downtown stores open evenings, tonight and tomorrow?"

"I think so."

"Well, I must have your father do a few errands for me downtown tonight."

After she left, Lizzie Lou sat at the kitchen table thinking about her. Unbelievable that this woman, who had been at their kitchen table in bathrobe and kid curlers, was the dramatic actress who could hold an audience spellbound with her acting and the magic of her voice. And she seemed to enjoy being here in their plain, ordinary house, a house so lacking in many conveniences possessed by those with more means. "Only those who love the real me ever get to see me like this," she had said. It was nice to have her speak like that. And Aunt Liz, beautiful and popular, and Uncle Mat, her eager suitor. It was a picture that even Lizzie Lou's lively imagination had trouble painting.

In the afternoon Lizzie Lou unwrapped the big turkey and put it in the kitchen sink. She set about pulling out the few pin feathers here and there and then washed it thoroughly. It was a big bird, eighteen or nineteen pounds. She must ask Aunt Liz about stuffing it, she wasn't exactly sure what you put in the stuffing. The turkey filled the big roaster. She opened the door to the cellar and carried the heavy pan downstairs. She put her burden on an old wooden table below and switched on the electric bulb that hung in the middle of the cellar room.

There was a cool, musty smell down here that was rather pleasant, for it was perfumed with the aroma from the apple basket. It was only when she walked into that far corner that her nose yelled, "Sauerkraut!" The smelly stuff was in a five-gallon crock, a plate on top weighted down with a heavy rock. Aunt Liz made delicious kraut. The canned-fruit shelves were further evidence of Aunt Liz's industry, filled with shelf after shelf of glass jars of peaches, cherries, tomatoes, green beans, corn, jellies, pickles, and preserves.

Lizzie Lou put the turkey in the coolest corner, where they kept their butter and milk in summer if they ran out of ice. There was a slight noise at the connecting door and Aunt Liz peered in.

"What are you doing?"

"Putting the turkey here in the cool corner."

"A turkey! Let me see."

Lizzie Lou removed the lid.

"Now whatever did you get such a big one for? It must have been very expensive."

Lizzie Lou looked at her aunt's iron-gray hair pulled back tightly into a severe knot on the back of her head, and tried to imagine it dark and surrounding a youthful face.

"Aunt Lou said she thought we ought to have a big one."

"Oh, she did, did she? You might know she'd have no consideration for anybody's grocery bill. Her and her extravagant ideas."

"But she did think of the grocery bill. Says she is going to pay it while she's here."

"She—she did?" Aunt Liz's indignant expression faded. She turned to the turkey and pinched the breastbone. "Not bad. You got a pretty good one, not too old. Shouldn't take long to roast."

"Will you tell me how to make the stuffing?"

"Of course. I'll bake the pies too. Where is she? Still in bed?"

"She was up for breakfast, but I took her lunch up to her. She still feels awfully tired."

"You keep her in bed, Lizzie Lou. She looked mighty thin and spindly when she came in Saturday. Does she eat well?"

"Pretty well. I think she could get over the flu, but it's grieving about her husband that keeps her from recovering as she should."

Aunt Liz nodded and as her face softened in sympathy Lizzie Lou could see traces of that beauty of which Aunt Lou had spoken.

After supper that evening, Father spent almost three quarters of an hour with Aunt Lou. He came into the living room afterward with his coat on, hat in hand.

"I'm going downtown," he told Lizzie Lou, "to do a few errands for Lou." His face had a warm glow of secrecy. Lizzie Lou wondered what the two of them had been plotting. Pleasant surprises she was sure, from the look of Father.

Next morning, Aunt Lou, propped up in bed, made clothes for Lucy's new doll, while Lizzie Lou unpacked the big wardrobe trunk standing in the center of the spare room. She felt a little giddy handling the finery of an actress. She looked at Aunt Lou propped up in bed, her hair in two braids, a shawl around her shoulders, and peering at a doll's tiny garments through spectacles. It was hard to believe that all this satin and velvet and linen belonged to her, she was so sociable and unpretentious. Lizzie Lou laughed and chatted with no self-consciousness at all. She held up an Alice-blue velvet dress.

"Oh, Aunt Lou, I'd love to see you in this."

Aunt Lou pulled off her glasses and looked at it. "All right, I'll wear it tomorrow, although it's a little dressy for Christmas Day

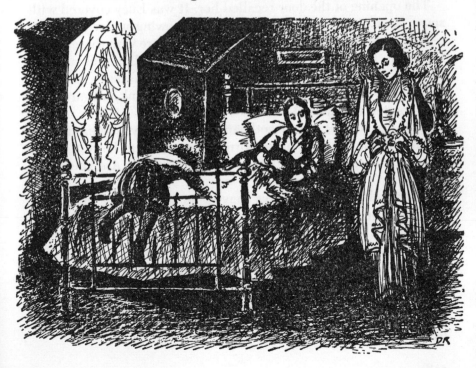

at home, but we'll forget what's proper and I'll dress up for you. I had that made for last year's play. It was quite effective in the second act. I wonder how the cast is doing in Chicago." She sighed and put her spectacles on again. "I always loved playing the Blackstone. I felt I could reach even the farthest row at that theater. Have you ever been to Chicago?" Lizzie Lou shook her head. "I'll take you some time and we'll do Marshall Field's together. I've never been able to decide which store I like better, Field's in Chicago or Lord and Taylor's in New York." Aunt Lou threaded her needle.

Lizzie Lou felt this must be one of those fanciful tales she often made up to put herself to sleep, tales full of gorgeous clothes and glamorous situations. With her arms full of lovely dresses, petticoats, and underthings and her ears filled with Aunt Lou's low, expressive voice, telling of plays, actors, and big cities, time stopped and she forgot that she was plain Lizzie Lou Jones with a family and household to care for.

The opening of the door recalled her. It was Lucy covered with snow. Aunt Lou hastily hid the doll and sewing under the quilt.

"Oh, Lucy, honey! You shouldn't come up here with those snowy things on. Here, let me wipe your nose." Lizzie Lou took a handkerchief from her apron pocket. Lucy blew vigorously, her eyes big above the handkerchief, taking in the open trunk and garments.

"I wanted to see Aunt Lou."

"You just look at me, sweetheart. Aren't I lazy, staying in bed so much? But you wait till tomorrow. I'm going to be rested so I can be downstairs and see what Santa brings you. Are you going to hang up your stocking?"

Lucy nodded. "Father says maybe he won't bring much this year because we had to buy that stove to keep it warm for you." She pointed to the flaming gas heater.

"Oh, Lucy!" Lizzie Lou exclaimed with a frown. Wouldn't you know that child would let the cat out of the bag?

Aunt Lou raised her eyebrows and took off her glasses. "Well, it's mighty sweet of you to get such a nice stove to keep me warm. But I wouldn't worry about Santa Claus, honey child. He's not likely to forget a good girl like you."

Lucy smiled at such reassurance and turned to her older sister. "I'm hungry, Lizzie Lou."

Lizzie Lou glanced at the clock on the dresser. "Oh, my goodness, it's twelve o'clock! Where did this morning go? I'll have to go fix lunch, Aunt Lou. I'll bring yours up and finish putting your clothes away this afternoon."

"All right. Lucy, why don't you take off your wraps and stay here and visit with me while Lizzie Lou gets lunch?"

Lizzie Lou helped her little sister get off her coat and rubbers and left her sitting on the foot of Aunt Lou's bed. She hoped the child wouldn't give away any more family secrets. But what if she did? Wasn't Aunt Lou family too?

On the stairs she gave a sigh of satisfaction at the sheer wonder of the turn her life was taking. Basketball, Armistice Day, and even Bill Monroe faded in importance before the brilliance and sweetness of Aunt Lou. She hoped Aunt Lou's husband was all right. She couldn't bear to have great sorrow come to so dear a person.

Only a faint gray light came through the bedroom window when Lizzie Lou opened her eyes Christmas morning. Lucy stood beside the bed shaking her shoulder.

"Merry Christmas, Lizzie Lou. Get up, get up, it's morning."

"Oh, you scalawag! It's so early. Get in here before you freeze." She pulled Lucy into the warm bed.

"But it's daylight, see? And listen, I hear Father shaking the stove, so he's up."

Lizzie Lou made a face at the child. "Poor man, I suppose Jimmy woke him up."

The door opened and that young man entered completely dressed. "Gosh, aren't you kids dressed yet? Hurry up. Father said I couldn't go down till the rest of you did."

About ten minutes later as Lizzie Lou and the others were at the top of the stairs, the door of the spare room opened and Aunt Lou appeared, her head wrapped in the red scarf, and a shawl clutched about her shoulders over the brown bathrobe.

"Merry Christmas! May I join you to see what Santa brought?"

"Oh, Aunt Lou, the house is awfully cold. It will be a little while before the living room will be really warm," Lizzie Lou warned her aunt.

"I pulled on some wool stockings and this shawl is very warm. I'll be all right and I'm as anxious as Lucy to see if Santa really got here."

In the living room the base-burner was doing its best to warm the atmosphere; tongues of blue flames darted up through the small black lumps of hard coal that Father had poured down from the top of the stove. The lighted chandelier showed evidence of Christmas magic to the children. There was no doubt that the room had been visited by some kind, thoughtful being and, be he fairy or human, he had, indeed, done well by the Joneses.

There was a Christmas tree, shimmering and sparkling in one corner, under it tissue-paper packages and objects too bulky for Santa to wrap. The stockings hanging on the wall back of the base-burner were full of interesting lumps.

After the first hush of discovery, pandemonium broke loose. Lucy jumped up and down in delight at sight of her doll, dressed in a full velvet skirt, satin blouse, and velvet jacket; Jimmy gleefully pushed his train along the strip of bare floor beyond the rug, and Peggy squealed for joy when she saw a silver mesh bag with her name on it.

Lizzie Lou was astonished at such a pile of presents. She had helped trim the tree last night, but Aunt Lou and Father must have brought all these gifts from a secret hiding place after she left for bed.

The children sat on the floor and read the names on the packages. Aunt Lou sat near the stove and watched them with happy eyes.

Peggy kept putting aside certain packages. "Why don't you open some, Lizzie Lou? These all have your name on them."

"For me?" Lizzie Lou knelt down and picked up a box tied with red ribbon. She untied the knot carefully to save the ribbon, opened the box and looked at the contents in wonder; two pairs of black silk stockings! She looked at her aunt.

"Aunt Lou, these are my first silk stockings! How did you know that I wanted them so much?"

Aunt Lou laughed gaily. "All girls love silk stockings, honey. Seeing you open them makes me remember the thrill of my own first pair."

The rest of Lizzie Lou's packages were as thrilling as the stockings, frivolous, luxurious, unnecessary gifts, things she had never expected to possess. There was a gold bracelet, gold beads, perfume, a manicure set, a silk taffeta petticoat, and a black purse of fine, soft, tooled leather. Receiving any one of these gifts would have been enough, but all of them, at one time!

She looked up at Father grinning down at her where she sat cross-legged on the floor. "Father, how did you ever do all this shopping in one night?"

He laughed. "It wasn't easy, but this sister of mine knew exactly what she wanted and made a very specific list. She suggested I take the list to the floorwalker at Saxon's department store. He went around with me, so I didn't waste any time. But I had to stop for a few items on the way home last night."

Peggy had put on her new red wool tam-o'-shanter, draped the matching scarf around her neck, the mesh bag hung on her arm, and, with one hand on a hip, she strutted back and forth in front of the stove. "How do I look, Aunt Lou, how do I look?"

"Perfectly elegant, Peggy. You'll probably grow up to be a fashion model. Pull your tam down on one side more. That's it, now hold up your head. That's the way." Aunt Lou laughed.

"Hey! Looky! Looky what's back here in the corner behind the piano," Jimmy yelled. Peggy and Lucy ran to see, Lizzie Lou put her gifts under the tree and got to her feet. It didn't seem possible that there could be another surprise.

"Why, it's a victrola!" Peggy exclaimed.

"You don't mean to tell me!" Father ejaculated in mock surprise, winking at his sister. "Santa really hid that present, didn't he? Here, I'll pull it out."

Lizzie Lou watched Father pull out a victrola in a tall shiny, mahogany cabinet. She helped him get it in position beside the front window. A black round record was already in place, he pushed a tiny lever and as the record started spinning he set the needle at the record's edge.

Jimmy and Lucy stood with their mouths open, Peggy's scarf hung over her arm. Aunt Lou's eyes sparkled at the sight of them, poised as they were on the edge of amazed anticipation. The music of Johann Strauss's "Blue Danube" filled the room.

Lizzie Lou walked to Aunt Lou, bent, kissed her cheek, and said softly in her ear, "Thank you, Aunt Lou." Aunt Lou took her hand and squeezed it. The sweet, gliding, rippling waltz played on. Lucy held her skirts at the sides and danced in the middle of the room with little, natural, childish movements. Lizzie Lou wished she could let loose and give vent to the joy she felt in such an uninhibited fashion.

The record finished; a voice from the dining-room doorway said, "Anybody ready for breakfast?" It was Aunt Liz, hands on hips, taking in the living-room scene, with its tree, gifts, scattered tissue paper, and victrola. She looked at the figure seated beside the stove and a look of disbelief at what she saw flashed across her face. Lizzie Lou suspected that Aunt Liz was thinking that the woman clutching a shawl over an ugly bathrobe couldn't be THE Louise Leander. Aunt Liz recovered from her surprise, gave a slight nod to Aunt Lou, and, disregarding the fact that she had ignored her coming until now, said, "Good morning, Lou. How are you feeling?"

Aunt Lou's eyes twinkled in merriment. She winked at Uncle Mat, who had come up behind his wife, and then began rocking slowly; holding her shawl close with one hand, she rubbed the arm of the chair with the other, pulled her features into lines of complaining wrinkles, and said in a cracked, old-lady voice, "Oh, jist tol'able, Liz, jist tol'able. My misery comes and it goes. But at my age I reckon I can't expect much else. Seems like a body's got jist so much pain to bear before he can shed this mortal coil."

Aunt Liz gasped and dropped her hands from her hips. Uncle Mat grinned, Lizzie Lou giggled, and Father smiled. Lucy clapped her hands.

"Oh, do it again, Aunt Lou, do it again! Make an old lady!"

Aunt Liz caught her breath. "Well, I never. You haven't changed a mite, Lou Jones. Always acting a fool."

Aunt Lou stood up. "Not changed a mite, Liz, not a mite. I smell bacon and coffee."

They went into the dining room, Lizzie Lou following Aunt Liz to the kitchen. "Aunt Liz, it was so good of you to get breakfast. I was so excited I forgot all about it."

"I don't wonder that you did. I never saw such an outlay of presents; and a victrola too. Did Lou do all of that?"

Lizzie Lou nodded as she pulled the big skillet to the front of the stove and began cracking eggs. She named all the gifts she had received. Aunt Liz shook her head. "Not a useful one in the lot. That's just like Lou, you needing practical clothes the worst way and she buys silk stockings and a taffeta petticoat."

Lizzie Lou started to defend Aunt Lou's gifts, but thought better of it. Aunt Liz probably wouldn't understand her delight in getting things she didn't actually need.

On their chairs each child found a package from Aunt Liz and Uncle Mat; dress material for each girl, shirt material for Jimmy. Peggy opened hers, it was a deep rose wool and would be lovely on blond Peggy. Lizzie Lou was almost afraid to open her own for fear it might be brown, but Aunt Liz had fooled her, it was a lovely blue.

"Oh, Aunt Liz, Alice blue! How did you know that I love this color? It's the color of your blue velvet, Aunt Lou. Oh, Aunt Liz how did you know?"

Aunt Liz smiled slightly, then pursed her lips. "Well, I'm not so backwoodsy, even if I haven't been to New York. I guess I know how stylish Alice blue is."

Lizzie Lou hesitated a moment, left her place and stood beside Aunt Liz's chair, then stooped and kissed that surprised lady on the cheek, whispering, "Thank you very much, Aunt Liz."

Aunt Liz's cheeks flushed. "Why, why, Lizzie Lou, what's got into you, kissing at the table! Good gracious!" But it was plain to see that she was pleased.

Lizzie Lou dropped a kiss on Uncle Mat's beaming face as she returned to her chair. Jimmy, Lucy, and Peggy followed her example, hugging Aunt Liz and Uncle Mat vigorously. Aunt Lou was right, Lizzie Lou thought, Aunt Liz was pretty, right at this minute anyway, with her cheeks rosy, her eyes soft, and a smile on her lips. Maybe what she needed was more affection from her family.

Still flustered from the unexpected kisses, Aunt Liz turned to Aunt Lou. "Give me your plate, Lou," she said in the tone she used with Jimmy and Lucy. "You must eat another egg. We've got to get some meat on those bones of yours."

Aunt Lou made her eyes round and her mouth innocent and trusting, like a child's, passed her plate, said in a small childish voice, "Yes, ma'am."

Peggy and Jimmy laughed. Lucy peered up in the actress's face. "Now you sound like a little girl, Aunt Lou. Do it again."

Uncle Mat and Father laughed and even Aunt Liz smiled as she took an egg from the platter and put it on the outstretched plate.

"Oh, Lou, you dunce. You don't act as old as Lucy." She put more bacon on the plate too.

Lizzie Lou looked around the table; they were all laughing, even sober Aunt Liz. What had happened to this family? Father jovial, talkative, and herself feeling free enough to go down there and kiss Aunt Liz before all the others.

What kind of magic was this that had entered their house this Christmas?

10. "Do You Fox-trot?"

Whenever Lizzie Lou thought of that gay, wonderful Christmas of 1918, she felt warm and elated right down to her toes. They hadn't had that much fun since before Mother died. Little Lucy had never known what a jolly, family Christmas could be like. The turkey had been perfect; there was white bread, and real butter, and plenty of sugar for the cranberry sauce. After the wartime restrictions imposed by Mr. Hoover and the limits of their own family purse, the bounteous dinner had seemed extra special.

Aunt Lou was lovely in the Alice-blue velvet; its princess lines made her look like a blue willow, slender and graceful. The cream-colored ruching around the neck and on the cuffs of the long tight sleeves matched the creaminess of her skin. She had piled her dark hair high in tiny puffs, as she had worn it in *Till We Meet Again*. Lizzie Lou found it difficult to connect this strikingly handsome Aunt Lou with the Aunt Lou of the brown bathrobe and kid curlers. But she had been just as much fun as she had been at the breakfast table, kidding Uncle Mat about his appetite, chiding Father because he didn't go to gym classes at the "Y" any more, complimenting Aunt Liz on her pies, and praising Lizzie Lou's roast turkey.

In the afternoon they had gathered in the living room to listen to the new victrola. There were Caruso, Galli-Curci, and Mc-Cormack records and popular music, too. Uncle Mat had liked especially "That Tumble-Down Shack in Athlone"; they had played it again and again. Peggy had done a few shuffling dance steps as she snapped her fingers to the "Ja-Da" record. Aunt Liz had looked disapproving and had said, "Margaret Jones, wherever did you learn such stuff?"

"Saw a girl dance like that at the vaudeville show Uncle Mat took me to."

Then Aunt Lou had put on "The Blue Danube" again and said, "Well, Liz—Mat, are you going to let that waltz go to waste, or have you forgotten the time you were crowned waltz queen and king at the Elks' carnival in Fort Wayne?"

Uncle Mat had grinned and then pulled protesting Aunt Liz to her feet, and before the astonished Jones children the two of them had waltzed about the living room. Lizzie Lou would never forget how lovely they looked, stately and graceful, gliding about as if the rippling music were a part of them, as though the notes flowed from their toes instead of from the flat black disc on the victrola.

Father had asked Aunt Lou, "Want to dance, Sis?"

"Don't believe I'm quite up to it yet, Warren," she had replied. "But why don't you ask Lizzie Lou?"

He had looked surprised. "But she doesn't dance."

"Don't be too sure. Ask her." Aunt Lou had winked at her. Then Father had held out his arms and Lizzie Lou had found herself waltzing too. Oh, what a good dancer Father was! So easy to follow.

"You dance beautifully, Daughter," Father had said as he whirled her about. "When did you learn?"

"Oh, from time to time with Mary," she had told him.

Aunt Liz and Uncle Mat had stopped dancing just to watch, as father and daughter ended with a big whirl, and a point of the toes. Aunt Lou led the applause at their performance.

"Bravo, Lizzie Lou!" Aunt Lou had cried. "Liz, that girl is going to be as good a waltzer as you are."

Aunt Liz had made a depreciative gesture. "Oh, Lou, I haven't waltzed for years; I'm awfully stiff and rusty."

"Liz, you and Mat should dance more," Aunt Lou had said. "Don't you belong to the Elks here in Medford, Mat?"

"Well, no, Lou. Somehow I never got around to it."

"You have lived here a long time; you two should have some fun." Aunt Lou had walked to the piano at that point, opened it, and run her fingers over the keys. "A little out of tune, Warren."

Then she had played and sung "My Belgian Rose," "Sometimes I Feel Like a Motherless Child," and last "Till We Meet Again."

Her fingers rested on the keys as she finished singing the last word and when she turned to them her eyes were full of tears. "If Jerry Logan had been here, this would be the happiest Christmas I have ever known. I'm awfully tired. Lizzie Lou, will you help me get to bed?"

Upstairs Lizzie Lou had hung away the blue velvet dress and put the gray shoes on shoe trees; then she pulled the rising-sun quilt over Aunt Lou's slender form.

"Honey, will you please get Jerry's picture from the dresser and put it here on the table. I like to have him near." She had closed her eyes a moment. "You waltz beautifully, Lizzie Lou. When I get stronger I'm going to teach you to fox-trot."

Yes, it had been a wonderful Christmas!

For the rest of the week Aunt Lou stayed in bed, worn out by the day's excitement. Father had Dr. Davis come in on Friday to see her.

Lizzie Lou took lunch up to the spare room after the doctor's departure. Aunt Lou was sitting up reading the letters that had arrived for her that morning. She took off her glasses as Lizzie Lou removed the napkin that covered the food.

"Ummmm. Looks good. What kind of soup?"

"Potato soup. My, you got lots of letters."

"Yes, every member of the cast wrote, bless their hearts. Jim Cassidy says Susan Barton is doing a good job in my Kitty Kimble part. But then I knew she would, she has true talent. My influenza is a real break for her. When she gets back to New York there will be any number of parts open to her after these reviews in the Chicago papers." Lizzie Lou put the tray on her aunt's lap. "Got time to visit with me while I eat?"

"Yes. The children and I have had our lunch." Lizzie Lou sat in the rocker. "What did Dr. Davis say about you?"

Aunt Lou tasted the soup and bit into a cracker. "He says I need a long rest. No more performances until I gain weight. Eat and sleep, sleep and eat was his prescription. He said I am to get up when I feel up to it but to go to bed the minute I feel the least bit fatigued. So, if you and the others can stand it, I guess you are stuck with me."

"Oh, Aunt Lou, we want you. Knowing you and having you in our house is one of the nicest things that ever happened to me." Lizzie Lou paused and looked out the window. "I can't explain it, but I can talk to you more easily than to anyone else. Aunt Liz is awfully good but she doesn't understand girls as you do. And until you came Father was so silent and standoffish all the time that I haven't felt at all free with him. I—I miss Mother more now, I think, than ever before."

"Of course you do." Aunt Lou finished the soup and started on the creamed turkey. "If I do understand girls, it may be because I have played so many different kinds. I'm a long way from girlhood myself, thirty-seven you know. I have tried to analyze each girl I have portrayed, tried to know how she feels inside. If you get the inside feel of a character right, the outside appearance and expressions will take care of themselves. I never worry about how I look if my inspiration seems natural for a part."

"But you never have to worry how you look, you are so beautiful."

Aunt Lou put down her fork and wiped her mouth with her napkin. "Me beautiful? Darling, I don't believe you've looked at this old face of mine. My nose is too big, cheekbones too prominent, and Jerry says no wonder critics compliment my voice, for it has such a fine big opening from which to pour forth. And, honey, when I was fifteen folks wondered what that Jones girl ever would amount to."

Lizzie Lou was startled. Aunt Lou's name *had been* Jones. "That Jones girl" had a familiar ring to it. She looked at the actress lying there under Mrs. Cameron's quilt. No, even when she looked at the long nose and the big mouth, Aunt Lou still didn't seem homely. Why was it? The expressive face, lighted by those large dark eyes, seemed the most beautiful she had ever seen.

"But speaking of girls," Aunt Lou went on, "I'm afraid my being here is spoiling your vacation, keeping your girl friends away and your beaux. You probably had to cancel some party dates on my account."

Lizzie Lou felt her face grow hot, she knew it was getting red. She got up and rearranged some magazines on the table. What would Aunt Lou think of her, seventeen, a senior who had never had a date?

"No, Aunt Lou, you aren't spoiling a thing. You're making this the most wonderful vacation I have ever had. I had no party dates, no dates at all," she added with a sigh.

Aunt Lou, sensing her embarrassment, changed the subject. "I received a letter from my agent, Andy Steiner. Ever hear of the new play, *Lightnin'* with Frank Bacon?" Lizzie Lou shook her head. "Well, it is a big hit. And success couldn't come to a nicer person than Frank. It seems his leading lady is leaving the cast in April and Andy says Frank wants me to take over the part. I'd love to do it, for the character is nearer my own age. Frankly I think a woman as close to forty as I am should give up girlish parts. But your Dr. Davis says I shouldn't return to the stage for six months, so I guess *Lightnin'* is out for me. Oh, well, if it lasts another six months, it might go on the road and I could do that. But it's awfully nice to have Frank Bacon want me."

"We want you too." Lizzie Lou took the empty soup bowl and plate from the tray as Aunt Lou started on the fruit jello. "You are wanted for an important part as sister and aunt in this family."

Aunt Lou put down the spoon and looked up. There were tears in her eyes. "Lizzie Lou, that's the best role I've ever been given. I won't have to act one bit to play it. And when I hear from my Jerry, this will be the happiest run of a play Louise Leander ever had."

Saturday afternoon Peggy took the two younger ones to the picture show. Aunt Lou urged Lizzie Lou to go too, said she would be fine, would read one of the new books Jim Cassidy had sent her. But Lizzie Lou said no, she wasn't keen on going, it was *Tarzan of the Apes* that Jimmy was set on seeing and she didn't think she would care for it.

While Aunt Lou took a nap, Lizzie Lou baked a cake. Even though Christmas Day had broken the ice between her two aunts, Aunt Liz still avoided the Jones's side of the house. Lizzie Lou found it exhilarating to work in the kitchen without supervision. If she made a mistake, there was no one to find fault, and making a mistake, she found, was a good way to learn what not to do. She had already learned how to avoid burning her hand on the tricky oven door and that too much milk in mashed potatoes kept them from standing up in fluffy white mounds. With Aunt Liz in the kitchen she didn't make mistakes, but she thought she didn't learn as much.

She wondered how she would manage when she had to go back to school on January sixth. Would Aunt Liz fix lunch for Peg and Jimmy when they came home from school and would she look after Lucy, or would she expect the Joneses to look after themselves? And how about Aunt Lou? Would Aunt Liz prepare her lunch? She would have to talk this problem over with Father.

The cake out of the oven, she left it on the kitchen table to cool. In the living room, she stood at the front window beside the victrola. She cranked it, put on the "Blue Danube" record, and turned the volume to "very soft." As the lovely music floated softly into the room, she looked up and whispered, "Why, I'd love to dance, Bill." She put her left hand on the shoulder of her imaginary dancing partner, her right into his left hand, and the two of them went gliding dreamily about the living room with only the glowing base-burner and Christmas tree looking on.

With her eyes half closed she fancied herself dressed in blue velvet, her hands soft and white, her feet dainty in high-heeled shoes, and her hair waved. The music stopped with a raspy sound of the needle on the record. Bill, the velvet dress, all vanished and she sighed as she turned off the machine. She knew exactly how Cinderella felt as she stood there in her gingham apron, heavy shoes, and her hair flat and straight. Only Cinderella was pretty, even in her rags, while she wouldn't be passable even if she were dressed in velvet. If she only looked like Aunt Lou, so poised, so lovely, so beautiful, instead of like herself.

Beauty was a strange thing, she thought. What was it anyway? Bonnie Mason was beautiful in a sort of picture-star way, dainty, well dressed, vivacious. And Mary Higgins was beautiful too, in a different way, when she looked up at you, with that sweet round face of hers, so believing, so interested in all you told her. Lizzie Lou sighed; if she could only be just a tiny bit beautiful she would be satisfied, but with a homely face and "tacky" clothes . . . Aunt Lou said as soon as she was able she would make up her new dress, maybe in an Alice-blue dress . . . No, it was too much to expect of a dress.

She gave herself a little mental shake. "Lizzie Lou Jones, quit feeling sorry for yourself and get out there and ice that cake," she said aloud. "You aren't the first homely, shy girl and not likely to be the last either. Bonnie Mason is right, you are a ninny!" The self-scolding made her feel better and she walked to the kitchen with firm steps.

The following Thursday, Aunt Lou came downstairs to breakfast. Her hair was combed neatly and she was dressed in a black tailored suit with a frilly white blouse.

"What time do the stores open downtown?" she asked at the table, after Father had left for work.

"At eight," Lizzie Lou answered, noting the sparkle of the diamond solitaire above Aunt Lou's wedding ring.

"Do you suppose you could go downtown with me to do some errands? I'm sure Peggy can wash the dishes while you get ready, can't you, honey?" She looked confidently at her curly-haired niece and smiled.

"Sure, Aunt Lou. I'll have lunch ready when you get home, too," Peggy replied brightly.

Lizzie Lou looked at her sister in astonishment. What sort of magic did Aunt Lou have that made Peggy agree to household chores willingly?

Aunt Lou said they would take a taxi downtown; she didn't believe she should stand out in the wind waiting for the streetcar. Lizzie Lou, aghast at such luxury, went to the Camerons to telephone for one. Mrs. Cameron was interested in hearing about the wonderful things that had happened at the Joneses since Aunt Lou's arrival. She said she wanted to call as soon as Aunt Lou felt able. Lizzie Lou told her how much Aunt Lou admired the quilt.

Seated in the taxi beside Aunt Lou in her black fur coat, Lizzie Lou wondered if Aunt Liz were watching them drive away and what she was thinking of such extravagance. Aunt Lou took a tiny notebook from her purse and glanced over her list of errands.

"Now where should we look for patterns, Lizzie Lou?"

"At Saxon's, I think. Aunt Liz always uses theirs."

"Take us to Saxon's department store, first, driver. And we'll want you to wait for us there. In fact I'd like for you to give us all your time this morning; wait for us at each place."

Lizzie Lou tried to figure what such taxi service would cost Aunt Lou, but having had so little experience with taxis, she gave up. At Saxon's, they sat at the pattern counter and looked through the fashion books. The pattern selected, Aunt Lou bought wide lace to make a bertha collar for the dress. It seemed so expensive that Lizzie Lou wondered if it wouldn't have been better to use that money to buy another dress, but she kept quiet. There was no doubt that Aunt Liz's frugality had rubbed off on her.

The next stop on Aunt Lou's list was the telephone office. "Next week," she explained, "you will be at school each day and I shall try my hand at running the household. I won't be up to doing the marketing in person, I'll need a telephone to order groceries. And then, too, if Andy should get any word from overseas about Jerry he could let me know at once instead of bothering Mrs. Cameron."

"But, Aunt Lou, Mrs. Cameron wouldn't mind. And—and we have never had a telephone."

Aunt Lou patted her arm. "Well, I think you'll enjoy having one all the more since you've never had its convenience."

Lizzie Lou was proud to be with Aunt Lou, she looked so distinguished, had such a nice way with the clerks in the store and the people at the telephone office. The man who filled out the telephone order in Father's name kept looking at Aunt Lou frequently. Lizzie Lou watched him and noticed his puzzled expression. At last he said to Aunt Lou, "You know, I have the strangest feeling that I have seen you before. Have I met you?"

"I'm afraid not," Aunt Lou answered, and as he turned to the form he was filling out she winked at Lizzie Lou. "Now how soon may we have the telephone?"

132

"Oh, at once, Mrs. Jones. Our man will be there tomorrow to install it." Aunt Lou rose, not correcting his assumption that she was Mrs. Warren Jones. In the hall Lizzie Lou laughed.

"Oh, Aunt Lou, he must have seen your play when it was here. Why didn't you tell him?"

The older woman shrugged. "Oh, it's nice to be a Jones once more. I used to get awfully tired of being Lou Jones when I was a girl, I felt it a handicap to have such an unromantic name. But being Louise Leander has had its difficulties too. Living up to what the public expects is awfully tough, Lizzie Lou, awfully tough."

Lizzie Lou opened the door of the building. "I don't like my name either," she confessed. "Are we going home now?"

"Just two more stops," Aunt Lou said as she got into the waiting taxi. "We want to go to the music store," she told the driver. "I want to get some victrola records."

At the music store the two of them sat inside a tiny booth to listen to the records they had selected at the counter.

"Now you decide which ones you want, Lizzie Lou," Aunt Lou said after they had played several. "We had better take 'Hindustan'; it's a good fox trot. I'll soon feel like dancing and we'll have you gliding around like Mrs. Vernon Castle in no time. What others would you like?"

"I like 'After You've Gone' and 'I'm Always Chasing Rainbows,'" Lizzie Lou answered, looking through the pile of records on the small table. "I wonder if there's a record of your song in the play, 'Till We Meet Again.'"

Aunt Lou smiled as she took a white linen handkerchief from her purse. "Why don't you go out and ask the girl at the counter?"

At the counter in the store the clerk looked up as Lizzie Lou approached. "Do you have a record of 'Till We Meet Again'?"

The clerk nodded and turned to the shelves behind her. "Yes, right here. The lyrics are sung by that actress who was here in the play recently." She looked at the label on the record. "Louise Leander is her name. It's been awfully popular here in Medford since the play. Did you see it?"

Lizzie Lou took the record and read the label. "Yes, I saw the play," she answered.

"Well, aren't you lucky. I heard she was gorgeous, simply gorgeous."

Lizzie Lou nodded. "Yes, she is, and a fine actress too."

Back in the booth she held out the record. "Aunt Lou, look here, you are right on this record." She told what the clerk had said. "May I tell her you are Louise Leander when we leave?"

"Oh no, honey. Let me be Mrs. Jerry Logan while I'm in Medford, at least as long as I can. Let that clerk think Louise Leander *is* gorgeous; no use spoiling her illusions."

Outside the music store Aunt Lou looked at her list. "Just one more place."

"Well, where to now, ma'am?" the taxi driver asked as his two passengers got in the back seat.

"To the Y.M.C.A.," Aunt Lou stated.

Lizzie Lou looked startled. "To the Y.M.C.A., Aunt Lou? Honest?"

"Of course. I want to buy a membership for your father. He needs to have some recreation. A gym class and swimming will be very good for him. He's getting round-shouldered and his color isn't good. Oh, honey, you should have seen him play baseball when we were young. He pitched for the Fort Wayne Bearcats and his pitching was really something. Some people thought he should be a professional."

"Father a baseball pitcher?" Lizzie Lou put the package of records on the seat beside her. What other startling revelations would Aunt Lou bring up? Aunt Liz and Uncle Mat prize-winning waltzers and now Father a baseball pitcher!

She felt strange and diffident as she followed her aunt through the Y.M.C.A. door. Somehow the "Y" had always seemed strictly masculine territory to her. At the far side of the lobby several boys were at tables playing ping-pong, and the cracking of billiard balls could be heard from the next room. A stairway descended at the back of the lobby and a sign read "To the Locker Room and Pool."

Aunt Lou walked to the counter and the man in charge stepped forward from his desk.

"I should like to purchase a membership for my brother," she told him.

Lizzie Lou saw the man give a start as he looked at Aunt Lou.

"Pardon me," he apologized, "but it is amazing the way you resemble that actress, Louise Leander, who was at the opera house in November. I saw the play and—why, even your voice sounds like hers. Are you a relative?"

Aunt Lou laughed and ignored the question. "I was at the play too. Perhaps I am a little like her. But I am Mrs. Jerry Logan and I want a full membership for my brother, Warren Jones."

Lizzie Lou watched the man as he filled out the blank for Father's membership. Every once in a while he would look up at the woman across the counter, shake his head, and murmur, "I have never seen two people resemble each other so much."

Aunt Lou would smile and nod as she answered the questions about Father. Lizzie Lou wanted to laugh right out. No one could play a scene like Aunt Lou and she was playing this one beautifully.

Lizzie Lou stood by the counter, facing the stairway, while Aunt Lou finished the transaction. There was a group of boys coming up. Lizzie Lou turned toward the counter; some of them might be from high school and she didn't want them to catch her looking at them.

The group passed by and she ventured a look at their backs as they sauntered toward the door. A flutter of embarrassment came over her as one of them turned and walked back toward her. It was Bill Monroe, his black hair slicked down from a recent swim, his basketball sweater open at the neck, and his cap in his hand.

"I thought that was you, Lizzie Lou," he said with a friendly grin. "What are you doing here at the 'Y'?"

"My aunt is getting a membership for my father," she answered.

Aunt Lou turned from the counter, putting the membership card and her change in her purse. She looked at Bill and then at Lizzie Lou.

"This is Bill Monroe, Aunt Lou," she said. "He is president of our senior class and is on our basketball team too," she added.

Aunt Lou smiled and offered her hand. "How do you do, Bill. I'm glad to meet a friend of Lizzie Lou's."

Bill took her hand and Lizzie Lou noticed that his face blushed slightly as he looked at stylishly dressed Aunt Lou. He gulped once and then stammered, "How—how do you do. Are you—are you the actress aunt Lizzie Lou told me about?"

"So—I am discovered!" Aunt Lou laughed. "I guess I'll have to plead guilty. I bet you've been swimming, Bill."

"Yes, I have, Miss Leander."

The man behind the counter gave a gasp. "I knew I couldn't mistake that voice," he said. "You were just wonderful in that play, Miss Leander, just wonderful."

Aunt Lou turned from Bill. "Well, thank you very much. I'm glad you liked the play." She turned back to Bill. "What position do you play on the team?"

"Center."

"Lizzie Lou, I hope you'll take me to a game sometime."

"I will, Aunt Lou. This month they are going to start playing in the big armory to accommodate larger crowds. Isn't that right, Bill? What's the date of the first game?"

"The twenty-fourth of January we play Hartsville."

They walked toward the door. "Could we drop you off anyplace, Bill? We have a taxi waiting," Aunt Lou said as Bill held the door open for them.

"No, thank you. I have to go across the street to the jewelry store to get my class ring. Had to have it made larger. Got the wrong size." He laughed. "Remember, Lizzie Lou, how I cautioned all the seniors to measure carefully for their ring sizes? And me, I just guessed at my size."

Lizzie Lou laughed. "I remember."

Aunt Lou put her hand on the taxi door. "We've been buying fox-trot records this morning. Do you fox-trot, Bill?"

Bill shook his head. "No, Miss Leander. I'm not much on a dance floor. I can two-step and waltz a little, but no fancy stuff."

"Well, you'll have to come over and have Lizzie Lou teach you," Aunt Lou said as she got into the back seat.

Lizzie Lou swallowed hard. What was Aunt Lou saying? She followed her into the car.

"Why, I'd like to," Bill answered as he closed the door. "Just tell me when, Lizzie Lou. Just tell me when."

Lizzie Lou managed to smile at him with what she hoped was a confident smile, but the pain in the pit of her stomach was one of utter misgiving.

"Oh, Aunt Lou, why did you say that? I can't fox-trot, and besides I don't know him well enough to invite him over, and besides that he wouldn't want to come to see me anyway." The words tumbled over one another as the car rolled away from the "Y."

"And why wouldn't he want to come to see a nice girl like you?" Aunt Lou wanted to know. "He seemed to know you well enough to call. And as for fox-trotting, you will pick it up quickly. You are graceful and have a beautiful sense of rhythm. I saw that when you waltzed with Warren. You can teach Bill, honey, don't fret yourself. As soon as I get all my strength back you must have some of your friends in for a dancing party. We'll roll the rugs back and you can have a gay time."

"But Aunt Lou——" Lizzie Lou began, then lapsed into silence. How could she tell Aunt Lou that she had so few friends, that she wasn't a party girl, that she was afraid and—— How handsome he looked, there in the "Y"! She teach *him* to fox-trot? Ridiculous!

11. *Beautiful Enough*

Back to school on January sixth and the teachers began piling on the work in preparation for semester examinations. Mary was full of questions about the Joneses' famous guest. When she could think of nothing more to ask she would say, "Well, just talk about her, Lizzie Lou, anything at all you can think of."

On Wednesday morning after senior meeting, Bill called to her as she started toward the door. "Lizzie Lou, wait a minute."

She paused and looked at Mary. "Did he mean me?"

"Of course. I'll go on. See you in English class."

Lizzie Lou felt panicky as Mary passed on with the other seniors. What did he want? What if he was going to say something about learning to fox-trot? What would she say? Aunt Lou had taught her a little last Saturday, but she didn't know enough to teach anyone else.

Bill picked up his books from the stand at the front of the room. Jim Buell was beside him. The two joined Lizzie Lou.

"I told Jim about meeting your aunt at the Y.M.C.A. last week, Lizzie Lou," Bill said as the three walked down the hall.

"Yeah, he did," Jim said. "How about you writing an article about her for the Medford High *News*, Lizzie Lou? You know, 'My Famous Aunt' or something like that."

Lizzie Lou looked straight ahead. It was a queer feeling walking down the hall between two prominent senior boys, president of the senior class and editor of the high-school paper. On ahead in the crowded hall she could see Bonnie Mason's blond head. What was it she had said? "I think she made the whole thing up just to get attention, especially Bill's."

"Well, how about it, Lizzie Lou?" Jim questioned her again.

Lizzie Lou took a deep breath, straightened her shoulders, and tossed her head in a way remarkably resembling Aunt Liz in moments of firm decision. "No, I can't write it. Aunt Lou is wonderful, but if I said so in an article it would seem that I was bragging."

"Aw, Lizzie Lou, no one could ever accuse *you* of bragging," Bill put in. "And besides your aunt is worth bragging about. Believe me, if she was related to me, I'd be telling the world."

"Sure, Lizzie Lou," Jim urged. "No one would say you were bragging."

Lizzie Lou saw Bonnie start down the stairs at the end of the hall. "Oh, wouldn't they?" She smiled to think how little these boys seemed to know about girls. She shook her head. "No, Jim. It's nice of you to ask me, but I won't do it."

"Well, O.K. How about me then? Do you suppose she would let me come over and interview her?"

"Why, I'll ask her." The three of them paused at the stairs.

"Hey, you know what?" Jim went on. "I work extra as a reporter on the Medford *Herald*. If I get a good interview, I'm going to show it to the editor. I bet he'd be glad to run it. Wonder if your aunt would have any pictures of herself. Say, come to think of it, it's strange that the *Herald* hasn't had a reporter out to see her before this."

"Only a few people know that she is here."

Jim took a pencil from his pocket. "Listen. Suppose you ask her when you get home. Ask her when I can come. I'll call you about five to find out what she says. What's your telephone number?" He held his notebook open to write down the information.

Lizzie Lou looked at Jim and a little smile flicked across her usually sober face. It seemed so strange that a boy should be asking for her telephone number; this time last week she wouldn't have had one to give him. Good thing she had memorized it. She repeated it to Jim, noting that Bill wrote something on the flyleaf of his geometry at the same time. Her eyes met his as he put his pencil back in his pocket. He grinned and she smiled back. Surely Bill wasn't writing down her telephone number too! This was a day! A real honest to goodness red-letter day!

Jim Buell interviewed Aunt Lou on Friday. He and Bill

walked home with Lizzie Lou after school. She was surprised how easy it was to talk to them. If she had thought about it beforehand, she would have been scared, wondering what she would say. It happened so naturally and casually; the boys kept the conversation going on school matters and she found herself so interested that she talked without embarrassment. When Bill brought up the subject of the senior play, she told of having read recently *Cyrano de Bergerac*. Jim knew of the play, but Bill had not heard of it.

No one would have been more surprised than Lizzie Lou Jones had she watched herself animatedly telling Bill Monroe and Jim Buell about the homely, brilliant, clever, swashbuckling Cyrano. Her enthusiasm for the character and the play crept into her voice and a flush into her cheeks as she described the plot. The boys were impressed not just by the play but also by the hidden Lizzie Lou revealed in this moment of unself-consciousness.

Bill glanced her way from time to time during the narration and he wasn't looking at the old made-over coat or the gray beaver hat, but at the sparkle in her eyes and the smile on her face as she tried to make them see Roxane, Christian, and the poetic Cyrano.

"Gosh, Lizzie Lou, you ought to be in the senior play. You're going to try out, aren't you?" Jim asked as she described the last scene.

Lizzie Lou gave a start. What had happened to her? She had been talking for the last three blocks, talking to Jim and Bill as though she were a Bonnie Mason. She felt her face get hot. What would they think of her?

"Oh no," she answered Jim. "I'm no actress even if I am related to one. I'd be scared to death on the stage."

Bill shifted his books to his other arm and grinned. "Like fun you would. Just now, as you were telling about that play, you forgot Jim and I were here. As soon as the committee chooses the play I'm going to have you read it and tell the story of it to the seniors. You really must try out for a part. I'd have put you on the senior play committee if I had known what a flare you have for the dramatic."

Lizzie Lou gave a self-conscious laugh. "Oh, I haven't really,

141

honest. I don't know what got into me, just got carried away by the tale of Cyrano, I guess."

In front of her home the three paused and Lizzie Lou wondered if she should ask Bill in too. Bill looked up at the house.

"So—this is where you live. Well, I'm going on down to the 'Y.' Hope you get a good interview, Jim. So long, Lizzie Lou. Don't forget now, you try out for the play." He touched his cap politely and continued down the street.

Aunt Lou looked lovely in a dark green dress, with a soft lace frill around the neck. Lizzie Lou was surprised to notice that the always-sure-of-himself Jim Buell seemed to lose his quick tongue in the presence of Louise Leander. But in a few minutes Aunt Lou had put him entirely at ease and the two were chatting like old friends, Jim taking notes on Aunt Lou's answers to his questions. Lizzie Lou excused herself, thinking it would be better to leave them alone.

Up in her room she looked in her mirror to see if she had changed any. Surely she wouldn't see the same homely face she had been looking at all these years. But there it was, just the same, the same dark circles under her big, funny eyes, the same colorless complexion, the same big mouth, and yet—— Slowly she spread her mouth into a smile. Did that help or did it only make her mouth look bigger?

How had she looked to Bill and Jim when she forgot herself this afternoon? Probably awful—and yet they both thought she should try out for the senior play. If they had thought her so homely would they have said that? Actresses had to be beautiful like Aunt Lou. She sighed and turned away from the mirror.

She took the calendar diary from her drawer and wrote under the date, January tenth—Bill—Jim—Cyrano—Aunt Lou.

Father was not home to supper. He had gone to his five forty-five gym class at the "Y" and Aunt Lou had suggested that he have supper with some of the other men in the class who always ate downtown after class. "You need to get out more, Warren," she had told him.

Now that Aunt Lou was managing the house there was a schedule posted on the kitchen wall showing the assignment of household chores. It was Peggy's turn to wash the dishes. It was queer the way Peggy would do things for Aunt Lou without grumbling. Aunt Lou certainly had a way about her.

·Father got home just as the younger children were going to bed. He seemed to have enjoyed his evening out, said he felt fine after the exercise and had enjoyed getting to know some of the men in the class. He thought he'd go over to the "Y" Saturday noon; some of the men played volleyball then. He'd like to learn that game.

Aunt Lou went to her room early; she still tired easily and had to rest frequently during the day. When Lizzie Lou went upstairs about an hour later she saw a light under the spare-room door. She paused a moment then tapped softly and went in at her aunt's invitation.

Aunt Lou was propped up in bed, her head wrapped in a scarf, a kid curler sticking out at one side; she wore a green sweater backward for warmth across her chest and arms. She put down her book and took off her spectacles.

"Come in, honey, and sit down." She rubbed her eyes. "I've been reading too long. My eyes hurt a bit. Get your Latin done?"

"Yes. What are you reading?"

"One of these new books Jim Cassidy sent, Tarkington's *Magnificent Ambersons*. Very good. Quite different from his *Seventeen*, which came out a couple of years ago. Have you read that?"

"Yes, but I didn't care for it very much."

Aunt Lou raised her eyebrows. "You didn't? I wonder why. I thought it quite funny. The play was done last winter with Ruth Gordon and Gregory Kelly."

"I didn't know there was a play. I didn't like the way the author kept poking fun at Willie. I felt so sorry for him, no one seemed to understand him, but somehow I felt I did." Lizzie Lou pulled the rocker beside Aunt Lou's bed and sat down.

Aunt Lou looked thoughtfully at her seventeen-year-old niece. "Yes, I expect you did."

Lizzie Lou took a book from the table. "What's this?"

"That's Willa Cather's new one, *My Ántonia*. Why don't you

read a little of it to me so we can get the flavor. She writes well. Do you like to read aloud?"

Lizzie Lou glanced at the chapter headings. "Yes, I do. I've read quite a lot to Peggy and Jimmy. Peggy has sort of taken over reading to Lucy. And you know, Aunt Lou, what I love to do?" She looked across at her aunt. "I love to tell moving pictures. You know, describe the scenes and give the conversation as I imagine it. I seem to live in the tale while I tell it to Mary or Peggy. It's a wonderful feeling." She paused. That must have been what happened to her today when she was telling Jim and Bill about Cyrano. Queer the way telling that tale had made her forget herself.

Aunt Lou reached out and patted her hand. "You have a fine imagination, Lizzie Lou. Read some to me and let's see what Willa Cather's imagination has done for *My Ántonia*."

Lizzie Lou settled back in the chair, rocked slightly, and began to read. The blue gas flame in the little heater sent out a pleasant warmth, Aunt Lou's ivory clock ticked quietly, and Lizzie Lou's voice rose and fell in the soft cadence of her appreciative understanding.

The story, as told by Jim Burden, had an easy, flowing style, and Lizzie Lou liked the feel of the words on her tongue, words that painted, with quick sure strokes, the picture of early days in Nebraska and most distinctly of all, the firm, strong, vital picture of Ántonia Shimerda, Bohemian immigrant girl. Lizzie Lou lost herself and lived with the characters.

Aunt Lou listened and watched the animated face of the girl in the rocking chair. She smiled appreciatively when Lizzie Lou gave special characterization and emphasis to conversational portions. After a time Lizzie Lou paused, put her head against the back of the chair and closed her eyes.

"Getting tired?" Aunt Lou asked.

Lizzie Lou opened her eyes. "No, just letting that last description soak in. Isn't it lovely, the way Willa Cather says things? Makes you see and feel?"

Aunt Lou nodded. "Did anyone ever tell you, honey, that you have a lovely speaking voice and that you read beautifully?"

144

Lizzie Lou's eyes widened. "Me? Oh, Aunt Lou, do you think so?"

"I do indeed. You have a real flare for dramatic emphasis and tone quality. Who taught you to read like that?"

"No one. It happens without my thinking. I'm sorry, but it is the only way I can read. I feel the story and—and it happens," Lizzie Lou finished lamely.

Aunt Lou laughed. "Well, don't apologize. It's a gift for which you should be grateful. Have you ever been in any plays at school?"

"Not very many, a few in grade school. But the teachers never gave me much to say. The prettier girls got the leading parts, the princesses, fairy queens, and the like."

Aunt Lou laughed again. "Sounds like some of my own little-girl experiences. I used to get so mad playing second fiddle to the pretty girls and I vowed that someday I'd show them all, show them the beauty I felt inside, the beauty that burned in me clear down to my finger tips. Sometimes, now, I feel grateful that my face was not perfect. If it had been I might not have worked so hard, and success in the arts comes to very few without years of painful labor."

"But, Aunt Lou," Lizzie Lou protested. "You could never have been homely. You're—you're so lovely. I'll never forget the beautiful picture you made in that white dress holding those red roses in the play."

"Just good theater, darling, just good theater. But getting back to you, don't they have any plays in high school?"

Lizzie Lou told of the senior play to be presented in April. After a moment's hesitancy she told of her walk home that afternoon with the two boys. She spoke of having read the play *Cyrano* because Father had said it had been Aunt Lou's first big success and how she had been carried away by the tale as she described it to Jim and Bill and that they had urged her to try out for the senior play.

"Do you really think I should, Aunt Lou? Do you think I *could* do a part?" She looked anxiously into her aunt's face.

"Of course you could, honey. With that lovely expressive face of yours, your beautifully modulated voice and your slender figure, you can do it with grace and charm."

145

Lizzie Lou put *My Ántonia* on the table and leaned toward the bed. "Aunt Lou, you can say the nicest things. And even though I know they aren't true, I begin to feel beautiful and all the other things you say."

"Who's to say what beauty really is? I think you have seen too many moving-picture stars who are only photographed in the most flattering angles and whose voices are never heard. Many of them, so publicized for beauty, wouldn't get far if they had to speak and let the public hear their voices. I think I have never seen women more beautiful than Sarah Bernhardt or Eleonora Duse; the Divine Sarah with her sweeping, conventional type of acting and Duse with her more subtle, natural approach. And yet if you study photographs of these two greats, neither would be considered a beauty in the usual sense." Aunt Lou picked up her glasses and put them in their case.

Lizzie Lou sat on the foot of the bed. "Have you really seen Sarah Bernhardt and Eleonora Duse?"

"Yes, Duse in Ibsen's *Doll's House* and Bernhardt in Rostand's *L'Aiglon.*"

"Rostand? That's the same man who wrote *Cyrano*. Oh, Aunt Lou, tell me about when you played Roxane. Did you wear beautiful clothes?"

"Yes, the costumes were lovely. I think, as I look back over my career, they seem the loveliest I have ever worn because that was my first big part. Want me to tell you how I got the part?"

Lizzie Lou nodded and pulled her knees up on the rising-sun quilt, careful not to get her shoes on it.

"Well, up until that time, I had had seven years of very small parts, most of them just walk-ons, no lines to say at all," Aunt Lou began. "One year I got nothing and had to take a job with a costume company for theatrical productions. I learned a lot there and was able to do a pretty good job on my own costumes afterward.

"I felt very fortunate when I got a small part in the Cyrano company. Edward Litchfield was playing Cyrano and Edith Todd, Roxane. I was doing a bit as one of the nuns in the last scene. This left me free to absorb the rest of the play. And how I did absorb it! In two months I knew every line, every movement, and every bit of stage business. Edith Todd was a lovely Roxane; she was old for the part, but you would not have known it. Every tilt of the head, every step of the foot, every gesture of hand spelled youth; youth, beauty, and grace. Edith Todd was one of the best." Aunt Lou sighed. "She died that same year, poor darling. What a Roxane she was!

"Edward Litchfield was younger. Within the last ten years he had become one of the best-known actors on the American stage. He was a worker and was forever striving for greater perfection in whatever role he portrayed. Although he was probably the handsomest man I have ever known, he never depended on his good looks to win an audience and never hesitated to take a part in which his personable features were entirely obscured, as in *Cyrano*.

"Well, as I said, I had been playing this nun for two months and one day Mr. Litchfield stopped me backstage and said, 'I see you in the wings often, Miss Leander. You should know the play rather well by now.' 'I do, Mr. Litchfield,' I replied. He looked me over from head to foot, gave a slight shrug of his broad shoulders, and said, 'You know, Miss Leander, you are extremely homely.' Well, before I could recover from this critical remark, he turned on his heel and left me."

"Oh, Aunt Lou, how rude of him. How could you go on after that? What did you do?"

"Do? Why, I stayed right there, gritted my teeth, so to speak, and played my nun better than ever. You see I was eating regularly, something you don't always do in the theatrical struggle, and I knew I must hang on to the job, for it looked as though it would have a long run. I had seen many exhibitions of temperament in other stars and I supposed this was just another turn it took sometimes, a star goading a bit player. And I still stood in the wings during every performance to learn all I could. I was young and had a great deal to learn and I knew it.

"Several days later, during a performance, Mr. Litchfield, pushing his sword back in its sheath, strode off the stage. He paused at sight of me standing there, grinned, put his big putty nose close to my face, and whispered, 'You really are homely, you know, young one.' Then he laughed and ran off to change his costume."

"Oh, Aunt Lou!"

"Yes, it was bad. I cried myself to sleep that night, wondering if I would ever, ever amount to anything, being so homely that Mr. Litchfield had to keep talking about it. Next morning I vowed that one more time and I would give him a piece of my mind and then he'd probably fire me, but I didn't care, I couldn't take any more.

"He didn't appear to notice me for a week or more. Then one day as I was walking toward the stage door, he came out of his dressing room, very debonair, handsome as a peacock, wearing a derby hat, spats, and carrying a cane. He stopped at sight of me, held up his cane, and gave an exclamation of surprise.

"'Well, as I live and breathe,' he exclaimed, 'if it isn't that ugly little nun. You aren't any better-looking in those street clothes than you are in costume.'

"Something inside of me snapped. I walked over to him and though my eyes must have been blazing I kept my voice low and put in it all the venom at my command.

"'Mr. Litchfield, my looks are no concern of yours! I am playing a nun in this company and doing it very well. From now on you mind your own business!' And I turned and almost ran for the door. Outside he caught up with me and took hold of my arm. I tried to withdraw from his grasp, but he held me firmly. When I looked up into his face I found him grinning and looking at me with twinkling, friendly eyes.

"'You've got spunk, Louise, you've got spunk. I wondered how long I was going to have to keep prodding you to see the sparks fly. Now, my fine little homely nun, do you think you could make yourself beautiful enough to play Roxane?'

"He stood still and turned me around so that he could look down into my eyes. Lizzie Lou, I was stunned for a moment and speechless as I looked up at his handsome face. Then my sixth sense, my sense of the dramatic, came to my aid. I tossed my head and replied, 'Of course, I can, Mr. Litchfield, since you are able to make yourself homely enough to play Cyrano!'"

"Oh, golly, Aunt Lou! Oh, golly!" Lizzie Lou's hands were moist, she had clasped them so tightly during the narrative.

148

"Well, that was the way I got my first big part. Edith Todd was to enter the hospital for an operation in four weeks and Mr. Litchfield had had his eye on me for some time. After my success in *Cyrano,* I never played bit parts again. But you see, honey, it certainly wasn't a beautiful face that got me the part. There were many better-looking actresses in the cast than I."

Lizzie Lou stood up, her hand on the foot of the bed. "Thank you, Aunt Lou, for telling me about it. This has been a night I'll never forget." She looked down at her hand on the bed. "It's so easy to talk to you and, oh, there is so much I want to say, so many questions I want to ask."

Aunt Lou put her spectacle case on the table. "We're going to have lots of good talks, honey. One of the prices I've had to pay for my career is not living a normal family life in the usual sense. Not having a daughter is my secret sorrow. Being here with you and the others is a great joy. And getting my thoughts so taken up by this family helps me forget the long months it has been since I heard from Jerry." She looked down at her wedding ring, then up at Lizzie Lou. "But I feel that soon some word will come from him. And now, honey, tomorrow's Saturday and you and I must have some more dancing lessons. You are getting very good, just a few more times on that tricky turn I do and you'll be ready to give that Bill Monroe some pointers."

"Oh, Aunt Lou, he wouldn't want to come here. He's too—too—well, too popular to ever want to date me."

"Now listen here, young lady, none of that. I wonder if you ever thought that Bill may want to be your friend, but that you have been so standoffish that you scare him?"

"But——"

"Next time you talk to him try to think about how he feels rather than about yourself. He's probably just as ill at ease at times as you seem to be." Aunt Lou pushed the kid curler under her scarf. "I was in my teens once and I remember very well how frightened I was of boys and of most other people too."

"It doesn't seem possible, Aunt Lou, that you'd ever be scared of anyone."

"Well, I was, and still am for that matter, though I can hide the fact better now. You must get to bed, honey, it's late."

Lizzie Lou glanced at the clock. "I should say it is!" She bent and kissed Aunt Lou's cheek.

In her room she walked softly to the window, pulled back the curtain, and looked out at the night.

"'Do you think you could make yourself beautiful enough to play Roxane?'" she repeated in a whisper. "O God, please give me the courage to try out for the senior play. If you'll give me the courage, I'll try to do the rest, oh, I will try."

12. First Date

Sunday morning it was Peggy who discovered it. The others were still at the breakfast table as she ran out on the porch and brought in the thick Sunday edition of the Medford *Herald*. There would be just time to look at the funny paper before she had to get ready for Sunday school. It was while she was pulling out the colored funnies that she spied the pictures of Aunt Lou on the front page of the society section. She ran out to the dining room with her discovery.

Father pushed back the dishes and spread the paper on the table. All gathered around to have a look. There it was: "Famous Actress Visits Medford Family" by James L. Buell, and pictures of Aunt Lou in three roles, Roxane, Juliet, and the recent Kitty Kimble.

Father asked Lizzie Lou to read it aloud to the rest of them. Jim had done a good job describing Aunt Lou, her charm, her friendliness, her unpretentious manner. He told of her relationship to Warren Jones and that she was staying with the family to convalesce from an attack of influenza. He told of her husband still missing in France and of her recent appearance at the Medford Opera House in *Till We Meet Again*.

But it was the last line that stopped Lizzie Lou in consternation. It read: "Miss Leander's eldest niece, Lizzie Lou Jones, is a prominent member of the senior class at Medford High School."

Why had he mentioned her at all? A prominent member, indeed! And her awful name sprawled right out there in print! How could she go to school tomorrow? The others might think she had something to do with Jim writing that. And Bonnie, what would she say? She could almost hear Bonnie's scornful remarks about bragging. And Bill, what would he think of her? He certainly knew the statement was untrue. Would he laugh at such an absurd assertion? She couldn't bear it if he laughed.

Aunt Lou began to clear the table. She smiled as she stacked plates. "Well, famous actress must get at dishes. Come on, famous senior, put away our publicity. Sunday school at nine-thirty, remember?"

In the kitchen she watched Lizzie Lou's sober face as the latter poured hot water into the dishpan. "What's the matter, honey? You look as though you'd lost your last friend."

"I probably will when they read that last sentence in your interview. Now why, Aunt Lou, did Jim have to mention me and call me a prominent senior? Why, I've never done a single outstanding thing in that class that would label me as prominent."

Aunt Lou poured bacon drippings from a skillet into a tin bucket. "Well, why haven't you?"

Lizzie Lou stopped rubbing the dishrag against the cake of soap and stared at her aunt. "Why—why, I—why, what could I do? I'm not good at anything. I study hard and my grades are fairly good, but—but——" She looked down at the dishwater beginning to froth with suds.

"Studying is very important." Aunt Lou put the skillet on the table. "You can't get anywhere without a well-rounded mental background. There's so much to learn and so little time to learn it. But how about other school activities? They are a part of your education too. Belong to any clubs?"

Lizzie Lou shook her head. "Mary wanted me to join the French Club, but Aunt Liz thought——" She paused. "No, it wasn't Aunt Liz's fault that I didn't join. I guess, I just didn't want to. I always feel so shy at places like that, shy and uncomfortable. I don't know why."

Aunt Lou shook her head and clicked her tongue. "You think too much about Lizzie Lou Jones, honey, and what people are thinking of her. You'll go right on being shy until you begin thinking of the other person. Try to show that you're interested in him, not just in yourself. What about games for girls at school?"

"There's a girls' basketball club after school on Tuesdays, but I'm not any good at games."

"Ever play any basketball?"

"No."

Aunt Lou looked at her niece speculatively. "You know, I believe you could be very good at it. And there's nothing like lively exercise to bring a good color to the cheeks and sparkle to the eyes. You would look awfully well in a gym suit."

Lizzie Lou laughed. "Aunt Lou, you make it sound as though the making over of Lizzie Lou Jones is a very simple project."

"Not the making over, my sweet, just the adding to, adding to her already many excellent talents. Here, I'll finish washing the dishes. You run along and get ready for Sunday school. I'm anxious to see you in that new blue dress."

On her way upstairs, Lizzie Lou went through the living room and patted Father's shoulder as he sat reading the paper. He looked up and smiled.

"We were so busy looking at Lou's interview that we failed to see this picture spread on Teddy Roosevelt."

Lizzie Lou looked down at the paper. "Is that a picture of his home?"

"Yes, in Oyster Bay, New York. I tell you, this country won't be the same without that man. When he died last Monday a great tradition passed out of existence."

"If he had been President instead of Mr. Wilson, do you think we would have got into the war sooner?" Lizzie Lou looked at the pictures of the Roosevelt family in the White House.

"No doubt of it, and it might have ended sooner, who knows? Teddy always said, 'Speak softly and carry a big stick.' I read here that President Wilson sent word from Italy that the flags in Washington are to be at half-mast for thirty days."

"I thought Mr. Wilson was in Paris for the Peace Conference."

Father folded the paper. "Well, I gather that he and Mrs. Wilson have been doing a little visiting around before the conference starts. I saw a picture of them the other day taken in Brussels with King Albert and Queen Elizabeth of Belgium. I certainly hope he's able to put across those Fourteen Points of his at that conference table. If he can, we may get a new world order."

Lizzie Lou looked closely at Father. How he had changed in the last few months. As she thought back it had begun with the advent of Aunt Lou in their lives. Now he was talkative, interested in evcrything and everyone. It seemed as though Father had done what Aunt Lou had advised her to do, forget self and think of others.

"When you clip that article about Aunt Lou, Father, why don't you cut out that about Theodore Roosevelt and I'll put it in our clipping box." She walked toward the hall. "Are you going to Sunday school?"

"No. I'm going to wait and go to church with Lou. She says she feels strong enough to go. Let me see your new dress before you leave."

Lizzie Lou felt that the new dress was the most becoming one she had ever had. Aunt Lou had made it beautifully and she realized now why Aunt Lou had insisted on the expensive lace for the collar. The lace extended over her shoulders and as she looked in the mirror it seemed that the soft, delicate, ecru-colored Venetian lace gave a creamy color to her complexion that was not bad, not bad at all. Seeing herself thus, her worry about Jim's unwarranted statement eased. After all, it was the last sentence in the article and few people ever read clear to the end of a news piece, anyway.

"Why haven't you done anything outstanding in the senior class?" Aunt Lou had asked.

She looked at herself again and held her head a little higher. Her neck seemed rather nice emerging from the beautiful filigree lace. Middy blouses hid most of her throat, this neckline really was becoming. Maybe she *could* do something at school and earn the right to be called a prominent senior. This lace was sort of like that on Bonnie Mason's black velvet dress. "You would look awfully well in a gym suit." She hadn't worn a gym suit since she was a freshman and had taken the one year of gym required for graduation. Some of the girls did look cute in their gym suits, she wondered if she . . .

Later in church Peggy sat between her and Aunt Lou, with Father on the aisle. Aunt Liz and Uncle Mat were in the pew behind them. It seemed as though Dr. Harter was preaching right at Lizzie Lou this morning. His subject was "The Light Under the Bushel," and his scripture "Neither do men light a candle, and put it under a bushel, but on a candlestick; and it giveth light unto all that are in the house. Let your light so shine before men, that they may see your good works, and glorify your Father which is in heaven."

Once Dr. Harter said, "Practically everyone has been given the ability to do something well if he will but take the trouble to explore his resources and use his talents. People seldom reach the highest point of their potential ability, but go on hiding their lights under the bushels of their own laziness, self-depreciation, or boredom. In the life of our late Theodore Roosevelt we have an example of an energetic man who was always striving to use his God-given talents and put his candle high on a candlestick."

Lizzie Lou looked over Peggy's head at Aunt Lou and caught her eye. Aunt Lou gave a quick smile and lowered one eyelid; Lizzie Lou knew she was thinking about her and her problems. During the silent prayer she prayed that she might discover her talents and then have the courage to use them.

It was after their one o'clock dinner. Lizzie Lou and Peggy had finished the dishes. Father and Uncle Mat were in the living room discussing the fabulous career of Teddy Roosevelt and what chance Wilson was going to have at the conference table convincing Lloyd George, Orlando, and Clemenceau of the value of his Fourteen Points.

Aunt Liz and Aunt Lou were seated at the dining-room table. Aunt Lou had asked Aunt Liz for a recipe for nut bread and Aunt Liz had brought over her recipe book. The two, bending their heads over the book, were enjoying one of women's greatest delights, the contemplation of various ways of preparing food.

"Oh, Liz, there's one for butterscotch pie! It's been ages since I have tasted any. How do you make it?" Aunt Lou put her finger on the page.

"Well, this is a pretty good recipe, though I cook the filling about three minutes longer than it says. I hate runny pie filling. And I use about two tablespoonfuls more of the brown sugar too." Aunt Liz picked up her pencil. "Here's the nut bread. I'll copy it for you."

Lizzie Lou took off her apron and watched them from the doorway. It was nice to have them so friendly. She didn't know quite how it had happened, but Aunt Liz was as nice as could be to Aunt Lou and gave her help and advice when she asked for it but did not interfere in the actual running of the Joneses' household. Something must have happened between them this past week while she was at school.

The ringing of the telephone caused Lizzie Lou to jump. It had rung so few times during the short period it had been installed that the sound was startling. The telephone was on the wall in the front hall. She heard Father answer it.

"Lizzie Lou, where are you? This call is for you." Father stepped to the dining-room doorway. Lizzie Lou looked dumfounded. "Well, go answer it. I said it's for you."

Her heart gave several extra beats as she walked toward the telephone. Who could it be? She had had only one call and that was last Wednesday when Jim Buell had called, but she had been expecting that. It couldn't be Mary because she didn't have a phone, unless she was calling from the next-door neighbor's.

Slowly she took the receiver from the little shelf under the mouthpiece, tilted her head up, and said a soft, "Hello."

A masculine voice said, "Hello. Is that you, Lizzie Lou?"

Her heart pounded now, for the voice sounded like—but it couldn't be. Why would he call her?

"Yes." Her voice was a bit stronger.

"This is Bill Monroe. I—I was wondering if you would care to go with me to Young People's meeting at our church tonight?"

Lizzie Lou gulped and couldn't say a word.

"Are you there, Lizzie Lou?"

"Yes."

"I know I'm calling rather late for a date. I—I—well, I wanted to ask you Friday, but Jim was along, and I work at a grocery on Saturday and I wasn't sure you would want to go and——"

It was plain to Lizzie Lou that Bill Monroe, who had always seemed so sure of himself at senior meetings and on the basketball floor, was ill at ease. Aunt Lou's words flashed across her mind: "Think of the other person."

"Why, it's nice of you to ask me. I'd like to go. Which church is it?"

"The Washington Street Presbyterian. Gosh, it's nice of you to go, as I called so late. It's a potluck supper at six-thirty. I'll come by for you at six. O.K.?"

"Yes. Shouldn't I take some food?"

"Oh no. My mother has made me a big dish of potato salad. You are a guest. . . . Well—then—I'll see you around six?"

"Yes."

"Well—good-by, Lizzie Lou."

"Good-by, Bill."

Slowly she returned the receiver to the hook and stood resting her head against the mouthpiece, her eyes closed. A date! She had a date! And with Bill Monroe! She hadn't dreamed that this beautiful thing could happen to her. Now she knew why fate had kept her waiting; it was so this first date could be with Bill.

O help her to find the right things to say, help her not act like a speechless nincompoop, she prayed fervently. She opened her eyes and looked down at her old green dress she had put on when she came from church. Should she wear her new one? Yes, she would. Should she have asked Father if she could go before giving Bill her answer? No, she was seventeen and surely she had the right to go to church in the evening. But she did hope Father approved.

In the living room she found him reading. Uncle Mat and Aunt Liz had left. Peggy was reading the funny paper to Lucy and Aunt Lou was looking over the music in the piano bench. Father looked at Lizzie Lou questioningly.

"It was Bill Monroe," she told him. "He wants me to go to Young People's meeting at his church. I told him I would. I hope you don't mind."

Father frowned. "Bill Monroe? Who's he?"

Aunt Lou broke in. "A very nice boy, Warren. I met him when Lizzie Lou and I were at the 'Y' getting your membership." She turned to Lizzie Lou. "Didn't you tell me he played on one of the teams?"

"He plays center on the basketball team." She watched Father's face anxiously.

"Oh yes. I remember seeing his name in the paper. Well, if you say he's a nice boy, Daughter, I guess it will be all right. But you do seem a bit young to start going with boys. I'll want to meet him before you go, of course."

Lizzie Lou nodded.

Aunt Lou smiled, walked over and rumpled her brother's hair. "Warren Jones, you old fuddy-duddy. Don't you realize your daughter is seventeen? Remember when you and Margaret started going together?"

Father gave a start, then looked at Lizzie Lou. "It's hard to remember, Lou, it seems so long ago."

Peggy, who had taken in all the conversation, dropped the funny paper and pointed a finger at her older sister. "Lizzie Lou's got a beau! Lizzie Lou's got a beau!" she teased.

Warren Jones spoke sharply to his second daughter. "That will be enough, Margaret. Quite enough."

Peggy returned to the funny paper. Lizzie Lou gave Father a grateful look and went upstairs. It was too early to dress, but she could use that lovely new Christmas manicure set and fix her nails.

At a quarter to six she was ready, wearing the new Alice-blue dress, her shoes shined, her hair neatly combed, face delicately powdered, nails buffed into glistening mirrors with the new buffer; Lizzie Lou Jones was as clean, neat, and shining as she had ever been in her life. Her glowing cheeks and sparkling eyes gave a hint of the excitement bubbling within her.

The family was at supper in the dining room. She had the hall light on but had turned out the one in the living room, so she could stand at the front window without being seen and watch for him.

She wondered if all girls felt as excited, thrilled, scared, and happy as she did before their first date. Her face felt hot to her hand. What if Peg and Jimmy came rushing in when he came; that would be just like them. Anyway Aunt Liz wouldn't be in to look him over. What would Father say to him? She watched the light go on in the Cameron's dining room. Mrs. Cameron must be putting supper on the table. It was a nice night, clear and cold, the stars were showing in the early dusk and the creak of the snow underfoot could be heard whenever anyone passed by. She started at every figure, wondering if it was he.

What would they talk about? Would she feel shy and tongue-tied? She hoped not. She must try Aunt Lou's remedy for shyness: think about the other person and help him not to feel shy. Bill had seemed sort of shy when he called, but why would he be, such a prominent boy! Still there was no knowing what went on inside a person. Who would ever guess all the beautiful daydreams that went on inside her own head just by looking at her plain, ordinary face?

Of late her daydreams were more often made up of realities, real people, real events. She found that she was resorting less and less to moving pictures and books for dreaming material. Was she perhaps growing up? It had been a long time since she had pictured herself as Lillian Gish or the red-costumed dancer. She clasped her hands together. After all, she didn't have to live another's life vicariously, she was having a life of her own. She was having a date!

The snow creaked and a figure turned up the front walk, a figure wearing an overcoat and cap and carrying a basket on his arm. There was a knock on the door. Lizzie Lou felt a pain in her stomach and a throb in her throat. O help her to say the right things! She stepped to the center of the room and turned on all three of the lights in the chandelier. She wanted the room to look bright. Slowly she walked into the hall; she must try to appear poised and at ease, he wouldn't know how fast her heart was beating. She opened the door.

"Hello, Lizzie Lou." He took off his cap.

"Come in, Bill." How casual the words sounded, as though she had been inviting boys into the hall for ages. He wiped the snow from his feet and stepped in.

"Come into the living room. I want you to meet my father."

"I'd like to. Sure good of you to go with me after I called so late." He followed her into the living room.

Lizzie Lou stepped to the door to the dining room. The eyes of the whole family were upon her as she said, "Father, won't you come in and meet Bill?"

Father put his napkin on the table and pushed back his chair. Peggy and Jimmy began sliding from their places, the gleam of curiosity in their eyes. Aunt Lou spoke quickly. "You stay and finish your suppers, Peggy and Jimmy."

"But I want to see——" Jimmy burst out.

"You will keep seated." Father placed a restraining hand on his son's shoulder, then joined Lizzie Lou at the door.

Bill had put his basket on the piano bench and stood beneath the chandelier. "Father, this is Bill Monroe." Lizzie Lou made the introduction with more ease than she had thought possible.

Father put out his hand and clasped Bill's. "Good to know you, Bill."

"Nice to meet you, Mr. Jones."

While Lizzie Lou went out into the hall to put on her rubbers and coat, the two conversed about the basketball team and the Y.M.C.A.

Father looked at her with a smile as she came back in the room. He turned to Bill. "What time will you be bringing my girl home, Bill?"

Bill picked up his basket. "Oh, comparatively early, I should say, sir. Before ten. You see I'm in training and have to be in bed by ten-thirty. Coach's orders." He smiled at Lizzie Lou.

"Well, have a good time," Father called after them as they walked through the door.

Lizzie Lou Jones was on her first date!

They got the streetcar at the corner; the ride seemed short. Bill told her the names of some other seniors who belonged to his church group, Pat Brandon, Frieda Hempstead, Miriam Hardin, Dale Gordon, and Jim Buell.

"Say, that was a good article Jim wrote about your aunt. I'd certainly like to see her in a play. Those pictures of her were great."

A question crossed Lizzie Lou's mind. What if he had called her for a date only because he was impressed by Aunt Lou, wanted to be seen with the niece of a famous actress? No, that couldn't be true. Bill wasn't like that, not a show-off. Careful, Lizzie Lou, she cautioned herself. Quit thinking about yourself.

"You should hear her tell some of her experiences in the theater," she said. "They sound like they came out of a book. She is a good storyteller."

"So are you. I'll never forget how you told Jim and me about that Cyrano fellow. It was good, really good."

The conductor called out, "Washington Street!"

The basement of the church was buzzing with young folks. The Young People's Society included those from eighth grade through high school. Tonight being guest night, there was a large crowd. Bill took Lizzie Lou to the room where the girls were putting their wraps. He took his potato salad to the kitchen.

Lizzie Lou hung her coat on a hook and removed her hat; carefully she placed her rubbers directly under her coat so she could find them easily. She took a clean handkerchief from her coat pocket and tucked it in her sleeve, admiring, as she did so, the deep lace cuffs around her wrists. She felt good in this dress, really good! Bill had said he liked it!

She turned to the big mirror where other girls were primping, and smoothed down a few stray hairs.

"Why, Lizzie Lou Jones, hello there!" Frieda Hempstead turned to her. "Have you joined our church?"

Lizzie Lou smiled, Frieda sounded so friendly. "No, I'm a guest."

"You are? Who brought you?"

"Bill Monroe." How she loved saying it!

Frieda raised her eyebrows. "Bill Monroe! Oh boy! Wait till I tell the girls. Most of them put off asking other fellows for tonight, hoping Bill would ask one of them." She looked at Lizzie Lou intently as though seeing her for the first time. "Say, I like your dress. That lace is lovely." She turned back to the mirror. "You know, I didn't know that you dated. I never see you around."

Lizzie Lou took out a hairpin and replaced it slowly. "I don't have time to date often," she said as casually as possible. She would not tell Frieda that this was her first date.

Some of the other girls whom she knew slightly at school spoke to her. There was so much chattering that there was no chance for her to feel self-conscious. She noticed one younger girl, a guest, holding her coat and looking uncomfortable.

Lizzie Lou smiled at her. "Here, there's room to hang your coat on this hook with mine." She took the coat and hung it on top of her own.

"Oh, thanks." The girl seemed relieved. "I've never been here before and I——" She looked around nervously.

"Neither have I," Lizzie Lou confessed. "Shall we go out together?" How well she understood this younger girl's discomfort. "Whose guest are you?"

"Max Thomson's. You probably don't know him. He's a sophomore. I'm Sue Allison, class of '21, too. You're a senior, aren't you? I've seen you at school." There was admiration in her voice.

Lizzie Lou nodded, feeling old and mature.

Outside the two parted. Bill joined Lizzie Lou and took her to meet his Sunday-school teacher and the minister. They were pleasant and cordial.

Down the middle of the room was a long table covered with food. What a variety! Baked beans, succotash, fruit salad, cabbage salad, Waldorf salad, potato salad, macaroni and cheese, escaloped potatoes, baked ham, cottage cheese, fruit jello, olives, pickles, celery, meat loaf, Parker House rolls, cakes, and pies.

Lizzie Lou and Bill joined the line passing by the table and began filling their plates.

"That's my mother's potato salad, right there." Bill pointed to a large glass dish. "But don't take any unless you like onions. She puts a lot in hers."

Lizzie Lou hesitated. Then she turned and looked up at him with a smile. "Are you going to have some?"

"If you do. I love onions."

"So do I," she confessed, and took a helping of Mrs. Monroe's potato salad.

"Do you like onions on hamburgers?" he asked as he took the serving spoon from her.

"Yes, those big sweet onions sliced real thin and with a little pickle too." Lizzie Lou took a piece of meat loaf.

"Fine, I knew you would be my kind of girl right along. I'd probably never speak to you again if you didn't like onions."

Lizzie Lou laughed and walked on. She hadn't dreamed it would be this easy to talk to a boy on a date. Imagine, talking about onions!

"Golly, look at those cakes and pies. What kind are you going to have?" Bill looked over the array of pastry with hungry eyes.

"You certainly know the war is over when you see those. This time last year we had sugar rationing and no one had enough to make stuff like that. I don't have any room on my plate for dessert, do you?" Lizzie Lou picked up a fork.

"I'll come back and get it when we finish this. Let's go find a place." He led the way to two chairs in the corner.

Afterward, Lizzie Lou could not remember exactly what she ate but she knew it was the best food in the world. The room buzzed with voices but she heard only one.

The food on the tables quickly disappeared. The girls washed the silverware and plates while the boys dismantled the tables and arranged the chairs. The minister led a short devotional service and they sang a few hymns.

Dale Gordon, president of the Young People's Society, led them in a sing. They sang "Keep the Home Fires Burning," "Pack up Your Troubles in Your Old Kit Bag," "Memories," "Roses of Picardy," "Smiles," "Over There," "Tipperary," "K-K-K-Katy," and, much to Lizzie Lou's pleasure, "Till We Meet Again." Jim Buell, on the other side of her, gave her a knowing nod.

Lizzie Lou knew she had never been so happy, sitting here beside Bill, relaxed, singing with the group. Having a date was fun, not at all the serious business she had thought. Picture shows never pictured anything as simple and ordinary as this and yet this was better than any show she had ever seen because she was living it herself, not just pretending.

After the sing they played games, musical chairs, charades, gossip, animal-vegetable-mineral, and wink'em. Wink'em was the one she liked best, it made her feel so special. The girls sat on chairs in a circle, with a boy standing behind each chair. One chair was empty and the boy behind it would try to get a girl to fill it by winking at one. However, each of the other boys, on the alert, would put his hands on his girl's shoulders and keep her from leaving his chair for the empty one. Lizzie Lou was winked at several times and knew the thrill of feeling Bill's firm hands on her shoulders. Once she eluded him and escaped to the chair on the opposite side of the circle and then was sorry, for Bill winked at Miriam and she sat in his chair. But when someone winked at Miriam he didn't seem to try at all to keep her. He grinned at Lizzie Lou and gave her a broad wink. It was good to be back in his chair again.

There was a mad scramble in the girls' room as the party broke up, finding rubbers, and gloves and getting a chance at the mirror to see if one's hat was straight.

Outside, the young people, mostly by twos, went off in various directions, a few toward town to catch streetcars, but more to walk.

"Shall we walk or catch a streetcar?" Bill asked.

"I'd love to walk on such a gorgeous night." She wanted to make this evening last as long as possible.

"O.K." He tucked a newspaper around the empty dish in his basket and offered her his arm. "Take my arm; it's kind of slippery."

Lizzie Lou put her arm through his and the two walked in step over the hard-packed snow. There was silence, only the creak of their heels. A flutter of fright came in her throat. Was she going to get tongue-tied now that they were alone? It had been so beautiful at the church with the others around. But now! What would he think of her? What should she say? Should she talk about the party, the food, or what? Was he feeling a little shy too? He hadn't said a word either. They crossed the street. This was awful. She had to say something. She opened her mouth.

"What are you——" came out just as he began, "What school do you——"

They both stopped and laughed. The laugh eased the tension.

"Go ahead. What were you going to say?" he urged her.

"I was going to ask what you are planning to do after graduation."

Bill sighed and shrugged his shoulders. "You shouldn't have asked that, Lizzie Lou. It's a long story and not very interesting, only to me. It would bore you."

"It interests me," she said softly. "Please tell me."

Bill looked down at her. "O.K., but you asked for it," and he launched into a description of his dream, that of becoming a doctor. It seemed to Lizzie Lou, as he went on, that he had been seeing himself as a helpful competent doctor pretty much as she had been seeing herself as a toe dancer or Lillian Gish. But his dream was more sensible; it was far more likely that he would be a doctor than that she would ever be a dancer or a moving-picture star. And furthermore he was doing something to make it come true.

Bill said his father could help him very little. Bill had two younger sisters and the family finances would not cover a medical education. But he was working and saving his money and intended to get a job when he went to college.

"It's going to be a long pull, Lizzie Lou, but when I put out my shingle, William R. Monroe, M.D., it will be worth it." He held his head erect and looked straight ahead. She watched him. Who would think when you saw him at senior meeting or on the basket-ball floor that his head was filled with such big thoughts? She could see him making house calls, reassuring mothers about their sick children. It was a fine ambition he had, really fine.

"You will make a wonderful doctor, Bill."

"Do you really think I can do it?" he asked anxiously.

"Of course." There was belief in her tone.

He took a deep breath. "You are a good listener. I've never told all that to any other girl. It's something pretty special to me. But golly, let's quit talking about me."

"I like hearing about you. Now I feel I know you better."

"What are you planning after commencement?"

"I don't know. I've thought some of taking a business course and getting an office job, but I expect I'll have to stay home and keep house for my father and the others. I don't know how long Aunt Lou will stay. She looks after things right now. Aunt Liz has looked after us long enough. It's time I took over."

"What would you really like to do?"

"I don't know. The things I've dreamed of sound so childish and impossible that I can't even repeat them."

He reached over and patted her hand on his arm. "Lizzie Lou, no dream is impossible if you're willing to do more than dream about it, but just dreaming won't make it come true."

"I know and I guess all my dreams are too fantastic. I've got to get down to earth. But the things I like to think about are bubbly, airy, gay, full of color and movement. I never have sensible thoughts like—well, like you wanting to be a doctor."

"One thing is certain, it doesn't sound like you belong in an office. You know what I think? I think you have been given a double dose of imagination. But I bet there is something you could find that would put that imagination to work."

"I wish I knew what it was," she answered slowly.

The walk from the church to her front door was the shortest her two feet had ever trod. She hesitated with her hand on the doorknob. Should she invite him in? The lights were still on in the living room.

"Would you like to come in?" she asked.

"No. It's nine-thirty and I have a few things to do for Mother when I get home. She thinks the world would stop if she didn't wash on Monday. I usually help her get the tubs ready."

Lizzie Lou smiled inwardly, remembering how self-conscious she had felt, speaking about helping with the laundry to Bill and Frieda on Armistice Day.

"Well, all right. I certainly enjoyed the party. Thanks for asking me."

"Well, thank *you* for going. And thanks for—for listening to my plans for the future. It was sure good of you."

"I liked hearing about it. Good night." She held out her hand to him, without planning to do so.

He took it and held it briefly. "Good night, Lizzie Lou and—and—thanks." And he was gone.

Her first date was over!

13. *The Storyteller*

Walking to school next morning, Lizzie Lou didn't notice the biting wind, gray skies, or bits of sleet stinging her face. Her collar pulled high, hat low, lunch sack, purse, and geometry hugged close, she bent into the wind and her thoughts raced about over yesterday's extraordinary and unprecedented events. Would she get to talk to him today? Would he walk in the halls with her? And most important of all would he ever ask her for another date?

He was going to be a doctor! If she was going to interest a boy with such ambitions, wasn't she going to have to do some better planning for her own future? You couldn't expect a smart boy like Bill to want to date a dumbbell.

Aunt Lou had been waiting for her last night and it was thrilling to relate the evening's events to such sympathetic ears. She had been surprised that Father wasn't home. He had gone to church and although it was way after time for services to be over he had not returned. Aunt Lou said she was urging him to join the church choir. Warren, she said, had a fine baritone voice and he should be using it. This morning at breakfast he said he had had a talk with the choir director and was going to choir practice on Thursday. How fine it would be to sit in church and see Father up in the choir loft.

Aunt Lou had looked sort of depressed this morning, though she tried to hide it. Lizzie Lou knew she was thinking about her husband, hoping for a telephone call, a letter, or a telegram. Once she had described Jerry Logan to Lizzie Lou. What a fascinating man he must be. She knew he was good-looking from the photographs Aunt Lou had about her room. Aunt Lou said he was gay, discerning, and a hard worker. He had started his life in the theater as an actor, then found producing plays interested him more. He had been producing for several years when he had met Aunt Lou. The combination of "Jerome Logan presents Louise Leander in . . ." had been very successful, both in the theater and in their private lives. She hoped Aunt Lou would hear from him soon. She disliked seeing circles under her eyes, showing that she was not sleeping well. Aunt Lou had recovered from the influenza, but she needed to gain weight and losing sleep was not good.

As she and Mary walked to first class, Mary spoke of the newspaper article about Aunt Lou. She squeezed Lizzie Lou's arm and exclaimed how thrilled she was, being friends with such a famous girl. A little later when Lizzie Lou told of her date the night before, Mary's eyes became big with admiration.

"Oh, Mary, you are wonderful. You make me feel so important even when I'm not," Lizzie Lou said as they reached Latin class.

"Bill Monroe wouldn't have dated you if you weren't important. Important to him," Mary maintained stoutly.

Lizzie Lou wished she could believe Mary, but—— All morning, though she tried to walk through the halls unconcernedly, she kept looking for him out of the corners of her eyes. She didn't see him in the cafeteria at noon. Perhaps he was absent. She hoped he wasn't ill.

No one but Mary mentioned the article in the paper about Aunt Lou. Evidently no one connected her with the Warren Jones family mentioned and had not read the last sentence in the piece. How silly of her to worry about that yesterday.

Several times during the day, when she wasn't mulling over last night, she remembered Aunt Lou's question, "Why haven't you done anything outstanding in the senior class?" She had less than five months in high school, what could she do in that short time? Commencement was on May twenty-third. She was going to have to dump her self-consciousness in the ash can, muster a lot of courage, and work like the dickens, if she was going to amount to anything. But why not? Hadn't she had a date? And hadn't he said she looked nice in her new dress? But where was he today?

As she turned from the main corridor, after the last period, toward her locker, her heart seemed to skip a beat. Beside her locker stood Bill!

He grinned as she approached. "Hi—there. Where have you been keeping yourself? I've watched for you all day."

"You have?" Her hand clasped her Latin grammar so hard the knuckles hurt. "Oh, I've been around."

"Well, I only have a minute. Coach has his car outside. He's taking the team down to the armory for practice. Less than two weeks till the Hartsville game and we've got to get used to that floor. But I wanted to give you this. It's the play the committee has chosen. I wondered if you could be ready to tell the class what it's like at senior meeting a week from tomorrow? You know, enough of the story so they can know what parts they'd like to try out for."

Lizzie Lou swallowed hard. Could she do it? Could she get up before all the others and tell the story of this play? She took the paper-backed book he held out and looked at it. *The Cavendish Pearls* she read on the cover. Among those listening to her would be Bonnie and her crowd; they would be critical and unsympathetic. Could she take it? Maybe this was her chance to do the something outstanding Aunt Lou had suggested. She raised her head and looked at Bill.

"Why, yes, I'll tell it." She straightened her shoulders and, with erect posture, felt more competent. "Is it a good play?"

"I don't know. I haven't had a chance to read it. Now I won't have to. I'll depend on you."

"Then you don't know what part you'll try for?"

"Oh, I won't try for any. I'm no actor. I'd be scared to death on a stage."

She smiled a little. "I can't imagine you scared of anything."

"If you knew me better, you'd find me out."

"I'd like to," she heard herself say, then died a little at her own boldness.

"Like to find me out?"

"No. Know you better." Could this be her own tongue saying these words? She shivered imperceptibly at her impudence. What had happened to her?

169

Bill laughed as though he liked it. "You shall, Lizzie Lou, you shall. I've got to get going. Coach will be on his high horse. Thanks for taking over the play presentation. See you tomorrow."

And he was gone. If Lizzie Lou had not been so engrossed with her own thoughts she might have noticed the many interested glances, of passing students, sent her way as Bill left. The student body was on the alert for signs of any new twosomes and Bill Monroe's doings were of interest to everyone.

"I'll depend on you," he had said. She placed her books on the shelf in her locker and put on her overshoes. She would go right home and read this play. She mustn't let him down. She looked around for Mary, but she was gone. Sweet Mary, a real friend if there ever was one. She wished Mary would get interested in some boy and he in her. Who would be right for Mary? How foolish could she be, trying to think of a romance for Mary, when she was so poor at having one for herself. Or was she? The way she had spoken to Bill just now, she hardly recognized herself. What one date could do for a girl! She went slowly to the front door and out into the cold.

She walked home as in a dream; inside her there was a warm glow, a singing, a happiness she had not known before. She had talked to Bill with a natural assurance she hadn't believed possible for her. And he had acted as though—as though—it was hard for her to admit it, but as though he thought her attractive. But how could it be? Did something magic happen to her plain face when she spoke to him? She knew that when she was with him she forgot how she looked; maybe that was the answer to looks as well as to shyness; forget yourself. Perhaps Aunt Lou did know what she was talking about. If she could forget herself completely at senior meeting when she tried to describe this play, maybe she could do a good job. She had to; Bill was depending on her.

A surprising scene took place when she reached home. Aunt Lou, dressed in her blue velvet dress, met her at the door, a radiant, sparkling Aunt Lou. Lizzie Lou thought she had never seen anyone as beautiful.

"We're waiting for you, honey. It's a party, a celebration. I've heard from Jerry!"

Aunt Liz, Peggy, Jimmy, and Lucy were gathered around the dining-room table. There was milk for the younger ones, tea for the others, and a plate of the thinly sliced nut bread Aunt Lou had baked that morning. Aunt Liz poured the tea while Aunt Lou told Lizzie Lou the details of the telephone call at noon from Andy Steiner, her agent in New York. Andy had received a cablegram from Jerry, who had been released from a German prison hospital and just admitted to a hospital in Paris. The cablegram had said explanations would follow.

"It's awful to know that he still has to be hospitalized, but, oh, the relief to know that he is alive. I keep wondering what's wrong with him, but whatever it is I'll help him adjust to the handicap and we'll go on together," Aunt Lou said excitedly.

"You should calm down, Lou," Aunt Liz told her. "You must concentrate on making yourself strong enough to care for him when he gets back."

"I will, Liz, I will. It was the uncertainty that worried me so. Now I'll be able to sleep better. And when I get a letter from him, I'll be fine. Please pass the nut bread. I feel very hungry."

After the tea, Aunt Lou put on a record and danced with Lizzie Lou. Said she had to work off some of her exuberance. Peggy got Aunt Liz to dance with her and Jimmy and Lucy danced up and down in one spot to join in the festivities.

"Lizzie Lou, you fox-trot very smoothly now. I think it's time you invited Bill over for his lesson, one of these days," Aunt Lou said as she turned the record over.

"He's pretty busy with basketball practice now. Getting ready for the Hartsville game. I don't think he has time to go out much."

"Well, we must keep it in mind. Nothing like a dancing party to have fun. Liz, why don't you waltz with Lizzie Lou, you do it so much better than I and we want her to be able to do all the steps well."

Aunt Liz looked pleased, put her arm about her eldest niece, and guided her about the room to the strains of a new record

Uncle Mat had brought home last Saturday, "I'm Forever Blowing Bubbles."

"Aunt Liz, you're wonderful!" Lizzie Lou exclaimed as the record stopped. "I felt almost like a bubble myself. You lead a waltz beautifully."

"Well, that's a good piece to waltz to. Mat Wallace knows his waltzes, all right. Shall we play it over?" Aunt Liz, her cheeks flushed and her eyes bright, wound the victrola and set the needle. "I do like to waltz. Don't know why Mat and I ever gave it up. Good thing you reminded us, Lou. Mat says he's going to get back in the Elks, here, so we can go to some of their spring dances."

Before she went to bed that night, Lizzie Lou finished reading the play. My goodness, how would they get all the props, scenery, and clothes for such a play? The main set, a fine living room in the mansion on the Cavendish estate, was supposed to be the essence of elegance and grandeur. They didn't have any scenery like that at school. She supposed that backdrop of woodsy landscape they had would do for the gypsy scene. But the fine clothes for the Cavendish family and the society wedding guests, where would they get those?

It was an interesting plot, beginning as it did with a proposal of marriage, a change from most plays, which usually ended with the proposal. The heroine, Diana Cavendish, was a delightful person, thoroughly unspoiled by wealth and position. Her mother was rather snobbish and "hoity-toity." Lizzie Lou was sure she would not want to try out for that part. The grandmother was an aristocratic, grand lady, stately and regal. The handsome hero, Malcolm Forsythe, was a young lawyer, exactly right for Diana. And the gypsy camp at the edge of the estate would give color and variation to the flavor of the play.

The gypsy girl, Carlotta, was a fascinating character. It was interesting, the way she got those family pearls, the night before the wedding. She was a strange, wild girl; whoever played her would have to be good at pantomime, for she was alone on the stage when she found the pearls.

That last scene would be lovely, with the wedding party

gathered in the spacious room before they started out for the garden where the ceremony was to take place.

Lizzie Lou closed the book and went upstairs. Seeing a light under Aunt Lou's door, she tapped on it lightly. Aunt Lou was reading in bed. Lizzie Lou gave her the playbook and told her a brief synopsis while Aunt Lou turned through the pages.

"Who is going to direct this?"

"My English teacher, Miss Tamer."

"Well, I don't envy Miss Tamer her job. This play is rather pretentious for a high-school group, costumes, scenery, and all. Your committee certainly has big ideas; an awfully big cast to handle. Of course, more people will be able to take part. But I repeat I don't envy Miss Tamer. What part are you going to try for?"

"I'll be satisfied to be a wedding guest or one of the gypsies at the camp scene."

"Oh, come, come, Lizzie Lou, be adventurous, try out for Diana Cavendish. You would look lovely in that bridal veil."

"Oh, Aunt Lou, I couldn't play the lead!"

Aunt Lou laughed at her niece's vehemence. "Want to bet? Well, you don't have to decide tonight. How about reading me a little from our book? Maybe your soothing voice will calm me down so I can sleep."

Lizzie Lou found their place in *My Ántonia* and began to read.

All week she thought about *The Cavendish Pearls*. She reread it until she knew several speeches word for word. She could see each scene plainly and the characters moving about. Mary said she acted as if she was bewitched, she talked so little. Lizzie Lou said that if she was to tell this story she had to feel it inside, and the only way to do that was to think about it a lot.

On Friday the Medford High *News* came out with Jim Buell's interview with Aunt Lou. The caption was, "Senior Has Famous Aunt." Some of the girls stopped her in the halls to talk about it; they said they'd love to meet the famous lady. Lizzie Lou told them to come over any time. Aunt Lou would like to know them. Once she noticed Bonnie Mason eying her curiously as they passed each other in the hall. Lizzie Lou wanted to make a face at her and say, "So there, Miss Smarty, I didn't lie after all." But she restrained from any such juvenile outburst and, instead, smiled and carried her head a bit higher.

She was feeling rather good that day, anyway, for she was wearing her hair a new way and the mirror had told her that it was becoming. She had watched Aunt Lou put her hair up on kid curlers several times, so she decided to try it herself. The wave that resulted was very satisfying. At Aunt Lou's suggestion she had parted her hair in the middle, made the ear puffs quite small and the knot low on her neck. She thought this arrangement gave her features a better frame, her face didn't look so broad. Strange what confidence this new hairdo gave her.

Friday she went down to the gym after school to see if she could get into the girls' basketball club. The girls' gym teacher, Miss Harrison, was cordial and remembered her from her freshman year. The beginners played at three forty-five on Tuesdays, she told her. If Lizzie Lou wanted to join the group, she should be on the gym floor in gym suit and sneakers at that time. On the way home Lizzie Lou wondered if she could still wear her freshman gym suit, bloomers and middy blouse. Aunt Liz had put them in the attic to save for Peg.

The suit was too small and next afternoon she went shopping with her aunts for material and patterns for a new one, while Peggy took the two young ones to see Tom Mix in *The Sage-Brush Kid.*

The purchases made at Saxon's, they went to the music store to listen to some new records. Aunt Lou got "Alice Blue Gown," "Dardanella," and "Swanee." She bought some sheet music too. Said it would be fun for them to play and sing some of the newer things.

Lizzie Lou looked at her two aunts as they listened to records: Aunt Lou so distinguished in her black fur coat, feathered hat, French heels, snug-fitting kid gloves, and fine black leather bag, she looked every inch the famous actress she was. And Aunt Liz, firm-lipped, outspoken, and energetic, dressed in a dark cloth coat and plain felt hat—well, she looked every inch the homemaker and manager that she was. Lizzie Lou felt lucky to have two such aunts. Somehow she had come to value Aunt Liz more since Aunt Lou had come. Perhaps it was because Aunt Lou appreciated Aunt Liz's accomplishments so thoroughly and never lost a chance to point them out to the family.

One thing Lizzie Lou was sure of, the two of them must have had long talks together, for there seemed to be complete harmony and understanding between them. Aunt Liz had mellowed a little; maybe she felt relieved to have someone share her responsibilities for her sister's children. Lizzie Lou decided she had taken Aunt Liz too much for granted.

When they got home, Aunt Lou spread the material on the dining-room table and cut out the gym suit before they had to set the table for supper.

The next day, Sunday, Jimmy and Lucy begged to stay through church service instead of going to children's church in the basement. They wanted to see Father in the choir.

Lizzie Lou felt very proud of him up there with the others, dressed in a long black robe. She had not realized how good-looking he was. She was sure she could hear his voice coming through, clear and strong. Last night at home Aunt Lou had played today's anthem and he had sung it for them. It was good to have Father interested in the church. It made her feel more a part of the congregation to have her father taking an active part. He said they were going to have choir practice twice a week from now on, until Easter, in order to prepare the Easter music. He did not seem to mind the extra rehearsal, in fact he seemed quite happy about it. Queer, but Father appeared to be getting younger, while she herself was growing older rather rapidly. This new hair style made her feel quite adult. She supposed it was Father's interest in his gym class and renewed interest in music that were clearing the sorrow lines from his face.

She looked at the clock while she was washing the dishes Sunday afternoon. It was this time last Sunday that Bill had called her. Would she ever dare ask him over to dance? She got along very well dancing with her aunts, but could she dance with Bill? She shivered a little thinking about gliding over the floor with his arm about her. She would never have the courage to ask him. Had he been this scared last Sunday before he invited her to the church party? Aunt Lou had said that she was sure boys were self-conscious, asking for dates, and that it must be a blow to them when they were refused. Yes, Lizzie Lou decided, it wasn't easy being a boy either. Growing up was tough any way you looked at it.

It wasn't long till Tuesday. She had to do a good job on the play. She went over the whole plot while she washed the dishes. She was so engrossed in reviewing the tale that she went ahead and dried them, forgetting to call Peggy to do her part of the job. Peggy, delighted at being forgotten, sank deeper into the pages of *Little Women*.

Monday evening the entire family gathered around to hear Lizzie Lou "speak her piece" as Lucy said. The machine work done on the gym suit, Aunt Lou sat sewing the stars on the collar of the white middy and Aunt Liz worked buttonholes on the waistband of the full navy-blue bloomers. Father put aside his newspaper and gave her all of his attention. She told the story as she had told it to herself many times. Peggy and Jimmy clapped when she finished.

Aunt Lou bit off a thread, tapped her thimbled finger on the arm of her chair. "I had the feeling that you were holding back, honey. That you were afraid of what we might think of *you*. Now forget yourself. The story is all that's important. Let yourself go free, and that tale will march right through at your listeners. It's as though you were a mirror and we could look in and see the characters, like a moving picture. Let it unroll on the screen of your mind and we'll see it too."

"Do you suppose I can forget myself tomorrow and do it any better?" Lizzie Lou sat down and turned through the pages of the play.

"Of course you will. Always difficult to perform for your family. And with a real audience in front of you, you will be inspired.

Every actress saves herself at rehearsals, waits for the real performance to give it all she's got."

"Oh, Aunt Lou, I'm no actress," Lizzie Lou protested.

"Now, I wouldn't say that," Aunt Liz interrupted. "I think you're
pretty good for a beginner. Lou, I think you are too critical. Don't
you think she expresses herself well, Warren?"

Father nodded and smiled at her. "Lizzie Lou, you amaze me.
If anyone had told me that you would get up before an audience,
I would have said he was mistaken. You have always seemed so
sort of shy and retiring. But, by George, you've got what it takes.
You really have. Lou, this takes me back to the time when I used
to play audience to your performances." He got up and patted his
daughter's shoulder. "You did fine." He walked to the piano. "Lou,
how about us singing a little before the children go to bed?"

They sang some of the popular songs purchased on Saturday.
"Oh, What a Pal Was Mary," "Let the Rest of the World Go By,"
and "The World is Waiting for the Sunrise." Aunt Liz wanted to
sing some of the old ones. Lizzie Lou felt happy and contented,
standing here singing these good old songs with her family. How
Uncle Mat enjoyed hitting some deep bass notes in "Old Black
Joe" and "We're Tenting Tonight."

She put her hands on Aunt Lou's shoulders. "Sing 'Till We Meet
Again,' Aunt Lou."

"All right, if Warren will harmonize with me. How about it,
Waddy? You know, like we used to?" She struck the chords and
the two of them began the sweet haunting words.

Lizzie Lou thought she had never heard two people sing so well
together. Her eyes stung a little. She had a nice family!

The next morning she got up half an hour earlier than usual and
tiptoed about the bedroom so that Peggy and Lucy would not be
wakened. She untwisted her hair from the kid curlers, brushed it
thoroughly, then combed it until the fuzziness disappeared and
only a wave remained. Her hair must look its best this morning.
She hesitated at the closet door; should she wear the new blue
dress? No, it would seem that she was showing off and besides
if she did a good job they wouldn't know what she had on. She

must make them see the characters in that play. She took out the navy-blue middy suit and brushed it well. In this comfortable old thing it would be easier to forget herself.

At the door before she left, Aunt Lou stopped her. "Now, don't forget, darling, I'll be sitting in the back row in spirit. Tell it right to me. Think only of your story and it will come through fine."

As she was stepping off the porch, Aunt Liz's front door opened. "Good luck, Lizzie Lou. I'll keep my fingers crossed for you," Aunt Liz called out. "Do it as well as you did last night."

She'd have to do better than last night, she thought as she reached the sidewalk, much better. Her throat ached and her stomach felt squashy. How could she do it when she felt so scared? She straightened up, took a deep breath, rearranged books, lunch and gym-suit packages, then set off at a brisk pace, trying to forget the ordeal ahead.

She and Mary sat in the front row. She had put her books on the floor so she would be free of them when Bill called on her. She took a handkerchief from her pocket and wiped the moisture from the palms of her hands. Mary wisely kept silent, but Lizzie Lou took comfort in the nearness of her sympathetic loyalty. They watched the other seniors file in noisily. Miss Tamer took a seat in the back. Bill rushed in at the last minute, put his books on the desk in front, and looked around. He sent a quick smile in Lizzie Lou's direction. The eight thirty-five bell rang and the room quieted.

"A few announcements before we come to the main business of the morning," Bill told the seniors. "Tomorrow a list of names will be posted on the bulletin board showing the time each of you is expected at the photographer's to have your individual pictures taken for our annual, the *Athenian.* If, for any reason, you can't keep your appointment, please notify the office. Group pictures will be taken the last week in February, but we want to get the senior pictures out of the way first."

Lizzie Lou put her handkerchief back in her pocket and fingered the knot in her tie. Her hands were like ice; she felt strange, scared, and her brain seemed a total blank.

"As you all know, the big event in April is the senior play. Last October I appointed a committee to choose our play. After months of reading many plays, the committee agreed on one. And this morning a member of our class is going to tell us the story of that play, *The Cavendish Pearls*. Lizzie Lou, the floor is yours." Bill nodded at her and sat down at the far end of the front row.

She couldn't feel her legs move and yet there she was, standing in front of the desk with a crowd of faces and a sea of eyes before her. She swallowed, raised her head, and looked at the tall windows in the back of the room. Aunt Lou was back there; she would tell it to her.

"Now, for generations, the brides in the Cavendish family had worn the famous Cavendish pearls on their wedding day." She was off! And, like a colt, nervous and uncertain before his first race, she found herself running the course of the tale more easily at every phrase, once the start had been made. As she described the scenes, characters, and situations a strange new feeling crept over her; a feeling of warmth, excitement, exhilaration. It almost seemed that the story was telling itself and that she was looking on from the side lines. Bits of dialogue came to her as she portrayed the sweetness of Diana and the snobbishness of her mother. Aunt Lou would have smiled if she could have seen the aristocratic bearing Lizzie Lou's body took on as she spoke for the grandmother.

By the end of the first act Lizzie Lou was enjoying herself and looking into the eyes of her audience without the slightest evidence of self-consciousness. She had a freedom she had never known before. It was as though the binding cord of her own shyness had been broken and a hidden store of power had been released and had rushed, hand in hand with her imagination, to re-create a world for these people before her. Lizzie Lou felt free, oh, she did feel free!

Her eyes took on a look of wonder as she told of the gypsy girl's awe when she saw the richly furnished room in the Cavendish home. Miss Tamer leaned forward with close attention to catch every word the storyteller spoke as Carlotta discovered the pearls.

Lizzie Lou came to the last curtain conscious of a great weariness. She had given it everything she had. She stood for a moment, motionless. There wasn't a sound in the room. She looked at those in front of her; the Cavendishes and gypsies vanished and there was only the sea of eyes. Had she made a fool of herself? Had she been a ham, a show-off? It was so silent now that the room wasn't filled with the voices of her characters. The clock on the wall gave a click and the big hand moved a notch to nine-ten o'clock. The bell rang and Lizzie Lou, divested of the disguise afforded her by imagination, walked self-consciously to her place beside Mary, sat down, and picked up her books from the floor. She wished she could run from the room, the silence was awful. There was a slight movement here and there as the seniors recovered from their astonishment at Lizzie Lou's unsuspected ability. Then they broke into loud applause. That Jones girl had given her first performance!

14. *Discouraged Basketball Player*

The rest of the day Lizzie Lou floated from class to class on a cloud of compliments. Whenever some senior who, heretofore, hadn't given her a second glance approached, her heart beat hard, wondering what nice thing this one was going to say to her. It was wonderful having people make a to-do about something she had done well! In her first study period that morning she sat, her French reader before her, not seeing a word on the page. Her thoughts raced round and round.

What had happened to her when she stood up there before the class? Whatever it was, she was as astonished as the seniors seemed to be; but how thrilling it had been. It was difficult to analyze the feeling she had had. It was as though she held those seniors in the palm of her hand, and all because of the power of the words coming from her, no, not the words exactly, but the way she said them.

Telling stories to the young ones at home, or describing picture shows had always been fun, fun to see their eyes grow bigger when she expanded an idea; but she had no notion that, with a larger audience, the pleasure would be so intensified. Was this the feeling Aunt Lou had when she was in a play? And if it was, could it be that she herself had acting ability too and might become an actress? A tingling sensation started at the base of her spine, crept up to her head, and suffused itself into a dizzy intoxication at such a thought. Might it not be that she had inherited dramatic talent from Aunt Lou?

She *would* try out for the play. And after the thing she had done this morning, it was possible that she might get the lead. Miss Tamer had been impressed and had complimented her warmly. She closed her eyes and could see the program headed by the words, Diana Cavendish . . . . Lizzie Lou Jones.

She wondered what Bill would say to her. She had been so surrounded by girls this morning after the class meeting that she didn't see him leave the room. She wished they were in some of the same classes. Perhaps he would be waiting for her at her locker at three-thirty. But she wouldn't be there, she had to stay for basketball club.

In the girls' locker room after school, she donned her gym suit and sneakers. She looked at herself briefly in the long mirror and wondered if she looked as well in this outfit as Aunt Lou thought she would. She retied her tie and went out into the gym. Miss Harrison hadn't arrived yet and the place hummed with conversation. She saw Mary on the other side, beckoning. Staunch, loyal Mary, she had walked beside her all day with admiring eyes and had listened to all the compliments with as much satisfaction as though they had been directed at herself.

"I wanted to tell you before I went on home," she said as Lizzie Lou approached. "When I got my coat, Bill was waiting for you by your locker."

Lizzie Lou's mouth curved into a pleased smile. "What did he say?"

"I told him you were playing basketball today. He said O.K. he would see you later; then Bonnie came by and they left together."

Miss Harrison blew her whistle and the smile left Lizzie Lou's face as she went to join the others.

When she got home at five, Aunt Lou was watching for her at the window. "Well, how did the storytelling go, honey?" she asked as Lizzie Lou hung her coat in the closet.

Lizzie Lou followed her into the living room. "It's hard to explain, Aunt Lou," she said. "I surprised myself so much that now I can't believe it was Lizzie Lou Jones up there talking to all those people. It was sort of like having a quiet, soft, little organ and suddenly you discovered you could pull out some stops and presto it became a big, powerful pipe organ. I don't know what happened, but all I can say is, I pulled out all the stops."

Aunt Lou smiled understandingly. "I know. I was sure last night that you would do well before an audience. Now, as soon as you get warm, you slip over to your aunt Liz and tell her about it. She is as anxious as I was to hear about your performance."

"She is? I don't understand it. Aunt Liz is so different since you came."

"Not different, but she has more time to relax and live her own life. She took her responsibility of raising you children so seriously that there was no chance for the real Liz to shine through. Now that she understands that I'm here to share that responsibility, she doesn't have to play such a heavy, exhausting role."

"I'll go over and talk to her now. But shouldn't I help you with supper?"

"Oh, Peg is getting supper tonight. She asked if she might."

"Well, will wonders never cease! Aunt Lou, how did you do it?"

"Now, now, don't underestimate Peg, she just needs a bit of stimulation now and then. I was downtown this morning and I got her a moving-picture magazine. In it was an article about Marguerite Clark, telling how she loves to cook. There were pictures of Miss Clark wearing a cute apron, beside her range, stirring some concoction in a big kettle. Peg read the article after school and then asked if she could get supper."

"Oh, Aunt Lou, you are the sly one, aren't you?" Lizzie Lou laughed as she left for the other side of the house.

Next day Lizzie Lou looked at the senior picture list on the bulletin board. She was to have hers taken Saturday morning at eleven-fifteen. Should she have it taken in her new dress? She would talk it over with Aunt Lou.

As the day passed, she felt let down because no one stopped her in the halls to tell her how good she had been at yesterday's class meeting. There was an emptiness about the day that was very disappointing. Even Mary didn't mention her wonderful performance. What was the use of doing something well if people forgot so quickly? And Bill, why didn't he find her and tell her what she wanted to hear? It was dull after yesterday's excitement.

Thursday morning there was a general assembly, a pep rally

for the Hartsville game on Friday night. The team, in colorful basketball sweaters, sat in a row on the stage with Coach Dawson. Lizzie Lou watched Bill. Only a week ago last Sunday she had that date with him. Her first date. Would he ever ask her for another? Probably not; after all, a boy who was going to be a doctor wouldn't be interested in a girl who had practically no plans for the future.

And yet since the magic of last Tuesday, wasn't a plan for the future evolving in her mind? If she had never found out about Aunt Lou, becoming an actress would probably not have appeared possible, but if Aunt Lou could do it, why couldn't she? But would that same exciting power come to her in a play? After all, on Tuesday she had been alone. Would that same feeling of living another life come to her in a real play with other actors on the stage?

But a doctor couldn't be seriously interested in an actress, could he? When a doctor married he needed a bright, alert partner to care for his home and children, not an actress traveling across the country on one-night stands. How confusing life could be! What did she want? And if she knew, could she make it happen?

She scarcely heard what Mr. Kingston was saying about the team. Ten years from now, where would she be, what would she be doing? Did her future include that tall center up there on the stage? She wished she knew.

As in a dream she rose with the others and joined the yells led by the cheerleaders. She thought how sweet Uncle Mat had been last night. He had come over after supper to say that he had tickets for all of them to the Hartsville game. Basketball, he said, had come to Indiana to stay, and this family must support the Medford team, especially since a certain young lady was interested in a certain player. She knew that she had blushed as Father laughed, but she had liked being teased about Bill.

Turning the corner in the hall at three-thirty, she saw him waiting at her locker. "Hi, Lizzie Lou. Will you wait for me at the front door? I have to go down to the gym to get some things."

"Sure, I'll wait."

"Good. I won't be long."

She watched him disappear down the stairs, then turned to see Mary putting on her rubbers in front of her locker.

"I'm going to wait for Bill, Mary." She opened her own locker and put in her books.

"Yes, I heard," Mary answered, slipping into her coat. "I'll go on. See you in the morning."

While putting on her coat, Lizzie Lou thought of that first time Bill had spoken to her on Armistice Day. "Say, you're a senior, aren't you?" he had said, and then had asked her name and hadn't seemed to notice at all that it was such a silly one.

In English they had had that Shakespeare quotation about a rose by any other name smelling as sweet. She giggled to herself as she wondered if Mr. Shakespeare would have said that if he had thought of a Lizzie Lou rose. What might not happen next, she was laughing at her own name. Wonderful what a date, a bit of acting for the senior class, and a boy asking her to wait at the front door could do for a girl!

Bill held the door open for her and they walked down the front steps together. He carried his gym clothes in a small canvas bag.

"Here, give me that book. There's room in my bag for it." He took her Latin grammar.

"Basketball practice, tonight?" she asked.

"Yes, but not till after supper. Coach wants us to get used to the lights at the armory. Since I didn't have to hurry there after school I wanted the chance to tell you what a fine job you did last Tuesday morning."

The sidewalk was horrid with slushy, melting snow, but it seemed to Lizzie Lou that she was walking on rose petals and pink clouds. He liked her! He thought she had done well.

"I'm glad you liked it," she said modestly. "I was afraid maybe I had put too much feeling in it; overacted, I believe is what Aunt Lou calls it. I got sort of carried away, I guess."

"Well, it was great, really great. Some of the fellows were awfully surprised at you. You know, because you are sort of quiet, not always showing off like some of the gabbier members of our class."

He grinned at her. "Of course, I wasn't surprised, because I know you and, after hearing you make that Cyrano guy come alive, I knew what you could do."

Lizzie Lou smiled her pleasure at him. How sweet to hear those words! Even better than praise of her storytelling was his statement, "I wasn't surprised, because I know you." And yet he didn't really know her, did he? If he knew how shallow and wishy-washy she really was, he wouldn't want to know her. And the conceited ideas she was getting, wanting to hear people praise her all the time. She'd better change the subject even though she loved having him say nice things.

"How's basketball practice going? Of course you're going to beat Hartsville tomorrow," she said.

"Well, the armory has a different feel about it, and with a big crowd there, I don't know how the team will react. But we'll try to win. Are you going?"

"Yes, my whole family will be there."

"Mine too. Say, you will try out for a part in the play, won't you?" He stepped behind her as she walked around a puddle.

"I guess so."

"You'll be good in it, that's for sure. How is your aunt, Miss Leander, feeling now?"

"Oh, much better, thank you. She heard from her husband. He's in a hospital in France."

"She is certainly a fine lady. Wish I could see her in a play."

"I wish you could too. She is wonderful on the stage, absolutely wonderful."

"I guess you must take after her." He hesitated and then gave a knowing nod. "You are pretty wonderful yourself in front of an audience."

Birds sang, flowers bloomed, rainbows arched, sunshine sparkled, breezes whispered, music played, all for Lizzie Lou on this gray, sloppy January day.

It got colder on Friday. The partial thaw froze and it was better underfoot. When they were ready to start for the game, Father wanted to phone for a taxi for Aunt Lou, but she preferred going on the streetcar with the rest of them. Said she'd be warm as toast in her fur coat, heavy shoes, and rubbers. They started early, for Uncle Mat said he was sure the streetcars would be jammed around game time.

Father was in a gay mood. He held Lucy in his arms as they waited at the corner, and on his lap after they were inside the streetcar. Lizzie Lou saw him whisper in the child's ear. Lucy laughed and reached up and patted his cheek with her mittened hand. How well Father looked, his eyes bright, smiling at his youngest.

"What's that they call the team? The Wonder Five?" Aunt Lou asked her.

"That's right."

Aunt Lou laughed. "Such publicity as basketball gets in your papers, more than a top New York play is able to get. But it's much better to read about young men playing games rather than about young men being killed in war," she added soberly.

"Just about this time last year our papers were filled with war headlines. Now everybody in town is interested in basketball."

"If they aren't they soon will be with all the news stories," Aunt Lou returned. "What about Hartsville? Do they have a good team?"

"Oh, the Hartsville team is one of the best in the state. Hartsville is a small town, but their team went to the semifinals in the state tournament last year."

It was seven-fifteen when they reached the armory, and already people were streaming in at every entrance.

"We're not a bit too early," Uncle Mat said as he got the tickets from his pocket. "Hope we get good seats."

Inside Lizzie Lou looked about. She had forgotten how big this place was! Bleachers slanting up from every side; it reminded her of a huge circus tent with the basketball court forming the center rings. Uncle Mat led the way to the bleachers. They found a vacant place and ascended. Lizzie Lou sat between her two aunts; Father, Uncle Mat, and the children in front of them.

"Now, Lizzie Lou, you'll have to explain the game to me," Aunt Liz said when they were seated. "I'm afraid I don't know much about it. How about you, Lou? Are you familiar with the game?"

"Not very. It's been a long time since I have seen it played."

By now the bleachers were pretty well filled. Down on the floor Lizzie Lou noticed two women and a man pause, the man pointed to the vacant spot beyond Aunt Lou. Slowly they climbed up, stepping carefully between those already seated. She saw that Father nodded to one of the ladies. She in turn smiled brightly at him. Now, who was she? Somehow she looked familiar. She was an attractive little woman, dressed in a gray astrakhan coat and light blue hat. When the three were seated, Father turned.

"Good evening, Mrs. Hubbard. I want you to meet my family." In turn he introduced them all saying, "Mrs. Hubbard sings in our choir, you know."

"Of course," Aunt Liz put in, "I think I met you once at a church supper. But I don't believe I ever see you at aid society meeting."

"I'm afraid not, Mrs. Wallace. You see I work in a law office and choir practice is about all I can manage. I'd like you to meet my next-door neighbors, Mr. and Mrs. Pendleton."

Introductions acknowledged, Mrs. Hubbard spoke to Aunt Lou. "Mrs. Logan, are you the actress sister of whom Mr. Jones told me?"

"Yes, I am."

"Well, this is very exciting meeting you. That was a fine article in the *Herald* about you. It made me sorry that I hadn't been able to see your play."

Aunt Lou smiled her thanks. "I haven't seen a basketball game in years. Lizzie Lou is going to have to explain the plays to me."

Mrs. Hubbard looked across at Lizzie Lou. "Maybe you'll answer my questions too. You see the Pendletons and I wanted to come because one of our neighbor boys is on the team. We have watched him grow up. He's such a nice boy. They don't come any better than Billy Monroe. He plays center, you know."

Aunt Lou laughed. "Do we know? Oh, how well we know, Mrs. Hubbard. Just ask Lizzie Lou."

Lizzie Lou's face grew warm and she smiled at her aunt. So, Aunt Lou did know how she felt about Bill.

"Oh, you know Bill?" Mrs. Hubbard asked.

"Yes. We're in the same year at high school, both seniors."

"Well, he's a fine boy, a very fine boy."

Lizzie Lou decided that Mrs. Hubbard was a very nice lady too.

By now the bleachers were well filled, and many small boys and girls sat on the floor in front of the first row. Some of them were romping and scuffling like puppies, throwing hats, and worrying their parents exceedingly, parents seated too far away to admonish their offspring.

The opposing team had brought such a big crowd of rooters that Father said there must be very few people left back in Hartsville. Lizzie Lou's spirits dropped when the visiting team came running out on the floor. What tall, big fellows they were. It looked as though every one of them had tried to outdo Indiana's famous tall corn in height. That center could practically stand under the basket and place the ball in it by just reaching out his arm. He was a good five inches taller than Bill.

As the Wonder Five rushed out, Ted Hinkle sprang into action in front of the Medford bleachers, shouting through his megaphone. "All right now. Let's give 'em the old locomotive. Come on now, everybody yell!"

Throwing the megaphone into the air, he went through his usual waving of arms, bending of body, and contortion of face, drawing out of the crowd a roar of sound to encourage the team.

M-e-d-f-o-r-d, M-e-d-f-o-r-d, M-E-D-F-O-R-D!
MEDFORD MEDFORD MEDFORD! YEA!

Lizzie Lou yelled as loud as she could.

"Well, I never," Aunt Liz said. "What do they want to make such a racket for?"

"That's to help the team, Aunt Liz," Lizzie Lou explained.

"I'd think it would help those boys more if it were quiet and they could think what they were doing. What are they doing out there now? Which one is that Bill Monroe you went out with?"

"They are warming up, taking turns trying to get the ball through the net. Bill is the tall black-haired one, the next one in line to shoot the ball. There, now he has the ball." Lizzie Lou felt proud as Bill tossed the ball easily through the basket.

"Well, I must say he seems good at it," Aunt Liz said. "Now what is the point of the game?"

Lizzie Lou explained.

"And you played this game last Tuesday in that new gym suit we made you?"

"Well, girls' basketball is a little different. There are six on a team instead of five and we can't play all over the floor as the boys can. And I wouldn't say that I played the game last Tuesday. I'm just learning and I'm not any good at it," Lizzie Lou answered.

"Now, Lizzie Lou, I expect you are doing fine," Aunt Lou put in. "Are those new uniforms the boys are wearing?"

"Yes. Don't they look nice? I love blue and gold."

The referee blew the whistle, but instead of the teams taking their places for the beginning tossup, they lined up facing each other on opposite sides of the center. Several men walked out.

"Now what's this?" Aunt Liz asked. "Are they going to start?"

"I don't know." Lizzie Lou was puzzled. "That's the coach, Mr. Dawson, and our principal, Mr. Kingston. Oh yes, that one in the brown overcoat is the mayor. I don't know the other two."

Aunt Liz leaned forward to ask Uncle Mat. "Mat says those other two are the presidents of the Rotary and Kiwanis clubs," she explained as she settled back.

It was evident to the crowd that some kind of a dedication ceremony was taking place out on the floor. But even though each man used a megaphone while delivering his speech, the people could hear only a few words; something about Medford's new basketball building, dedicated to good sportsmanship. There was something about the Wonder Five too, but Lizzie Lou couldn't catch it.

"I do hope," Aunt Lou said when it was over," that someday they will invent something so people can be heard in a big place like this. I hate missing lines."

"Well, that's not likely, Lou, not likely at all," Aunt Liz said.

"Oh, I don't know; whoever would have thought man could fly or go under water in a submarine?"

Lizzie Lou knew from the moment Hartsville got the first tip-off that the Wonder Five were outclassed. Those tall farm boys ran rings around the home team. Medford was blocked at every turn. She answered the questions of her two aunts with difficulty, she was so disconsolate at the way the game was going.

It was awful watching Bill out there, playing his level best and to no avail. The new blue jerseys with the gold letters were wet with sweat at the end of the first quarter.

With a pain in her throat, she watched the Wonder Five sink exhausted to the floor when they called time out. She watched Bill talking to the others seriously, earnestly emphasizing his words with clenched fist. This was awful. She joined the others, yelling their throats out, trying to hearten their losing team.

"Those boys are worn out," Aunt Liz said with concern, as the whistle blew and the Wonder Five leaped to their feet. "They should have a longer rest. Do they have to go on playing?"

"Yes, until the half is over."

"Well, they should rest longer. Look at those other boys, not a bit tired, they look as fresh as daisies," Aunt Liz observed.

Yes, just look at them, keeping the ball down around their basket all the time. Bill had the ball. Now if Medford could keep it and get it down the floor. Bill passed to Tim, while Pat raced toward their basket, a tall guard after him. The ball sailed through the air over the guard's head and Pat connected with the basket. The Wonder Five had scored at last! Aunt Liz and Aunt Lou shouted approval along with their niece. As Bill ran back to center for the tossup, Lizzie Lou saw him give Pat an appreciative slap on the back.

Uncle Mat turned to Lizzie Lou. "Now we're going places. Just needed that first one to break the jinx."

But at the end of the half the score was 27 to 2. It seemed hopeless to Lizzie Lou.

"Well, thank goodness, those poor boys can get a longer rest now," Aunt Liz said as the teams retired to the dressing rooms. "Warren, do you play this game at the Y.M.C.A.?"

Father turned around. "Sometimes. It's a Y.M.C.A. game, you know. A 'Y' man, name of Naismith, invented it."

"Well, I had no idea you could cavort around like these boys."

Father laughed. "Our game is much slower, Liz, much slower, but it's a fine game for men as well as boys."

"And don't forget us girls, Father," Lizzie Lou put in. "I'm not good at it yet, but it's fun trying."

Mrs. Hubbard turned to Aunt Lou. "I feel so sorry for Billy out there, working hard and yet not able to make baskets. From what I read in the papers, Medford expected to win this game. Isn't that right?" She looked at Lizzie Lou.

"Yes. The team did so well against Kokomo."

"Well, only one team can win and the way it looks now that team is not going to be the Wonder Five," Uncle Mat said ruefully.

"Oh, Mat, don't be so pessimistic," Aunt Lou admonished. "Just wait till the second half."

But Uncle Mat was right; though the Medford boys came back with renewed vigor and determination, Hartsville's lead was too much to surmount. The score at the final gun was 39 to 8.

Lizzie Lou stood up amid the victorious yells of the Hartsville visitors. She saw Bill run up to the other center and shake his hand. She wished she could tell Bill what a fine game he had played and that she thought he was wonderful. She had a great urge to brush his hair up off his forehead. Imagine even thinking such a thing! She must be careful or she would be getting as bold as Bonnie. There had been a time when she would have thought that good, but from several casual remarks Bill had made, she gathered that he didn't admire the bold type. And she wanted Bill's approval more than anything else in the world.

Saturday morning she was dusting the dining room, trying to get finished in time to go down to the photographer's for her appointment. The telephone rang and Peggy, who was supposed to be dusting the bannister rails but in reality was seated on the stairs reading *Lady Jane,* answered it.

"Somebody wants you, Lizzie Lou," she shouted.

Lizzie Lou pulled her dust cap up from over her ear as she took the receiver and said, "Hello."

"That you, Lizzie Lou?"

She shoved the receiver hard against her ear. "Yes. Sounds like Bill."

"Right. I wondered if you would like to cheer up a poor, tired, discouraged old basketball player tonight?"

She clasped the wooden shelf of the telephone tightly with her right hand. "Why—I—why, yes, of course."

"Well, my boss gave me the evening off here at the grocery and I thought maybe you would like to go to a picture show. I need to forget about last night."

"Why, I'd like to go. What time?"

"How about seven? Maybe if we get out of the show in time we could dance a little at your house afterward." His voice hesitated. "Would that be all right with you?"

"Yes. You'll be here at seven, then?"

"Righto. Got to get back to work. See you tonight. So long."

"Good-by, Bill."

Would it be all right with her? Would it ever! A picture show and then—dancing with him! She turned and saw Peggy grinning, Peggy who had listened to every word, but she was too happy to scold. Instead she grabbed her astonished sister about the waist and waltzed her into the living room.

15. *"I Never Knew"*

The new semester began on February third, began so auspiciously that Lizzie Lou knew this was going to be the best semester of school she had ever had. She and Bill were in the same civics class! Now she would be sure to see him every day and not have to depend on a chance passing in the halls or meeting on the way to or from school. This class period she could count on, no chance about it.

She had had two dates with him! She would probably never forget that first date. As she looked back on it, it seemed that a new spirit had begun to blossom within her that Sunday evening.

The second date had been wonderful! They had gone to the Bijou to see Douglas Fairbanks in *Bound in Morocco*. Walking downtown she had done her best to cheer Bill, tried to tell him what a fine game he had played the night before. The picture was marvelous. The way that man could leap from high places and escape from his enemies, the way he could swing down, hanging onto a rope or a piece of drapery and knock down his pursuers, the way he would run and leap on a horse. Bill said Douglas Fairbanks was a fine athlete. He would have to be to do all the stunts he performed in his pictures.

And when they got home, the lights in the living room were still burning, but her family had disappeared. Probably Aunt Lou's doing. Bill had looked through their records and had put on a waltz first, "I'm Forever Blowing Bubbles." They pushed back the chairs, he turned down the volume. Her left hand had trembled a bit as she placed it on his shoulder, but her right hand felt steady, held in his firm grasp. They glided about the room. She would always remember his remark as the record finished. "Say, we do all right together. You're light as a feather on your feet, Lizzie Lou." Then they had put on "Hindustan" and she had tried to pass on what Aunt Lou had taught her about the fox trot. Before he had left they were doing rather well with that combination of two-step and one-step. "I didn't think the fox trot would be this easy, Lizzie Lou. You are a good teacher," he had said, when he left at eleven.

And now they were in a class together! February was going to be a good month. Basketball club was fun. Mary had joined too and Lizzie Lou found it easier, having her friend there; they could laugh together at their mistakes.

It had been a good day too when Aunt Lou received that long letter from overseas. Her eyes were like stars the rest of the week. It was easy to see how much she loved Jerry Logan. Lizzie Lou wondered if she would ever be able to call him Uncle, he seemed such a hazy figure in her mind.

And then there was that evening when Aunt Liz and Uncle Mat had gone off to their first dance at the Elks' club. Aunt Liz had a new dress and Lizzie Lou could tell she was excited about the whole affair.

Father's interest in the "Y" and the church choir was doing him a lot of good. He was lively and told a lot of jokes at mealtime. He went to a party that Mrs. Hubbard gave for the members of the choir. It was surprising, he said, Mrs. Hubbard had such a big house. One would think she would want to sell it, since her husband had been killed overseas in 1917. Lizzie Lou had wanted to ask him if Mrs. Hubbard had showed him which was Bill's house in the neighborhood. But she didn't; it seemed sort of a silly question.

Mary was working on the *Athenian* staff now. Jim Buell was editor in chief of that annual publication. He had given Mary a special assignment, to select a suitable quotation for every senior, the quotation to appear under each picture. Mary searched through books of quotations every free bit of time she had, and her conversation to Lizzie Lou was filled with, "What do you think of this one for Dale Gordon?" or, "I think this fits Mark Johnson to a T. What do you think?"

"Mary! You're going to have quotations coming out of your ears before this thing is over," Lizzie Lou told her.

"Well, I've got to do a good job. Jim thinks I can do it."

"Of course you can. Jim's nice, isn't he?" Lizzie Lou remembered what a good listener he had been to her tale of *Cyrano*.

"He's wonderful," Mary answered with firm conviction.

It was Aunt Lou who suggested that Lizzie Lou have a Valentine party.

"But—but, Aunt Lou, whom would I invite?"

"Why not invite the girls and let them invite the boys? I wonder whom you would invite for yourself?" Aunt Lou laughed.

"Oh, Aunt Lou, do you suppose he'd come?"

"I wouldn't see why not. He has taken you out twice. Valentine's day comes on Friday. There's no basketball game that night and he won't be working at the grocery Friday after supper."

"What girls would I ask and would they want to come?"

"Of course, every girl likes an excuse to take the initiative and invite a boy to an affair. Why don't you start with Mary? She seems to be your best friend."

"But Mary doesn't date."

"Well, it's time she did. We'll help her get started. From that one time I met her, I imagine she won't have any qualms about inviting a young man. She seems like a girl who gets things done, once she makes up her mind."

Aunt Lou was right. A pleased expression appeared on Mary's face when Lizzie Lou told her about the party. She gave her head a slight nod.

"That's wonderful, Lizzie Lou. And I know exactly the boy I'll ask—Jim Buell."

"Jim Buell? But do you know him well enough?"

"Well, I will after the party. Who else are you inviting?"

"Frieda Hempstead, Velda Conner, and Sara Duncan. There will be five couples. That's about as many as can dance in our living room."

"Of course you are asking Bill."

"Yes. Right after civics class. I wish you were taking civics."

"Couldn't fit it into my schedule. Sorry to miss that course. I always thought it would be fun in that class when Mr. Faulkner has you write a paper on the kind of person you'd like to marry. Milly Stover told me about it last year. She said Mr. Faulkner read some of them in class, not giving names, of course."

Lizzie Lou thought that over as she walked toward Room 106 for civics. The kind of person she wanted to marry! Would anyone ever want to marry her? It didn't seem possible, for she had so many faults. And yet hadn't she had two dates with the nicest fellow in school? But marriage was a long way off. First things first. Would Bill think she was too bold, asking him for a date? No, of course not. Lots of girls asked boys to things, she knew that. She remembered early last fall the Kappa Zeta Phi sorority had given a progressive dinner and the girls had invited the boys. She had wondered at the time how girls could muster the courage to ask boys to escort them. And now here she was, Lizzie Lou Jones, about to invite the president of the senior class to be her partner for an evening. How she had changed.

Bill was not at his desk when she entered 106 but dashed in just as the bell rang. Mr. Faulkner called the roll. Before he had a chance to start his usual questions on the day's assignment, Walter Johnson waved his hand in the air. Bill looked at Lizzie Lou and winked; she grinned back. They both recognized this old trick of Walter's; he had used it in other classes when he was unprepared.

"Mr. Faulkner, what do you think of the Prohibition Amendment ratified in January?" Walter asked, knowing that Mr. Faulkner was a "push-over" for a topic on current events.

"Walter, that is an excellent question. I'm glad to know that you read the newspapers." Mr. Faulkner rose and walked over by a window. "Personally I am undecided. It's probably good for the people. But I can't for the life of me see how they'll have enough officers to enforce it. People have a habit of not wanting what's good for them. Of course it doesn't go into effect until January of next year, so we'll have to wait to see how it works."

Lizzie Lou remembered hearing Father and Uncle Mat discussing the pros and cons of prohibition. She didn't know much about it, since neither Father nor Uncle Mat drank. A few times she had seen men staggering on the streets downtown and had been frightened and repulsed. But since it was no problem in her family she had not given it much thought.

Walter certainly had known the question to ask. Mr. Faulkner talked on and on. Then someone asked about the possibility of passage of the Nineteenth Amendment, giving women the right to vote. Lizzie Lou saw Walter sit back and relax, it was well-known that this was Mr. Faulkner's pet peeve, the fact that the women of the United States were not permitted to vote.

"The women of Finland have voted since 1906." The teacher ran his hand through his hair, a characteristic gesture. "Why we have to be so inconsiderate of women in this country, I don't know."

Lizzie Lou looked at the clock, only fifteen more minutes; they wouldn't get to the assignment today. This was more interesting than the details of city government anyway.

After class Bill joined her at the door and they walked toward the stairs. "Well, old Walter did it again," he laughed.

"It was interesting though. Say, Bill, I'm having a Valentine party on Friday. Will you be able to come?" She was surprised how easy it was to ask him.

"Friday? Why, yes, I'd like to come if you don't mind my leaving early. Saturday night is the Anderson game at Anderson. What time is the party?"

"About eight. There will be five couples. I thought we'd dance and maybe sing. Aunt Lou has quite a lot of sheet music."

"Sounds like a good evening. I'll be there."

Later she invited the other three girls, who accepted with alacrity. Now that the die was cast she worried. What would the rest of her family do while the party was in progress? Of course Jimmy and Lucy went to bed at eight-thirty, but there would be Peggy, Father, and Aunt Lou. She worried most about Peggy; one never knew what embarrassing thing she might say.

When she got home, she and Aunt Lou did some planning about refreshments. At supper they told Father about the party.

"Well, now, that's too bad, I won't be able to make it. The choir director is having a little get-together at his home after choir practice that evening. But I expect you will be able to get along without me." He smiled at Lizzie Lou. "That long-legged center going to be here?"

"Oh, Father, he's not long-legged. He's just tall."

Peggy put down her fork, gave Lizzie Lou a mischievous look, and began to sing.

> *"He was just a long, lean, country gink*
> *From away out West where the hop toads wink.*
> *He was six feet two in his stocking feet*
> *And he kept gettin' thinner the more he'd eat."*

Lizzie Lou gave Father a beseeching look.

"That will be enough, Margaret!"

"Yes, Father." Peggy picked up her fork.

Lizzie Lou's appetite left her. What if Peg did something like that at her party? If she did, Lizzie Lou knew she would die of embarrassment, absolutely die. What did you do with a family when you had a party and the house was small? The upstairs was too cold for them to go up there until it was bedtime. Aunt Lou smiled at her reassuringly.

On Friday evening, dressed in her new blue dress, hair neatly combed, Lizzie Lou surveyed the living room. It wasn't quite seven-thirty. Father had gone to choir practice. Jimmy and Lucy were in the kitchen "helping" Aunt Lou. Aunt Liz had endeared herself to her eldest niece by inviting Peggy to her side of the house for supper and to spend the night.

Lizzie Lou walked to the victrola and touched the crank to see if it was wound. She sat down on the piano bench and leafed through the sheet music Aunt Lou had discovered in the bottom of her trunk. She picked out the melody with one finger and sang, "Down Among the Sheltering Palms." It had been a long time since she had heard that one. Here was "Pretty Baby" and "Poor Butterfly." She wished she could read music quickly and play things right off, but it had been so long since she had had lessons. Velda was a good piano player. She played with the school orchestra. She would be able to play these.

She got up and went to the dining room and turned on the

light. Aunt Lou had put on the best linen tablecloth and made a centerpiece of red hearts. There were red candles in the candlesticks. Lizzie Lou gave a sigh of satisfaction at the whole effect. She was lucky, having two such aunts: Aunt Liz, who had taken care of them all for so long, and now Aunt Lou to provide an imaginative touch to make life extra sweet. She touched the tablecloth to feel the ironed slickness of it. How nice her hand looked, nails filed into rounded points and shining from recent buffing. Her hands were soft and white too. Aunt Lou had given her an old pair of kid gloves and some special cream with instructions to apply the cream and wear the gloves every night. The result had been sheer magic.

Sounds of singing came from the kitchen. She found Aunt Lou and the two children seated at the kitchen table. Aunt Lou was playing checkers with Jimmy and singing Mother Goose rhymes with Lucy.

"Now let's sing 'Jack and Jill' again, Aunt Lou." The little girl noticed her sister. "Lizzie Lou, Aunt Lou knows two verses that aren't in my book."

"It's your move, Aunt Lou," Jimmy reminded his aunt.

"It's nice of you, Aunt Lou, to keep them out here." Lizzie Lou put her hand on her aunt's shoulder.

"Oh, we're having fun. Now, honey, the sandwiches are wrapped in a clean towel there in the breadbox and the dish of jello is in the roaster on the back porch. Those cookies Aunt Liz made are there in that crock on the cabinet. There's plenty of milk if you want to make cocoa."

Lizzie Lou took the lid off the crock and looked at the cookies. They were heart-shaped with pink icing. "These cookies are beautiful. I have two of the nicest aunts." She walked toward the dining room. "Oh, Aunt Lou, do you think everything will be all right?"

"Of course, honey. You just act natural and try to see that everyone has a good time. You look very nice. So don't worry about yourself."

"Will you come in and meet them? They are all anxious to see you. You already know Mary, Jim, and Bill."

"I'll come in for a moment after the children go to bed. But I'll not stay. This is your party."

There was a noise from the front of the house, a knocking on the front door. The party had begun.

"Thought I'd come early," Bill said as Lizzie Lou opened the door. "Maybe I could help in some way."

"Well, that's nice of you. You can put your coat here in the hall closet. Aunt Lou took the family's things upstairs, so there's room." She gave him a hanger.

Bill put his cap and a large flat package on the closet shelf and removed his coat. "Don't let me forget that package before I go home. Hmmmm, got on that pretty blue dress again. I sure like it."

She led the way to the living room. "I'm glad. Do you think we should move the chairs back before the others come?"

"Let's do. How about some music while we work?" He went to the victrola and looked through the records below, then put on "Swanee." They began pushing the furniture to the walls. Bill whistled with the music. Lizzie Lou thought chairs had never seemed so light. The floor space was empty in a trice.

Bill snapped his fingers, swung his shoulders, and did a couple of steps. "Come on, gal, what are we waiting for? The music is a-wastin'." And Lizzie Lou found herself swung into a fast one-step.

By the time the others arrived she and Bill were really "goin' to town" as Bill said.

Jim Buell brought some of his records. They played them all. "For Me and My Gal" and "Everybody Ought to Know How To Do the Tickletoe" were favorites, but "Ja-Da" they played again and again until it was a wonder the record didn't crack. They sang it as they danced:

> "Ja-da, Ja-da
> Ja-da, Ja-da Jing jing jing."

Mary found Aunt Lou's record of "Till We Meet Again." After they played it Velda said, "Lizzie Lou, are we going to get to meet your famous aunt?"

"I think she is upstairs. I'll call her."

Lizzie Lou was proud as she introduced Aunt Lou, she looked so pretty in a black and white, tiny-checked, gingham dress; a plain dress, but the white organdy collar and cuffs gave it an air of style or maybe it was Aunt Lou who provided the style. Anyway she looked charming and her simple, friendly manner put the young people completely at ease. After a few pleasant remarks she turned to go back upstairs.

"Oh, Mrs. Logan, won't you sing something for us before you leave?" Frieda asked. "We played your record and it's lovely."

Aunt Lou smiled and went to the piano. "All right, just one." She sat down, took the stack of music on her lap and turned through. "I'll do this one. I'm a sentimental fool when it comes to any song about Indiana." She set the music of a popular song about Indiana before her, played a few chords, and sang in her rich, full voice. When she finished she looked over her shoulder. "Come on, sing it with me."

They came closer and joined in on the nostalgic song, enjoying its sentiment with real Hoosier fervor. Lizzie Lou knew she had never enjoyed herself so much, standing behind her aunt, between her best friend and, though she wouldn't have said it, she thought it, her best, her one and only beau.

They begged Aunt Lou to sing some more, but she said no, Velda could take over at the piano. Lizzie Lou squeezed her hand as she left the room to go upstairs. She hoped the squeeze would tell her what a wonderful time she was having, not knowing that her pink cheeks, sparkling eyes, and curved lips had already told Aunt Lou a great deal.

Velda played and they sang. They danced some more. Although she hadn't planned to, Lizzie Lou asked if they would like to help get out the food. What a stroke of genius that was!

The kitchen had never been so full of people, fun and laughter. Everything was funny. Lizzie Lou hadn't known things could be so funny. Jim said he could make dandy cocoa, so he and Johnny Hanly took over. Jim found an apron and Lizzie Lou's dust cap in the pantry. He came out wearing them and putting on an uproariously funny act. The girls set the table and lit the candles; Ben Zeigert and Don Temple got out the cookies while Bill brought in the jello and held the dishes while Lizzie Lou filled them.

Jim insisted on wearing the dust cap to the table. Lizzie Lou and the others laughed until they ached. Bill told him instead of becoming a newspaperman, he should think of going into vaudeville. Jim said he might just do that.

There was very little food left when they finished. Lizzie Lou was surprised that Bill didn't leave, but he showed no signs of it. He seemed to be waiting. They danced some more after the food. It was a little after eleven when the others left to get the eleven-fifteen car at the corner. Bill was still there.

As she closed the front door he came into the hall and started toward the hall closet. She thought he was going to get his coat but instead he took down the package from the shelf and handed it to her.

"This is sort of a—a—well, a Valentine present for you." He spoke slowly. She took it. "It's a record," he went on. "The music store only got it in today. I kinda liked it and thought you might too. Shall we play it?"

Walking back into the living room, murmuring a thank-you, she took the record from the paper and looked at it. Bill looked over her shoulder.

"No, not that side. It's the other side that I bought it for, 'I Never Knew.' Put it on. Here, I'll wind it up."

As the tune filled the room, he said, "Let's see how it dances."

Lizzie Lou fell into step with him. After an evening of dancing together she followed him easily, recognizing each change of step, anticipating each turn. Now the orchestra played more softly and a male vocalist was singing the words. Lizzie Lou's heart seemed to beat double time. Was she hearing right? Were those words saying what she thought they were? Had he chosen this record because of the melody or the words?

The record finished. He looked down at her. "Like it?"

"It—it's lovely. Thank you very much." She turned off the victrola. "Shall we play the other side?"

"No, I have to go. I shouldn't have stayed this late. Coach won't like it." He started toward the hall and she followed. She was silent as he put on his coat. He held out his hand and took hers. "Thanks for asking me, Lizzie Lou. I've had a great time. Really great."

"Thanks for the record. And—and good luck for tomorrow's game."

"Thanks. Good-by."

He was gone!

She stood there a moment. She glanced at the hall closet. Father's hat and coat were there. He must have come in while they were eating. Slowly she went to the victrola, wound it, set the record spinning and put the needle down. She stood, head erect, listening; then as the vocalist began she bent with her ear close, that she might not miss a word.

> *"I never knew I could love anybody,*
> *Honey, like I'm loving you.*
> *I never realized what a pair of eyes*

And a loving smile could do.
I can't eat, I can't sleep
I never knew that anyone could be so sweet.
I never knew I could love anybody,
Honey, like I'm loving you."

She put her hands to her face. Bill had given her this record! But of course it didn't mean anything. Most popular music was about love. It didn't mean a thing. He probably hadn't even noticed the words.

She stopped the victrola and pulled the furniture back into place. She went to the kitchen and put the dishes to soak. She would wash them in the morning.

She went back into the living room and played the record again. She turned out the lights and stood at the window. She didn't feel a bit sleepy, though it was way past bedtime.

Whoever would have thought that she could have had such a party and such fun. And she hadn't been afraid, she hadn't been scared at all. She sang softly:

"I never knew I could love anybody,
Honey, like I'm loving you."

16. *Spring*

When she got to be an old, old lady, Lizzie Lou knew she would remember this spring of 1919, the year spring began on February fourteenth. The air was sweeter, the sky bluer, birds came earlier, and the first crocus in March was so deeply purple that it made her throat ache. It was as though she had not seen spring before. This year she not only saw it but felt it, felt it to the tips of her fingers and down into her feet, feet that seemed to dance even when she walked. On her way to school each day she held her head high, watched for buds on trees, listened for a robin's song, hummed bits of tunes and, when no one was in sight, she whistled "I Never Knew." Spring was in her thoughts, in her heart, and in her soul.

A few afternoons when he didn't have to attend basketball practice Bill walked home with her. They had a great deal to talk about, for there were so many senior activities going on. Lizzie Lou felt that she had become another person since Bill had come into her life. That scared, shy, self-conscious, self-critical person seemed very immature and childish as she looked back. Was this— this thing that had happened to her—love? She had heard it said and read it again and again that high-school affairs were only puppy love. She couldn't believe that. Perhaps freshman or sophomore crushes might be, but if one waited until one's senior year, as she had, surely it had to be the real thing.

She felt, deep within her, that her life was bound to be linked with Bill Monroe's. But it wouldn't happen if she didn't do something about it. She would have to make herself the kind of girl he could admire. She would have to set herself some goals in life just as he had. No boy would want a girl he might be ashamed of later on when he got to be a fine doctor. She would have to be able not only to keep up with him but also to inspire him to reach the highest point of his own abilities. It was a full order, she knew, but this spring anything seemed possible.

One evening, after the children had gone to bed, Aunt Lou brought up the subject of Lizzie Lou's future. Father seemed surprised when Lizzie Lou said, "I would like to go to college."

"You would? Why, I thought, well, you spoke of going to business school here in Medford. I can manage to send you there, but college—well, I don't know about that. What made you change your mind?" Father put his book on the table.

"Oh, I don't know, so many things, Father. I've discovered that there are lots of books down at the library that are way over my head. I'd like to be able to read more widely and to read with understanding."

Aunt Lou smiled and put a marker in the play she was reading. Her agent was sending new scripts every week or so, hoping she would find one to her liking for the coming season. "That's my girl! Warren, your daughter is becoming a woman, fast. Have you noticed?"

Father rubbed his chin. "Uh-huh. But college, Lou—I'm not sure that I——"

"That you can afford it? Well, Warren, I've been thinking about this ever since I came. I've written Jerry and he agrees that since we have no daughter of our own it would give us great pleasure to help our niece get to college." Aunt Lou looked at Lizzie Lou. "In fact Liz and I have already written to a lot of schools asking them to send their catalogues. Liz agrees with me that you should go away to school, honey."

"She does? But I thought—I thought she wanted me to take over here at home."

"That was some time ago. I think Liz has changed about a lot of things since she and Mat have started having some fun."

"But, Aunt Lou, when your husband gets back, I mean when Uncle Jerry and you return to New York, Aunt Liz will have the same responsibilities again, unless I——"

Father rose and walked to the window, pulled back the curtain, and peered out. Aunt Lou watched him.

"Don't worry about that, Lizzie Lou. Who knows what will happen by summer?" Aunt Lou smiled knowingly. "When are those tryouts for the play?"

"Not until the week of March twenty-third. The play is to be given April twenty-fourth and twenty-fifth. Miss Tamer says she will start rehearsals on March thirty-first after the state basketball tournament is over. No one could get his mind on a play with basketball in the air. Wouldn't it be wonderful if we got to play in the state tournament at Indianapolis? If we can just do as well at the regionals next Saturday at Lafayette as we did last week at the district tournament. Did I tell you that Miss Tamer is wearing an engagement ring? It's Mr. Dawson, the coach, you know. She'll probably have trouble getting her mind on the play even when basketball is over."

"I shouldn't wonder. Warren, how is the Easter music coming along?"

Father turned from the window. "Oh, first rate. Would you mind going over some of it with me? I have a small solo bit and I need practice."

Lizzie Lou watched them, seated on the piano bench. My, what it had meant to Father having Aunt Lou here, after those years of separation. How lonely he would be when she returned to the stage and if she herself went off to college next year. She couldn't bear to leave him.

The Wonder Five lost to Huntington at the regionals the following Saturday and basketball was over in Medford for another season, over as far as high-school games were concerned. But the spell of the game continued. Big boys, little boys, girls and men, all over town, went right on tossing balls through hoops, from regulation hoops in gyms to barrel hoops nailed on barns and sheds. It was a fascinating game and the Hoosiers "took" to it.

Lizzie Lou found Bill rather quiet on the Monday after the regionals. Losing his chance to play in the state tournament was a great disappointment, for, as he told her, his program at the university would be a heavy one and he wouldn't be able to go out for the team, could only play in intra-mural games.

But Lizzie Lou found there were compensations to losing the

tournament; Bill walked home with her every afternoon. Of course it was never prearranged; she would just happen to be strolling down the steps casually at three thirty-five, after tossing her books in her locker, grabbing her coat and racing down the hall in order to assume that casual appearance before he got there. He would step up from behind and say softly, "Carry your books, Miss Jones?" She sometimes wondered if he too hurried at his locker so that he could arrive on time at this seemingly chance meeting. No matter how it happened, it was wonderful.

He listened thoughtfully when she told of her prospects for college. He discussed with her the various colleges as her catalogues began to arrive. He came over one Friday night and they looked the catalogues over together. They danced, too, after her family had gone to bed. Bill sang "I Never Knew" softly in her ear. Was there ever such a spring? Such a spring!

On the Sunday afternoon before the play tryouts, Lizzie Lou

went upstairs to her room, took off her good dress and shoes, put on her bathrobe, turned the covers down on the bed, piled the pillows up, and crawled in. She had to be alone and it was too chilly up here unless she got in bed. Now, she must think and concentrate. She had not thought of the play for weeks, her mind had been filled with spring and Bill.

At the senior meeting last Friday Miss Tamer had said that since the play had been told so well they undoubtedly had the characters well in mind and that she would let them read lines for the character they chose to try for in any scene they liked.

Lizzie Lou leaned back against the pillows and closed her eyes. She visualized Diana Cavendish moving across the stage toward her fiancé wearing a dress of pale green chiffon. Diana Cavendish wearing a long black cape at the gypsy camp to have her fortune told. Diana Cavendish in a pink silk negligee receiving the Cavendish pearls from her grandmother. Diana Cavendish in her wedding dress and veil holding her father's arm. Which scene should she read from? She could do any of them well, but which would be more effective?

She wished Bill would try for a part. Rehearsals would be so much more fun if he were there. She repeated some of Diana's lines that she remembered. Should she make her just sweet or a little haughty? No, not haughty, but genteel and aristocratic, very aristocratic. Saxon's department store was going to lend the costumes. It would be fun going down there and being fitted in all of Diana's clothes. Almost as good as getting ready-made clothes of her own.

That scene with the grandmother seemed best, that's the one she would ask to read. Miss Tamer had been so complimentary about the way Lizzie Lou told the play, surely she had a good chance of getting the Diana part.

It was good to have this confidence in herself. It was Bill and spring and Aunt Lou that did it. She turned her class ring on her finger and let herself sink into the best of her current daydreams.

The following day she walked slowly from her last class toward the stairs. No need to hurry since she was staying for tryouts. She would have time to powder her nose and comb her hair. Miss

Tamer had said three forty-five. She had felt good today in a gingham dress. Nice to get out of wool. She had spent a lot of time on Saturday fixing and pressing her cotton dresses. Father had gone to Mrs. Hubbard's for supper, last night; he said the minister and his wife were among the guests. It was good, having Father do things like that, being interested in people. It had taken him so long to get over Mother's death, but now, at last, she believed he had.

Bill was waiting for her at her locker. "Wanted to wish you luck before I left," he said.

"Well, thanks. I wish you would try for a part."

"Nope. The stage is not my meat. When there's a play I want to be sitting on the other side of the footlights."

She smiled. "It takes people on both sides to make a play. The audience is as important as the actor."

"You can count on me to be out there clapping my hands off. Well—so long. See you tomorrow."

"Good-by, Bill." She unlocked her locker and put her books on the shelf.

"Well, Lizzie Lou Jones, as I live and breathe!" Mary grinned as she stopped at the next locker. "Usually all I see of you at this time of day is a brief glimpse of your coattails as you are whisking downstairs. Care if I go to the auditorium with you?"

Lizzie Lou looked surprised. "But you said you weren't trying for a part."

"Changed my mind last period in study hall. I didn't have anything to do, so I just sat there and thought about the play and the more I thought of it the more I thought I'd like to do that maid. She has some funny lines. Who knows, maybe I'm a comedian at heart."

Lizzie Lou grinned knowingly. "And of course the fact that Jim Buell said he was trying out for the butler part had nothing to do with it. Several good scenes there between the butler and maid."

Mary knelt to retrieve a pencil.

The auditorium was buzzing with the voices of would-be actors when the girls walked down the aisle. It looked as though a good half of the senior class was there. Mary and Lizzie Lou sat in the third row behind Janet and Bonnie.

"Hi," Bonnie turned and smiled at them. "Where's your shadow, Lizzie Lou? I didn't suppose you ever went anyplace without him."

Lizzie Lou returned the smile. Was Bonnie being catty or did she want to be friendly? She would give her the benefit of the doubt. She could afford to be magnanimous.

"Bill isn't trying for a part. What part are you trying for?"

"Diana Cavendish. It's the only part I'm suited for. I tried on my mother's wedding dress and veil yesterday and it looks lovely on me. I thought it would look old-fashioned but it didn't at all. What part are you reading?"

"I'm not quite sure, yet." No use telling her.

Janet turned and looked at her. "After the way you told us that play, I'd think Miss Tamer would give you any part you asked for. You certainly were good."

"What's happened to your actress aunt?" Bonnie asked.

"She's still at our house."

"She is? I wouldn't think she'd want to stay in this dull town when she could be in New York." Bonnie shrugged her shoulders.

"She's recuperating from an illness and says she likes living in a large family." A picture of Aunt Lou propped up in bed, hair in curlers, spectacles on and reading, crossed her mind. Bonnie probably wouldn't believe that glamorous Louise Leander could look so homely. But then Bonnie didn't know the real Aunt Lou as she did, the Aunt Lou who was so beautiful inside that it shone through in spite of curlers and spectacles.

Miss Tamer came out on the stage. The noise ceased. "I have a list of your names here and shall call you alphabetically. Anyone disturbing the tryouts will have to leave and relinquish any chance of a part."

At first, watching was interesting. Miss Tamer had four on the stage at a time, seated near her. She made notes after each reading. However, since those seated in the auditorium could hear nothing but a faint mumbling from the stage, it soon got to be boring. Lizzie Lou wished J was not so far down in the alphabet. She squeezed Mary's hand encouragingly as Mary went up with

Frieda Hempstead, George Harvey, and Tim Hamilton. She hoped Mary got to be the maid.

When it finally came her turn, Lizzie Lou joined the group of four seated around the attractive teacher. Mark Johnson read for the leading man's role, Diana's fiancé. He did rather well, Lizzie Lou thought. Miss Tamer smiled at her.

"I know pretty well what you can do, Lizzie Lou, after your storytelling, a few weeks ago. What part do you want to read?"

"Diana Cavendish."

Miss Tamer wrinkled her nose. "Oh dear, you too? We have had twelve girls read Diana already. Looks as though I'm to have a whole cast of leading ladies. All right, go ahead, what part? You just as well be the thirteenth."

Lizzie Lou read Diana's long speech after her grandmother gave her the pearls. She thought she did it well. Miss Tamer nodded appreciatively as she finished. Would she get the part, she wondered? But she *was* the thirteenth and Bonnie was still waiting to try for Diana. . . . It was disconcerting.

Mary was waiting for her and they walked part way home together.

First thing next morning, Lizzie Lou looked at the bulletin board outside Mr. Kingston's office. There might be something about the play. There was, but it was disappointing. It stated: "Tryouts for senior play to be continued at three forty-five, today." So—they hadn't finished yesterday.

All day she found it difficult to keep her mind on her work. She kept seeing Bonnie as Diana and, though the idea was painful, she admitted that Bonnie would make a beautiful Diana. But could she act? For that matter, how did Lizzie Lou know she could? All she had to base her belief on was the special feeling she had had that once when she spoke before the senior class. Acting in a play would probably be a lot different. But she had always been able to pretend so well, surely that would carry over onto the stage. Or would it?

She was very quiet as she walked home with Bill that afternoon.

The next day while she and Mary were eating in the cafeteria, Jim Buell brought his tray over and sat across from them.

"Just saw Miss Tamer putting something on the bulletin board as I came down. Was too hungry to wait to look at it."

Lizzie Lou dropped her partially eaten apple into the paper bag and pushed back her chair. "Excuse me. I'll run up and get the bad news."

"Well, I like that, running off the minute I get here," Jim complained.

"Oh, you don't mind and you know it. Mary's not anywhere near through. So long, you two. See you in French class, Mary."

Lizzie Lou dropped her wastepaper in the basket on the way out and hurried upstairs to the first floor. From the end of the hall she could see a crowd of seniors gathered about the bulletin board. She slowed her pace, trying not to seem too anxious. She couldn't quite read the paper from where she stood behind the others. She heard Delitha Smith murmuring something about Frieda and Dale looking cute together. Those in front withdrew and she was able to get closer.

Now she could read. The heading was, Principal Characters. Mrs. Cavendish—Janet French; Mr. Cavendish—John Kelly; Grandmother Cavendish—Grace Vincent; Malcolm Forsythe—Dale Gordon; Diana Cavendish—Frieda Hempstead. That was all. Her name was not there.

A great pain of disappointment filled her chest and throat. The vision of herself as the graceful Diana burst and she felt the hurt of a child whose airy, wind-tossed circus balloon has been pricked and scattered about him in pieces of curled, ugly bits of rubber.

Slowly she turned away and walked toward French class. It was fortunate that she had told only a few that she had hoped for that part; just Mary, Bill, and Aunt Lou. She thought of Aunt Lou's stories of her years of disappointment in getting parts before she got that break in *Cyrano*.

Room 203 was empty. It would be fifteen minutes before time for the bell. She sat at a desk and rested her head in her hands. Come to think of it, Frieda would make a good Diana. Since she couldn't have the part she would rather Frieda had it than anyone else. . . . Frieda was attractive and had a friendly charm which would suit Diana. Probably Miss Tamer's choice was the right one. She wondered if Bonnie would be as disappointed as she was.

She got up and walked to the window. A few more days and that forsythia bush out there would be a mass of yellow blossoms. She gave a long sigh and the pain in her chest eased. Disappointments could come and go but there was always spring to bring comfort and promise of future achievement. And there was Bill, he wasn't going to be in the play. After all, she had no right to complain, she had spring and Bill; what more could any girl ask? "A part in the play," a tiny voice whispered. She stifled the voice, went to her desk, and opened her French grammar.

Later in English class, Miss Tamer told how hard it had been selecting a cast for the play. "There is so much good talent in the class. I had some very difficult decisions to make. I'll post the minor characters tomorrow. Of course we all know that the success of any play depends as much on the performance of the bit players as it does on the leads."

As Lizzie Lou was leaving after class, Miss Tamer called to her. "Will you stay a few moments, Lizzie Lou?"

When the others had gone, she stood in front of the teacher's desk and thought how pretty Miss Tamer looked.

"Lizzie Lou, I expect you wondered why I didn't cast you in the part of Diana, for you must have known how beautifully you read the part."

Lizzie Lou looked into Miss Tamer's eyes and felt a pleasant warmth at the praise but did not reply.

"Ever since you gave that excellent, dramatic presentation of the play," Miss Tamer went on, "I have been able to see you in only one part and that is the role of Carlotta, the gypsy girl." Lizzie Lou gave a start of surprise. "When you spoke of and for the gypsy," the teacher continued, "your face became vivid with the girl's awe and excitement at the beautiful furnishings she discovered there in the house and her delight when she found the pearls. All her emotions were written right there on your expressive face. It is a difficult part, and though she doesn't have many lines, the whole plot of the play hinges on her. There's no one else in the class who would be able to do the pantomime of this part necessary for a complete understanding of the play. It is a rich role for a good actress and you can do it beautifully. I hope you won't mind not doing Diana. I couldn't bear giving you anything but the Carlotta part."

Lizzie Lou smiled a short smile and took a deep breath. "I expect you know best, Miss Tamer. I was a little disappointed at first," she admitted. "But I'll do Carlotta, the very best I can." She picked up her books.

"Good. I knew I could count on you. We'll talk about your costume later. Saxon's won't have anything suitable for a gypsy."

Bill was waiting at the front door after school. He took her books and they walked down the steps. She looked at him; he was frowning.

"What's the idea of Miss Tamer not giving you a leading part? Doesn't she remember how you gave us the whole play? What's the matter with the woman? Probably thinking too much about Coach."

"She talked to me after seventh period. I am to have a part." Lizzie Lou liked his concern for her.

"You mean she knows she made a mistake giving Diana to Frieda?"

"No. She wants me to do the gypsy girl."

"The gypsy girl!" He thought a moment. "Well, that is a good part and you did her awfully well, but she doesn't have much to say."

Lizzie Lou repeated what Miss Tamer had said about the importance of pantomime in the part.

"Well, of course I know you can do it well, but then you could do any part well in that play." They turned the corner and he gave her a long look. "You'll make a beautiful gypsy, your eyes are so big and dark. I like brown eyes," he added.

Lizzie Lou's heart sang. It was best of all, being a gypsy. Spring was beautiful! Very beautiful!

17. *The Actress*

The rest of the cast for *The Cavendish Pearls* was posted next day. Bonnie Mason was furious; her name appeared opposite Dorothy Madden, second bridesmaid. Janet French told Lizzie Lou that Bonnie had informed Miss Tamer she couldn't be in the play, so small a part was not worth her time. Mary was delighted that she was to be the maid and began at once practicing an Irish brogue. The fact that Jim Buell was cast as the butler added to her pleasure.

On Friday Miss Tamer gave the cast their books so they could read the play before first rehearsal on Monday.

At home Lizzie Lou found Aunt Lou excited and smiling. There was a letter from France saying it wouldn't be long until Uncle Jerry would be released from the hospital. He said he had only a slight limp, which would be an asset really, for it would give him an excuse to carry a cane, something he'd always wanted to do. He wasn't exactly sure when he would sail, but as soon as he saw Andy Steiner, her agent, in New York, he would be on a train for Indiana.

He had made a friend, he went on, a young fellow in the moving-picture business, Jack Barstow. He and Jack had spent hours exchanging ideas on show business, both pictures and the legitimate stage. Jack's obsession was talking pictures; he was sure that within a matter of ten years or so they would be a reality. He wanted him, Jerry, to come to Hollywood, so that they could be among the first to produce pictures with sound. Jack said that the whole picture technique would change when the actors' voices could be heard and Jerry's experience in the theater would be worth a lot of money to the industry.

"'I may go out to Hollywood and investigate the situation,'" Aunt Lou read on. "'It might be a good idea to be in a business where we didn't have to travel and could have that home we've always dreamed of. You and I will soon be pushing forty, old girl, it's time we made some of our dreams come true. How would you feel about acting in pictures? Jack even has some stories in mind for you. Wants to do some classics like *Anna Karenina, Bleak House, Macbeth, Romola,* and *Cyrano.*'"

Aunt Lou dropped the letter to her lap and smiled at Lizzie Lou. "That crazy, sweet Jerry, thinking he can make a moving-picture star of me."

"But wouldn't you like it, Aunt Lou?" Lizzie Lou could see the posters in front of the Bijou, "Louise Leander stars in . . ."

"I wouldn't be much good in pictures. My biggest asset is my voice and I think I'll be too old by the time talking pictures are perfected. I don't imagine the public would pay to see my face in a close-up. Motion pictures call for youth and beauty and I have neither."

"Oh, but Aunt Lou, you have something better than either of those," Lizzie Lou protested.

Aunt Lou rose and looked down into Lizzie Lou's eyes. "And what could be better than youth and beauty, honey?"

"Well, it's hard to explain, but there's something inside you that shows through; it gives you kind of a shining quality and it makes you seem young and very beautiful. It makes me feel good whether I see you on the stage or"—she hesitated—"or in curlers and your brown bathrobe. I guess it's just a special Aunt Lou magic."

Aunt Lou bent and kissed her. "You sweet thing. I've had lots of nice things said about me, but that's the nicest." She looked at Lizzie Lou's schoolbooks on the table. "I see you have brought home *The Cavendish Pearls.* I think we better get to work on that gypsy girl. I want you to know her, how she thinks, how she looks, how she walks, and how she speaks. Know her so well that when you walk on that stage you will *be* Carlotta in truth."

At first rehearsal Lizzie Lou was the only one who knew her lines, but then of course she didn't have many. Twice she would have the stage alone and her success in the part depended on stage business and pantomime.

They read the play through in a short time, seated around Miss

Tamer on the bare stage. Then she placed folding chairs about to designate doors and explained the entrances and exits of the first act. They had three and a half weeks of rehearsals, she told them, and the sooner they learned their lines the more polished performance they could give.

On Wednesday Miss Tamer talked to Lizzie Lou about her costume. A full, bright-colored skirt, blouse, bolero jacket, wide sash, and lots of beads, she said. She could wear a bright handkerchief on her head or let her hair hang loose and wear flowers in it, whichever she liked best. Lizzie Lou said she would talk it over with Aunt Lou.

Aunt Liz wanted to go right down to Saxon's and buy sateen for the costume, when Lizzie Lou described the outfit.

Aunt Lou looked up from Jimmy's black-ribbed stocking she was darning. "Liz, I don't believe a gypsy's clothes should look new. Bright colors, yes, but a little shabby and worn. What do you think, Lizzie Lou?"

"But what will we make it out of?"

"There are some things in the attic." Aunt Liz hesitated. "Some things that were Margaret's. I've never been able to use them. But somehow, I think Margaret would want them used for your play, Lizzie Lou."

The three of them went to the attic. A strong smell of moth balls floated up to Lizzie Lou as Aunt Liz opened the trunk and took a layer of newspaper from the top.

Remembrance of things past assailed her when she saw Mother's blue silk Sunday dress. She could feel the softness against her hand as she sat beside Mother in church. She could hear the rustle of the taffeta petticoat Mother had worn beneath it. She could see Mother at the head of the table, dressed up because they had the minister to dinner.

Aunt Liz held up the dress. "Lots of nice material in this dress."

"Oh, let's not use that, Aunt Liz. I want to keep it, just as it is," Lizzie Lou protested.

Aunt Liz nodded appreciatively, folded the garment, and laid it on the newspapers. Farther down they found a long blue serge cape, its high collar trimmed in red military braid and lined with red silk, which had faded in places with the years.

Aunt Lou thought the lining would do for the skirt and Aunt Liz decided she would make Peggy a spring coat of the serge. Aunt Lou said she had a black velvet stole; it had been very elegant once with feathers all around the border, but she had used the feathers on a hat and the stole looked sick without them. The velvet would do for the jacket. Lizzie Lou could picture Aunt Lou making an entrance in the second act with the feather-bordered stole worn dramatically over a sparkling evening dress.

The other girls in the cast had spoken of wearing French-heeled pumps in the play, the new kind with those beautifully pointed toes that made feet look so dainty. Lizzie Lou mentioned this, hoping her aunts would suggest that she should have some. However, Aunt Lou said a gypsy wouldn't wear French heels, but she had a pair of soft, black sandals that she had worn for a dancing class once; she thought they would do nicely.

Although her part was small, Lizzie Lou attended every rehearsal, sitting out front, watching and listening. Before the second week was over she knew every line and movement. When she got home she would stand in front of the mirror and say the lines of the other characters, trying to fit facial expressions to the thought. She hadn't done this for a long time, pretend she was another, a person from a moving picture or book. She had been so busy being Lizzie Lou Jones that there was no time.

She missed walking home with Bill, but she saw him every day in civics class. In the last issue of the Medford High *News* an item had appeared that she never tired of reading; got a new thrill every time she read it. It said, "A certain class president is mighty sad these days. Has to walk home all by his lonesome every afternoon. Too bad she is so busy with dramatics, Prexy!" There it was right there in print and everyone knew that it meant Bill and herself. Life was very full and wonderful.

On Saturday, a week before Easter, Father, Aunt Lou, Peggy, and Lizzie Lou had gone down to Saxon's department store. They selected a new dress and hat for Peggy and a navy-blue suit for

Lizzie Lou. Father paid for Lizzie Lou's suit. Aunt Lou said she wanted to get the accessories. The accessories were as exciting as the suit; a navy-blue, beaded georgette blouse, a perky black straw hat, black French-heeled pumps, black kid gloves, and a black grosgrain bag with a cute mirror in the round top. Lizzie Lou was glad that Easter came late this year, April twentieth; it should be warm enough to wear a suit. Those wonderful French-heeled pumps! Her very first high heels.

Almost everyone knew his lines by Monday the fourteenth and Miss Tamer rehearsed them hard. They would rehearse after supper on Thursday and Friday she told them. Bill said he would like to see how the play was coming along; he would walk over with her if she didn't mind.

Walking to school on a spring night, the stars so bright, hanging in a sky of soft dark blue, the smell of moist earth and opening buds, the chill breeze blowing, Bill holding her hand, what could be sweeter?

They talked about the *Athenian,* out in a few weeks, about the picnic the seniors were planning, and the way tickets were selling for the play. Almost all the seats were sold and the play still a week off. She told him about Uncle Jerry and what he had written about talking pictures.

"Talking pictures? It doesn't seem possible that there could ever be such a thing. But I suppose nothing is impossible. I only hope that medicine will advance and lots of new cures be discovered. I guess I haven't told you but I've decided definitely on North-western for my pre-med work."

"Northwestern? That's near Chicago, isn't it?"

"Yes, in Evanston. Have you decided yet?"

"Father favors I.U., Uncle Mat, Purdue, Aunt Liz, DePauw, and Aunt Lou says I must decide for myself."

"You couldn't make that Northwestern, could you?" He gave her hand a squeeze.

"I don't know, I hadn't thought of it."

"Well, think of it, Lizzie Lou, think!"

"O.K., I will," she said softly. "Bill, I've often wondered what your middle name is, what the R stands for."

"That, Lizzie Lou, is a cross I bear, a secret I tell to few, but if you'll never give me away, I'll tell you. It's Reginald. Mom had a favorite uncle and she had to saddle me with his name."

Lizzie Lou laughed. "But you can hide that with a nice unrevealing initial, but Lizzie Lou I have to wear right out in the open."

"But I think that's a cute name. I like it and it fits your quaint, interesting personality. I wouldn't have you named anything else."

Lizzie Lou sighed. "That helps. That helps a lot."

Long after she went to bed his words sounded in her ears. "A cute name, fits your quaint, interesting personality, I wouldn't have you named anything else." The name Lizzie Lou wasn't bad, not bad at all.

Easter was warm and sunny. As she took her place between Aunt Lou and Aunt Liz in church, she tried not to think of her new finery, tried to think of the significance of the day. But, being seventeen, and having felt well dressed so few times in her life, she could not resist looking at her smoothly gloved hands or peering down at the pointed toes of her new pumps. The calves of her legs hurt a little, she was not used to wearing high heels; but the pain was ignored as a small price to pay for dainty-looking feet.

The choir's music was beautiful and when Father came in with his solo bit it made tears come to her eyes. She looked at Mrs. Hubbard standing with the sopranos; she looked lovely in her black robe with the severe white collar. She too was watching Father on the opposite side of the choir loft. Lizzie Lou liked Mrs. Hubbard; she was going home with them to dinner after church.

When they got home, Aunt Liz shooed Lizzie Lou out of the kitchen, told her she was too dressed up to work, told her to go read the funny paper to Lucy. Aunt Lou gave Mrs. Hubbard an apron and the three women had dinner on the table in a short time. Lizzie Lou didn't change her clothes because she had a date at three to go "kodaking" with Bill, Mary, and Jim. Bill and Mary both had Brownie cameras and they were going out to the city park to take pictures.

They sat down to dinner and Father pushed Mrs. Hubbard's chair in for her. She looked up at him and said quietly, "Thank you, Warren." Father replied, "You're welcome, Jane." Lizzie Lou saw Aunt Liz raise her eyebrows and Aunt Lou smile as she tied Lucy's napkin.

Lizzie Lou felt a little stunned. What if—but no, it couldn't be, she had just imagined that special tone in their voices. Had she been so taken up with Bill that she had missed this? Was Mrs. Hubbard the reason for Father's new outlook on life?

Only partially, she decided; it was Aunt Lou's coming that had worked wonders on all of them with that special Aunt Lou magic. Aunt Lou was a fairy godmother and today Lizzie Lou felt like Cinderella at the ball, in her snappy, stylish Easter outfit. She was glad Bill was going to see her in it.

When Bill came at three, Mrs. Hubbard, dish towel in hand, came in from the kitchen to speak to him. It was nice having the whole family know Bill. Mrs. Hubbard called him Billy and asked about his mother.

Lizzie Lou liked Bill's mother; Mrs. Hubbard had introduced Mrs. Monroe to Aunt Lou and herself one day, when they met downtown.

Lizzie Lou felt very smart and well dressed as she walked down the street beside Bill, pulling on her kid gloves, her new bag hanging on her arm. Downtown they would meet Jim and Mary at the streetcar station and take the car to the city park.

Bill looked at her. "Boy! You sure look great in that outfit!"

Lizzie Lou laughed and looked up at him. "Well, thank you, Mr. Monroe. You look pretty grand yourself in that blue flannel suit. New, isn't it?"

"Yeah, it's my graduation suit."

On the streetcar she wondered at herself, speaking so easily and confidently to a boy. Was it having nice clothes and a beau that did it? Not entirely; there was something inside her, a feeling of exuberance, a singing, a strength that was overcoming her shy nature, something that made her look out at others instead of in at herself.

They had a hilarious time at the park, walking along paths, taking pictures beside rocks, blossoming trees, and the river. Mary and Jim rehearsed their scenes in the play and Jim kept them roaring with his overdone British accent as the butler. He put Mary's hat on sideways and stood on a fallen log with his right hand thrust in his coat à la Napoleon. Bill took his picture. Jim was really funny, a born comedian, the others decided.

Bill and Lizzie Lou found a bench in the sun and sat there awhile. He put a blossom in her hand and told her to look down at it, then held his camera close to her face and clicked the shutter. "I hope that gets your eyelashes, you have such nice long ones. But I suppose no picture can really do you justice and see what I see."

Lizzie Lou looked up into his clear blue eyes. He looked down at her steadily, with a smile. The world stood still; all life, all time, all future springs flashed like a golden promise between them. They knew something momentous had happened to them, had happened because they were young and it was spring.

Monday Miss Tamer announced that dress rehearsal would be after supper on Wednesday and that they would get through the whole play if she had to keep them there all night.

Lizzie Lou's costume had turned out well, she thought; a yellow sash showed vividly against the red skirt and Aunt Lou had sewed sequins on the velvet bolero. They had decided she would let her hair hang free in the back, in curls. Aunt Lou had a new electric curling iron which did wonders in making long curls. Aunt Liz took a bright red rose from an old hat of her own and said she thought it would be just right for Lizzie Lou's hair.

It was during the last period on Wednesday that Lizzie Lou was called to the office. Miss Tamer was there looking hollow-eyed and agitated. "I'll never coach another play as long as I live," she was saying to Mr. Kingston as Lizzie Lou came in the door. Mr.

Kingston looked helplessly at Lizzie Lou. What could be the matter?

"Lizzie Lou, an awful thing has happened. Mrs. Hempstead just called to say that Frieda has laryngitis and can't speak above a whisper. The doctor is working on her and is hopeful that her voice will return before tomorrow. Will you look over her part and read it at tonight's rehearsal? The rest of the cast can't rehearse without a Diana."

"I know her lines, I think, but I'll review them before I come tonight. But, Miss Tamer, what will we do if she isn't able to play tomorrow night?"

"Heaven only knows!" Miss Tamer exclaimed, shaking her head in despair.

Lizzie Lou reviewed the Diana role with Aunt Lou cuing her. She did know the part. "If Frieda doesn't regain her voice you could do it tomorrow night, but I'd hate for you to give up Carlotta. That is such a rich part."

Bill went with her to rehearsal. As president of the senior class he was much concerned about the crisis in the play. "But if you do have to do Diana, who will do the gypsy?"

"I've been thinking about that. Madge Downey is dark and about the size for my costume. I could work with her tomorrow, there aren't many lines for Carlotta, mostly stage business. You know, it's strange. I wanted to get the part of Diana so badly and now that I might do her, I don't want to at all. She seems sort of namby-pamby after Carlotta. I was looking forward to sort of letting loose and putting lots of fire into that girl."

"And you're just the girl who could do it, too. Well, we'll just hope Frieda gets her voice back before tomorrow night."

Dress rehearsal went as badly as most dress rehearsals. Lizzie Lou felt strange in the beautiful clothes Frieda was to have worn. She knew the lines but she didn't feel at ease in the part and the others muffed their lines again and again. They left out Carlotta's solo scenes and Lizzie Lou did the scene at the gypsy camp still dressed as Diana. It was confusing.

At a quarter to eleven Miss Tamer spoke to the cast. "This has been the worst dress rehearsal I have ever lived through. I shall arrange for us to have supper here in the cafeteria tomorrow. So come in the morning prepared to stay through. We'll rehearse again tomorrow afternoon. If Frieda isn't here, Lizzie Lou will have to do her part. Thank heaven she knows the lines and we'll have to teach Carlotta's part to someone else, perhaps Madge Downey. Now go home and try to get some restful sleep. We'll need all the energy we can muster to get through a believable performance tomorrow night."

Aunt Lou's bedroom door was open when Lizzie Lou came upstairs. "Well, how did it go, honey?"

"Awful, simply awful. Miss Tamer is almost crazy. I bet she will be glad to give up teaching school and be a wife and housekeeper." Lizzie Lou sat on the bed. "I won't be home tomorrow afternoon, we're going to rehearse right through and have supper at school."

Aunt Lou put aside the play she was reading. "Well, in that case you and I must get up early so that I can curl your hair before you go. If you do have to do Diana you can pin the curls up. I have fixed a small box of make-up for you to take. For Diana use lighter tones and blue eye shadow instead of the dark you had planned for Carlotta. Miss Tamer will be glad I have taught you to put on your own make-up. She'll have her hands full. Will she have some help?"

"Yes, some of the other teachers. What play have you been reading?"

Aunt Lou picked up the book. "It's *Beyond the Horizon* by Eugene O'Neill, a tragedy of American farm life. O'Neill is a comparatively new playwright, but it's quite evident after reading this play that he's going to be one of our greats if he keeps doing plays like this. Andy Steiner wants me to come to New York to read for the feminine lead. Richard Bennett is pretty certain to do the male role. But I don't know; with Jerry having this Hollywood bee in his bonnet, I hesitate to make any decisions until he gets here."

"When do you think he'll come?"

"Who knows? Jerry is unpredictable and full of surprises. You better get to bed. Tomorrow is your big day."

228

Lizzie Lou started to school next morning with her hair hanging down her back in curls, curls which Peggy said were as lovely as Mary Pickford's. At the door Aunt Lou and Aunt Liz wished her luck. Aunt Lou said, "We'll be out front, honey, and pulling hard for you. If you feel scared, and what actress doesn't, take a deep breath and tighten the muscles of your abdomen. That has helped me many times. Whether it's Diana or Carlotta for you, we know you'll do a bang-up job."

There was excitement in the air at school. Bill met her, asking if she had heard from Frieda. They went to Miss Tamer's room and found members of the cast about her desk. She was talking to Madge Downey, and looked up as the two entered.

"Lizzie Lou, if we don't hear from Frieda by eight forty-five, I have arranged for you and Madge to be excused from classes the rest of the day. You can try to teach her the lines and business so she can rehearse the gypsy with us this afternoon. Bill, suppose you go on down to the office and call the Hempsteads and see what's what? We just as well know where we stand."

"Sure, right off, Miss Tamer." As Bill reached the door he stopped, looked down the hall, and began to grin. "Look, everybody. Look who's here."

Frieda appeared at the door.

Miss Tamer stood up, face full of smiles. Frieda's voice had returned. She said her doctor hadn't been sure whether it was laryngitis or stage fright; anyway, she was all right this morning and was sorry she had caused so much trouble.

Lizzie Lou went off to class, grateful that she didn't have to give up Carlotta. Now she could think about her all day and get in the mood, imagine her in other situations besides those in the play. She didn't do much work in study hall that day.

At three-thirty Bill told her, "I'll see you next from the other side of the footlights, be sitting fourth row, center. And you knock their eyes out, kid, you can do it." He squeezed her hand.

They treated Frieda like a piece of delicate china at rehearsal.

Miss Tamer told her to speak in low tones and save her voice for the evening performance.

Supper in the empty cafeteria was fun. Lizzie Lou sat with Mary and Jim. Jim kept the whole table laughing so, they didn't have a chance to get stage fright.

By seven the women teachers' lounge, just off the stage, was bedlam, full of girls in all stages of dressing. Lizzie Lou dressed quickly in her gypsy costume, folded her other clothes neatly, and put them in her suitcase. She took her make-up box and got out of the room. Across the hall, in Room 124, Miss Tamer and two other teachers were working feverishly with eyebrow pencils and rouge on the long lineup of actors. That room was also bedlam. Lizzie Lou hesitated at the door, then made her way toward the stairs, up to the dark second floor and to the girls' room. She flipped on the light inside the door and put her make-up box on the shelf beneath the mirror.

This was nice, so quiet, and she had plenty of time to do a good job on her face. How those blue-green sequins sparkled on her jacket and the many strands of beads showed up well too. She looked at her face critically. Same old face; it surely needed a good job done on it to make Carlotta the vivid beauty she imagined her.

She opened the box and took out two towels; one she fastened about her head, drawing her hair back to the hairline, and the other she pinned about her neck to protect the costume. She rubbed cold cream into her face, then wiped it off with the cheese-cloth Aunt Lou had provided. She took a dark, skin-tone stick of grease paint and blended it on with the tips of her fingers. Her face took on the dark complexion of the outdoor-living gypsy. Aunt Lou had experimented on her several times and she had practiced on herself. Now her fingers worked deftly, blending the dark eye shadow on the eyelids, making a line below and extending it at the sides to make her eyes look larger. She applied lip rouge with her little finger, following the full curve to each side of the upper lip, using it more sparingly on the lower one. How lucky she was to have Aunt Lou teach her all these tricks to bring out the best in her features.

She powdered her face lightly, removing the excess with a soft brush. Having the proper tools made this business easier. She stood back and looked. She removed the towels, took a comb, and smoothed her hair, pulling her curls over her shoulders for inspection. How well they had stayed in; she had been very careful all day. She pinned the rose just above the right ear.

She stood back across the room from the mirror and raised herself on her toes. Her feet felt light and free in Aunt Lou's soft sandals. Her heart beat in excitement at what she saw at this distance. At last, at last, Lizzie Lou Jones was beautiful! It had taken some real doing with eye pencil and paint, but there it was, plain as a nose on your face, she was a vivid, exciting, gypsy beauty. Her accented features, colorful costume, curls, and red rose combined to make one plain girl into a person she scarcely recognized.

She flashed herself a smile and liked the way her white teeth shone from the red lips. She whirled about and the full red skirt rippled. But she must tame down now and forget how she looked, her looks would need no more thought; the main thing was to concentrate on the character. She put away the make-up and walked slowly down the dark hall to the stairs.

In Room 124 she found Miss Tamer working on Jim Buell. Mary, very pert in her maid's costume, was watching. Miss Tamer paused and looked at Lizzie Lou.

"Am I all right, Miss Tamer?" she asked.

The teacher smiled. "Yes, Lizzie Lou, you'll do. You'll do very well."

Jim turned and gave a long low whistle. "I'll tell the world, she'll do. Gosh, she's a knockout, isn't she, Mary?"

Mary put her feather duster on a desk and stepped back to look at her friend. "Lizzie Lou, you are as beautiful and fascinating as Theda Bara, have the same gorgeous eyes."

"Hope I'm not as wicked as that moving-picture vamp." Lizzie Lou looked at the clock; four minutes to eight.

"There, Jim. Let's see to the stage and you two get ready to open the first scene." Miss Tamer wiped her hands and picked up the play script. "I want to start on time."

Lizzie Lou stood in the wings, feeling breathless and excited as Mary got set on the stage, for, at the first curtain, the maid was discovered dusting the drawing-room furniture. Miss Tamer gave a nod. Bob Cunningham, at the switchboard, pulled the switch for the house lights as he pushed up the footlights, and the curtain rose on the first act of *The Cavendish Pearls*.

Lizzie Lou clasped her hands tightly; she could hear Mary humming as she flicked her duster here and there, she could see her eyelids blink as she looked out at the audience. Jim entered, stately and dignified, dressed in a long-tailed coat, holding his head haughtily in the air. Tim Hamilton, dressed as the gypsy chief, stood beside Lizzie Lou, his thumbs thrust in his broad red sash. "Pipe those sideburns, will you? Old Jim is really laying it on," he whispered.

"Sh," she whispered back. "They're doing great."

As Mary and Jim proceeded with the scene Lizzie Lou's heart beat more normally. It was going all right. The audience laughed at the right times and there was scarcely even a cough. Mary made her exit and stood by Lizzie Lou.

"You were fine, just fine," Lizzie Lou whispered as she squeezed her friend's hand.

Mary's eyes sparkled with excitement. Now Frieda and Dale were on, Frieda looking lovely in a chiffon evening dress.

"I saw Bill out there," Mary told Lizzie Lou.

"Right in the center?"

"Yes. Right next to Bonnie."

Now Lizzie Lou was not listening to the love scene between Dale and Frieda. She left the wings and walked out into the hall. He hadn't told her he was bringing Bonnie. He had said his family was coming and she had just supposed he was coming with them. She felt a slight stinging of her eyelids. She exerted her will power, she must not let any tears come—with this make-up, it would be disastrous. Surely he meant those things he had said last Sunday, but if he had brought Bonnie tonight, well, what——

Jim walked to her, pulling at the stiff collar torturing his neck. "It's going great guns. Got a packed house. Saw old Bill grinning up at me. He's out there with his folks."

"But I thought he—that is Mary said he was with Bonnie."

"Take it easy, kid. She came with her family too. They just happen to be sitting next to each other."

The hurt in her throat subsided. Frieda dashed off stage and into the dressing room to change into her negligee. Lizzie Lou returned to the wings and gave her attention to the play. She could hear Janet and John Kelly doing the Mr. and Mrs. Cavendish scene. Janet was doing a good job on Mrs. Cavendish, making her very snobbish and "snooty." Lizzie Lou could see her as she walked upstage, with her head held high and looking very haughty. Good for Janet.

Frieda stood beside Lizzie Lou. "Gosh, I'm scared. Aren't you?"

"Not yet," Lizzie Lou answered. "But maybe I will be when I get on."

Grace Vincent, hair piled high and powdered white, came close, listening for the cue for Grandmother Cavendish. In her hands she held the box containing the pearls.

All through the scene between Diana and her grandmother, Lizzie Lou stood erect, breathing deeply and tightening her abdominal muscles, as Aunt Lou had suggested. She must not be afraid when she got out there, she must leave Lizzie Lou in the wings and take only Carlotta onto that set.

There, Frieda said her last line, as Grace made her exit. Now Frieda was looking at the pearls. She closed the box, Miss Tamer rang the bell for the telephone, Mary went to the archway and called Miss Diana to answer. Frieda put the jewel box on the table and left the stage.

Lizzie Lou counted four, then stepped to the window, cupped her hands on each side of her face and peered in. The footlights were so bright that the audience seemed only a shadowy mass beyond. Slowly she pushed the window inward, put a hand on the window seat, and looked about. Assured of the emptiness of the room, the gypsy crawled through.

She stood looking about; awe and wonder at the rich furnishings showed on her face as her eyes grew larger and her mouth opened slightly. The audience was quiet, not a cough, not a shuffling foot. Lizzie Lou felt a thrill go through her at such concentrated attention. She didn't look at the audience and yet she could feel its presence, its warmth, its close interest in her every movement. It was as though she was filled with some magnetic power that drew these people to her.

Now that she felt them close and sympathetic, she forgot them and was one with Carlotta. She touched a lamp shade, rubbed her hand over a brightly upholstered chair, pulled out the fullness of a gold-colored drape at the window and held it to her body as though admiring it for a skirt for herself, and then she discovered the large mirror above the fireplace.

A little murmur of appreciative laughter rippled through the audience as the gypsy intruder looked at herself, whirled about on one toe, and looked again. She walked upstage center looking curiously about. Now she found the jewel box Diana had left on the table. She worked at the catch, got it open, and the pearls were in her hands. The box dropped to the floor as she ran to the mirror, holding the pearls first at her throat, then draping them across her hair, admiring the effect. She gave a laugh of glee, held them high in one hand, and twirled about looking up at them.

Voices were heard off stage. The laughing gypsy became taut and wary; putting the pearls in the folds of her wide sash, she ran to the window and disappeared into the darkness beyond.

The audience burst into spontaneous applause. Lizzie Lou's pantomime had come across the footlights convincingly and she had not made one sound other than laughter.

She ran through the wings to the hall and stood there, her heart beating hard, as she heard the applause. Oh, the thrill of it; she had played a part and they had understood.

Jim came toward her after his exit. "Say, girl, you're some actress. You really wowed 'em. You put in stuff that you didn't do at rehearsals."

"I know. It just came to me when I got out there."

"Well, it sure was O.K. I had to hold up my entrance for your applause. Say, who's the good-looking man sitting there with Miss Leander and your father?"

"I don't know. I didn't look at the audience."

"Come over in the wings on the other side and you can see."

From the other side of the stage Lizzie Lou could see her family. And there was a strange man between Aunt Lou and Father. He was handsome and had an air of distinction. It must be Uncle Jerry. He had arrived unexpectedly as Aunt Lou had predicted. She had performed before the New York producer, Jerome Logan. She was glad she hadn't known he was there before she went on.

In the gypsy-camp scene the stage was darkened and she had several opportunities to look at the audience. She could see Bill and his family. She could see Lucy on Uncle Mat's lap. Uncle Jerry looked as though he was enjoying the performance. He *was* good-looking. She could see Mrs. Hubbard seated on the other side of Father.

Her scene with the gypsy chief and the sheriff went well, except the sheriff forgot his lines and Tim had to prompt him. She had a feeling of exhilaration as she delivered her speech to the sheriff, smiled up at him flirtatiously, and then pointed a finger accusingly at the villainous chief, who, earlier, had taken the pearls from her. Her face took on a look of malicious glee as the sheriff found the pearls on Tim and clapped handcuffs on his wrist.

She knew she would never forget this night. The unsuspected dynamic force of her imagination, which she had been able to project across the footlights, was a thrilling and exciting discovery.

The applause after the last curtain was deafening. As the cast took a curtain call she could see Bill clapping and looking straight at her. She gave him a smile, a Carlotta smile. She could see Uncle Jerry clapping enthusiastically, Aunt Lou looking at her proudly, Aunt Liz smiling and saying something to Uncle Mat. Father was applauding and nodding his head at something Mrs. Hubbard was saying.

She did love acting! She was sorry the performance was over. But there would be another tomorrow night.

The young actress was ecstatic. She knew she had done well. She squeezed Mary's hand as the curtain came down.

18. *The Graduate*

It took a very long time for her to get to sleep that night. She felt as though she had drunk a whole pot of strong black coffee. Again and again she could see herself out on the stage and hear the applause. Then there was the heady excitement of having Aunt Lou bring Uncle Jerry to see her. Uncle Jerry had held both her hands as he said, "You have a real spark and flair for it, my dear. You aren't the niece of Louise Leander for nothing. Cut over the same pattern, I'd say. You even look like her and you couldn't resemble a finer woman." He had turned and given Aunt Lou an affectionate look.

Then Bill arrived and she forgot Uncle Jerry. Bill had said, "You were great, really great. I couldn't believe that quiet Lizzie Lou could turn herself into that vampish Carlotta."

Now she could understand why Aunt Lou had defied her family and run away to go on the stage. The stimulation and fascination of acting was a powerful force when it got in your blood. It would be a difficult feeling to forget. Was she going to be able to ignore it?

Next day at school compliments on her ability came from all sides. Jim Buell brought a clipping from the morning paper. His boss, editor of the *Herald,* had seen the play and written the review. Jim had underscored the lines he had written about Lizzie Lou. "Lizzie Lou Jones gave an extraordinary performance in a bit part as Carlotta the gypsy girl. She was not only excitingly beautiful but acted the part with a skillful technique seldom shown by an amateur actress. We predict the young lady will follow in the footsteps of her famous aunt, Louise Leander."

Lizzie Lou felt as though she were in a dream and would wake up any minute. "Excitingly beautiful!" What magic make-up could bring. Too bad she couldn't wear it all the time.

Bill walked home with her. "It's a good thing you have a level head," he said. "Otherwise you would be getting ideas about going on the stage with all these compliments. I'm glad you're the sensible type. Stage-struck girls get my goat."

Lizzie Lou didn't tell him that she was fast becoming a very stage-struck girl.

The world seemed tasteless to her the Saturday morning after the second performance of *The Cavendish Pearls*. Oh, to do it again, to feel that wonderful sense of power. It was good that things started popping at home to get her mind off her past glory.

First there was the excitement of having Uncle Jerry in the house. What a fascinating character he was; full of tales about his experiences at the war front and in the German prison hospital. And he kept talking about the plans he and Jack Barstow had made for working together in Hollywood. He was meeting Jack in Chicago and going out there next week.

He was so nice to the children. He let Jimmy play with his cane and roared with laughter as Jimmy gave his imitation of Charlie Chaplin, walking with his feet out to the sides, then running and making that special hopping, on one foot, around a corner, so typical of the little mustached comedian. All little boys tried to walk like Charlie; Uncle Jerry said Jimmy did it better than most.

"Warren," he said to Father, "it seems to me you have a whole family of hams here. Peggy wants to be a picture star, Jimmy a comedian, and Lizzie Lou with a lot of talent for the stage." He looked down at Lucy on his knee. "And what do you want to be, sweetheart?"

"I just want to be a mama."

They all laughed, but Lucy's answer had a sobering effect on Lizzie Lou. That picture of herself at the window of a little house and a young doctor nailing up his shingle on the white picket fence flashed into her mind. What *did* she want to be?

Uncle Mat was late getting home to supper that night. Aunt Liz came over to ask if he had phoned. He didn't come until seven.

At eight the two of them appeared in the Joneses' living room, Aunt Liz looked worried and Uncle Mat excited. The company he worked for wanted to transfer him to their Fort Wayne factory. The war being over, the demand for the output of the specialized Medford plant had decreased and they needed Mat Wallace in Fort Wayne where they manufactured peacetime products.

Lizzie Lou knew at once why Aunt Liz looked worried. She was concerned about them. After Aunt Lou left and she went off to college who would look after Father and the children? She hoped Aunt Liz wouldn't get one of her nervous headaches; this was the sort of thing that brought them on.

Maybe she wouldn't be able to go away to college to get educated and keep up with Bill. Was that what she wanted? Aunt Lou hadn't gone to college and she had done well on the stage. But if she, Lizzie Lou, had to stay home and keep house for Father she couldn't do either one. She would end her days cooking, cleaning, washing dishes, the spinster of the family, while Peggy went on to a Hollywood career with Uncle Jerry. Lucy and Jimmy would marry and she would be just old Aunt Lizzie Lou to their children. Her eyes stung with tears of self-pity at the picture of her dull future.

The others were talking, talking. She scarcely heard them. Uncle Jerry and Father were asking Uncle Mat all sorts of questions about the new job. Lizzie Lou took Lucy's hand and led her upstairs to put her to bed. She just as well get used to devoting her life to other people's children since that was to be her lot in life.

How depressing life could be at times. The play was over, in four weeks commencement would be over, Aunt Lou and Uncle Jerry would be gone, then Bill would be gone, and she would be left with stacks of dishes to wash and a million garments to iron. What good did it do to know that she could act if she never had a chance to use the ability? It might have been better if she hadn't found out that she could; then she wouldn't feel so wasted doing homely chores.

If she hadn't been afraid of disturbing Lucy she would have thrown herself down on the big bed and had a good cry. If she only had a room of her own, all by herself, where she could get away from everyone and be as miserable as she felt. Instead she dabbed at her moist eyes and went downstairs.

Father was at the phone in the hall and was saying, "I'll be over in half an hour." He turned to his daughter as he hung up the receiver. "I'll be out awhile, Daughter; hope you're still up when I return." He took his coat from the closet and was gone without stating his destination.

The living room was quiet. Peggy and Jimmy were reading the library books they had borrowed that morning. Peggy's eyes were darting quickly from line to line as the story of *Secret Garden* unfolded. Jimmy paused in his reading frequently to look at the pictures in *The Dutch Twins*. Upon being questioned Peggy mumbled that Uncle Jerry and Aunt Lou had gone for a walk.

They probably wanted to be alone, Lizzie Lou decided. They had lots to talk about and who could be alone in this house? Not even an alone place in which to cry.

She picked up a volume of Richard Sheridan's plays. She had taken it from the library this morning, thinking an actress should be familiar with all famous plays. She tried to read *The Rivals* but it seemed dull and Mrs. Malaprop's lines didn't appear as funny as Aunt Lou had said. She closed the book, she was in no mood for reading. Promptly at nine she sent Peggy and Jimmy off to bed in spite of their complaints.

Now she could be alone in the living room and be as miserable as she liked. She turned off the lights and threw herself down on the couch and tried to shed the tears she had wanted to weep a short time before. Nothing happened.

She tried to escape into the soothing comfort of seeing herself as the toe dancer in scarlet chiffon on the softly lighted stage with the velvet backdrop. It had been a long time since she had tried this trick of bolstering up her ego. It didn't work. What had happened to the old dream?

She tried to see Carlotta on the stage of the high-school auditorium, but Lizzie Lou, a college graduate, a doctor's wife, kept intruding on the scene. Bill would need a good steady person to run his home and take care of his children. She almost wished she had never heard of *The Cavendish Pearls*. That play had given her all these new, strange yearnings that were destroying her other beautiful dreams.

She got up and walked to the window. Becoming an adult hurt deep, inside. If one only knew what dreams upon which to concentrate. If it could just be ten years from now when she would be twenty-seven, really old, and everything would be decided; her life pattern would be cut out for her then and she could start living without any worries. Maybe by that time she wouldn't even mind not being beautiful; old people never seemed to think much about their looks. However, she must admit that not being beautiful had bothered her less and less since Bill had started paying attention to her. And she did look beautiful on the stage, everyone said so.

Everyone was gay and talkative at Sunday dinner except Lizzie Lou. Mrs. Hubbard was with them and, amidst the chatter and laughter, no one seemed to notice Lizzie Lou's silence. She hadn't heard one word of the sermon. She knew it was foolish to keep on feeling sorry for herself, but when the words kept dinning in her ears, "No future, no future at all for you," how could she help it? And then, too, to be so undecided about what kind of future she wanted even if she could have one; that didn't help either.

She and Aunt Liz had just served the lemon pie and Lizzie Lou was filling coffee cups when there was a lull in the conversation. She picked up Mrs. Hubbard's cup, filled it, and set it back in the saucer.

"Thank you, dear." Mrs. Hubbard smiled up at her. There was a warm compassionate look of understanding in that smile. Could it be that Mrs. Hubbard had some intuition about her mixed-up mental state? She murmured, "You're welcome," and swallowed the lump in her throat. It was nice to know that someone had noticed her.

Everyone but Father had picked up his fork and started on the pie. What was the matter with Father? Lemon pie was his favorite. He looked at Mrs. Hubbard with a questioning look, she smiled and nodded. Father cleared his throat.

"I think this is as good a time as any to give you folks the news.

We weren't going to tell you till June, but since Mat's going to be transferred to Fort Wayne, I thought it would set your mind at rest, Liz, about the children. They'll be in good hands. Jane and I are going to be married in June."

There was a moment of silence. Lizzie Lou put her fork down slowly. Aunt Lou smiled as though the news didn't surprise her at all. Aunt Liz frowned, then her forehead cleared and she looked relieved. Uncle Jerry and Uncle Mat got up to shake Father's hand. Aunt Lou kissed Mrs. Hubbard and Aunt Liz patted her shoulder. Peggy and Jimmy looked at their elders, then grinned at each other. Lucy listened to the talk, got off her chair, and crawled onto Mrs. Hubbard's lap. Looking up she said, "Will you be my mama?"

Mrs. Hubbard's eyes filled. "I'd love to, honey, I've always wanted a little girl, just like you." She hugged the child close. Raising her head, her eyes met Lizzie Lou's, who still hadn't spoken and whose face was sober. "Lizzie Lou, you haven't said a word. How do you feel about my becoming a Jones?"

Lizzie Lou looked into the older woman's anxious eyes, and gave her a warm, sincere smile. "I think you are one of the nicest things that ever happened to this family."

Mrs. Hubbard glanced at Father. "I told you, Jane," he said. "Jane was worried about whether you children would want her."

"Well, it's a great responsibility becoming a stepmother to four children. Warren has told me, Mrs. Wallace, what a wonderful aunt you've been, keeping his family together. As you know my husband was killed in 1917. It was my great sorrow that I had no children to comfort me. I haven't enjoyed living in that big house alone and I find I'm not a career woman at all. I love to keep house. Warren and I seem to have the same interests. We were attracted to each other the very first time we met at choir practice."

"Well, I know I was," Father laughed. "But I didn't think a fine lady like you would ever notice me." He looked at Lizzie Lou and then Peggy. "Jane thinks we should give up this house and live in her larger one. What do you children think about that?"

Mrs. Hubbard looked anxiously from one to another. "My house was built for a large family. I had always dreamed of having lots of children to fill it. I hope you won't mind living there."

Jimmy licked the pie from his fork. "I think I'd like that."

Lizzie Lou smiled at Mrs. Hubbard, so anxious to win all of them. "Me too," she said.

Her outlook improved as she and Peggy washed the dishes. They discussed the changes Father's marriage was going to make in their lives.

"And you'll be living close to that Bill Monroe, who walks home with you." Peggy hung up the dish towel. "I bet you'll like that."

"Uh-huh." Lizzie Lou poured out the dishwater. "I'll take out the garbage, I know you're dying to get back to your book."

"Gosh, you're nice, Sis." Peggy grinned. "Sometimes, that is," she added impishly as she dashed out.

Lizzie Lou walked out past Aunt Liz's garden to the garbage pail. She paused on her way back to see if anything was up yet. The sun was warm and she sat down on the old bench beside the coal shed. Blossom-laden branches of the cherry tree next door hung over the fence. How fresh and delicate those blossoms. Spring, there was nothing like it, absolutely nothing. She felt the tired worries slip away from her as she looked at the tree.

The back door opened and Aunt Lou, a shawl about her shoulders, came down the walk. "I was looking for you. Soaking up some sunshine?"

"Soaking up spring. Spring is so beautiful, it hurts me inside, makes my throat ache."

Aunt Lou sat down beside her. "I know, honey. Are you pleased about your father and Mrs. Hubbard?"

"Oh yes. I think she will be a very good mother for the children. Peg, you know, is getting to that age where she needs a lot of understanding and mothering." Lizzie Lou leaned her head back against the shed and looked up at the blue sky.

"Jerry and I were talking about you last night. Decided where you want to go to school yet?"

Lizzie Lou hesitated. "Aunt Lou, what would you say if I told you I didn't want to go away to school, but wanted to go on the stage?"

Aunt Lou gave her a steady look. "I'd say it's no more than I expected after you had done well in your first amateur performance. Every girl gets stage-struck sooner or later."

"Oh, but, Aunt Lou, while I was on that stage it was like there was a fire burning inside of me and I must try to make the audience feel its warmth and see its flame."

"I know, darling, how well I know. But being in the world of the theater is so much more than just that wonderful moment of being one with the audience. The theater has been called the school of hard knocks and no one knows that better than I. There is so much to learn in technique even if you have talent." Aunt Lou paused.

"Now everyone said nice things about your performance at high school," she went on. "But suppose I should begin to tell you what was wrong with your work, would you still be sure you were destined to be a great actress? As an amateur, you did well, to be sure, but if you were under the supervision of a real director, he would tear your performance to shreds. Do you suppose you could take that? Could you cope with other actresses doing their best to spoil your scenes to make themselves show up to advantage?

"I tell you, honey, being an actress isn't all dressing in lavish costumes, smiling, taking curtain calls, and listening to applause. It's walking, walking on hard pavements, trying to get bit parts, it's living in cheap rooming houses, it's traveling across country on one-night stands with small stock companies, learning the tricks of the trade. And even after you reach what the world calls success, it's one continual battle to hang on to it."

Lizzie Lou's eyes opened wide at her aunt's vehemence. "But, Aunt Lou, does all that have to happen to everyone? Couldn't you, couldn't a girl go to an acting school and learn some of those things there?"

Aunt Lou's face relaxed. "A school of acting? Well, someday a good school of drama may develop, but so far——" She shrugged her shoulders. "Learning elocution does not give one a background for work in the theater."

"Then you think I can't become an actress?"

"I didn't say that. There's no doubt in my mind about your talent. Would being an actress make you happy, I wonder? I would rather see you leading a normal life as a wife and mother. It is very evident that you have wonderful talent for that. If I could only make you know what delight these months here with your family have brought me. What I have missed not having a normal family life! I'm luckier than most actresses, for I have Jerry and I wouldn't change him for any man, but I must confess to you that I envy Jane Hubbard and her newly found family."

Lizzie Lou bit her lip, perplexed. "But, then, what do you think I should do?"

"You'll have to make up your own mind. If this acting bug is so strong that you have to do something about it, why you must try to get in a stock company. I'll give you letters of introduction to certain persons, but I shall not say anything about our relationship. You will be better off on your own. You must have a play ready if they should ask you to read for them. You must be prepared for indifference, for long waits in offices, and long days of loneliness."

Lizzie Lou shivered in the warm sun. "Golly, Aunt Lou, you make it sound awfully grim."

"I want you to know what you are getting into. This desire to act is a rather new idea to you. It may be that my coming has fostered it. I don't want to be the cause of a lot of unhappiness for my eldest niece. There are many actresses who never should have taken the profession, their ability assigned them to mediocrity from the beginning. I wouldn't want you to be anything but the best."

"You think I should go to college?"

"The more education an actress has, the better she can understand and portray life. If you do have talent, going to college will encourage it and there are always dramatic groups putting on plays in which to try your wings. And then if you decide to marry some nice young man instead of following the stage, well, a good education would make you a better wife and mother. Any career you follow, education would stand you in good stead."

Lizzie Lou sighed and relaxed. "You're right. I don't believe I'd have the courage to face those casting directors. Maybe after four years of college, if I still feel the same, I could do it."

Aunt Lou patted her hand. "Just remember, honey, an actress is sort of like whipped cream; she makes a dessert delightful on special occasions, and, like whipped cream, folks can get along without her, but teachers, librarians and especially wives and mothers are meat and vegetables, absolutely necessary to sustain the good life. With a well-trained mind you can tackle any problem, in schoolroom, library, home, or the second act."

"I know, Aunt Lou. You're good to—to—well, to talk to me like a Dutch uncle. I needed it, needed someone to set me straight."

The back door opened and Peggy yelled, "Lizzie Lou, that Bill Monroe is on the phone."

Aunt Lou grinned. "Good for Bill. He enters right on cue, doesn't he?"

Lizzie Lou smiled happily as she went in to take the call.

Aunt Liz finished the machine work on Lizzie Lou's graduation dress the following week. Aunt Lou put the hem in by hand and sewed on the narrow lace edging. Aunt Lou said the senior girls' decision on dresses was a good break with tradition; instead of the usual white they chose to wear pastel colored organdy. Lizzie Lou's was a very pale green. It reminded her of spring, fresh and delicate.

Aunt Liz had suggested pink or blue when they were choosing material, but Aunt Lou had held the green up to Lizzie Lou's face and said that color did a lot for her. Now that the dress was almost done, she could see that it did.

Before Uncle Jerry left for Hollywood, he told her of the graduation present he and Aunt Lou had planned for her. After commencement she would spend two weeks with them in Chicago at the Blackstone Hotel. They would show her the great city, take her to plays, and visit some college campuses nearby, Northwestern, the University of Chicago, the University of Wisconsin at Madison, and others. Aunt Lou spoke of the advantages of Lizzie Lou's going to a school near Chicago so she could see all the good plays during the year and come to know the work of the best actors. This way she would learn the competition she was up against and know how good she would have to become if she decided to follow a stage career. Lizzie Lou wondered what she had ever done to deserve such a gift.

On May fifth the yearbook, the *Athenian*, came out. During lunch hour the steps and grounds around high school were sprinkled with students, their heads bent over the fascinating book. Mary and Lizzie Lou sat on the steps to the side entrance. Lizzie Lou looked at her picture; it wasn't bad, her hair was curled a little and nicely arranged. She was glad she had worn her navy blue middy when it was taken, it seemed so typical of her senior year. It didn't flatter her, but then, after all, she had faced the fact long ago that she was no beauty. That was a nice quotation they had given her. "Her voice was ever soft, gentle, and low—an excellent thing in woman."

She turned to Bill's picture. He was certainly good-looking. She marveled that he payed attention to her. His quotation was, "This was the noblest Roman of them all." She agreed, heartily. Mary's was cute. She wondered if Jim Buell had suggested it: "Just as high as my heart." Bonnie's fitted her all right: "If ladies be but young and fair, they have the gift to know it." And Jim's was wonderful, "I am not only witty in myself, but the cause that wit is in other men." Amazing—Shakespeare, his work, written so long ago, fitted people exactly, today.

It was fun getting everyone's autograph and laughing over the pages of crazy snapshots.

Baccalaureate sermon was on Sunday afternoon, May eighteenth. Lizzie Lou wore her new blue suit and black straw hat. Mr. Faulkner and Miss Melby lined up the seniors alphabetically by twos in the hall; they would march into the auditorium at two forty-five. Lizzie Lou's partner was Fred Jenkins. She tried to see where Bill was but didn't spot him. Just as the line began to move, there he was.

"Fred, you find another partner, I'm going in with Lizzie Lou."

Fred grinned, stepped out of line, and Bill fell in step beside her. "Didn't mind, did you?"

She smiled and shook her head. This would be another golden moment to store in her memory. Now that she had decided not to try for a stage career until after college, she put the acting bug away for the time being and enjoyed being a senior and most of all enjoyed being Bill's girl. He was so obvious in his preference for her company that she knew it was so.

The sermon was dull; about them being at the threshold of life, they were the future leaders of the country, the future parents of the race, etc., etc. What a lot of responsibility! She was glad it was going to take her a while to get over that threshold and into her life's work, whatever it turned out to be. It was good being seventeen, finished with high school, a new life ahead at college, and sitting beside Bill. That was best of all.

Commencement day, May twenty-third, was perfect; flowers in bloom, grass green, leaves fresh and new, and sunshine to warm the spring air. There was no school that day; Lizzie Lou got her clothes in order for the trip to Chicago on Monday. Every once in a while she would sit down on the bed and look off into space and tell herself that today she was graduating from high school. Difficult to realize that those four long years were over at last, and she, Lizzie Lou Jones, was on her way, on her way to that great unknown future of hers.

She felt mature and rather wise too, although she supposed when she became a freshman in college this confidence would melt before the new scholarly courses to be mastered.

She got dressed early that evening. The seniors were to be at school by seven-fifteen. She came downstairs at six-thirty. Peggy and Aunt Lou were finishing the dishes. Father stopped her in the living room. "Let me look at you, Daughter. What a picture." He looked at her softly waved dark hair, excited brown eyes, the pale green organdy dress, which gave her face and neck a soft creamy glow, her feet dainty in French-heeled white kid pumps. "Lizzie Lou, you really are lovely. How I wish Margaret could see you. She would be so proud."

"Thanks, Father. I guess I'll run over and show Aunt Liz and Uncle Mat."

"Do that. I think Uncle Mat has something for you."

On the other side of the house she had to turn around slowly so the Wallaces could admire her from every side. Uncle Mat gave her a florist box containing lavender sweet peas.

"Lou said that was the color I should get. I was going to get red roses, but she said your flowers should be pale lavender to go with the color of your dress."

"Oh, Uncle Mat. They're perfect. The first bought flowers I ever had." She kissed him, then turned to Aunt Liz, hugged her tight, and whispered in her ear, "Thank you, Aunt Liz, thank you for everything."

"You're a fine girl, Lizzie Lou," Liz Wallace said huskily, "one of the very best."

Aunt Lou was waiting with a light spring wrap of her own for Lizzie Lou to wear. Peggy, Jimmy, and Lucy watched her admiringly as she walked down the street.

It was still light and she had plenty of time; she could think, remember, and dream on this last walk to high school. Her feet burned a little in the stiff new shoes, but they looked so pretty, who cared? She held the coat open a little so that Uncle Mat's sweet peas, which she wore, wouldn't be crushed.

How good the air smelled, of flowers and freshly cut grass. As she turned at Franklin Street she could see a few other seniors strolling toward the building. There was Mary waiting for her at the steps, Mary looking like a rosebud in her pink dress.

There was something sad about walking into school for the last time with your best friend. Neither girl mentioned it, but the bonds of confidences shared, of hours together, of sympathetic understanding of the other's problems, of joy at each other's successes, these bonds held them close. Lizzie Lou knew she would never have another friend like Mary. And after tonight it would never be the same again.

The back halls near the stage were soon filled with chattering, excited seniors, the girls flushed and animated in their delicate hues of organdy, the boys talkative and very conscious of their new dark blue suits. As president of the senior class, Bill was everywhere, checking on the program, conferring with Mr. Kingston, asking Miss Tamer's advice. Lizzie Lou thought he didn't see her, he was so busy.

She knew they couldn't sit together tonight, for they must be seated alphabetically in order that each would receive his own diploma and J was a long way from M. The long line was already moving to the stage when he paused beside her as he was about to take his own place farther back. "Wait for me, afterward," he whispered.

She nodded and walked onto the stage completely happy. She sat in the second row; that was good, now she could cross her knees or put her feet on the rungs of the chair in front. They would be sitting here a long time and it would probably get tiresome before it was over.

As the curtain went up she heard a soft ripple of pleasure go through the audience; she supposed they did look sort of nice, the pastel shades of the dresses and the dark hues of the boys' suits. There was her family down there. Little Lucy was sitting between Father and Jane. Little Lucy called Jane "Mama" already. Poor baby, she had never known what it was to have a mother.

She looked at her two aunts and wished she could be like both of them, each was so fine in her own special way. Why couldn't she? She was not Liz, she was not Lou, she was Lizzie Lou; maybe she could be a little of both.

The program was a long one, a vocal solo, a piano solo, a short speech by William R. Monroe, class president, a much too long valedictorian address by Frank Bannerman, a speech by the superintendent of schools, medals presented by the D.A.R., the Kiwanis Club and the County Historical Society, each accompanied by a speech. Two scholarships were awarded, more speeches. Lizzie Lou saw that Lucy was asleep on Father's lap. The seniors moved restlessly on the uncomfortable folding chairs.

What a relief it was to see Mr. Kingston approach the table of diplomas and begin to call out names. Lizzie Lou's right foot was asleep; it had a million pins in it as she walked across the stage after Mr. Kingston called, "Lizzie Lou Jones." She had to laugh when she heard him say, "William Reginald Monroe." Bill wouldn't like that; now everyone knew what the R stood for.

He was waiting for her off stage. "How about walking downtown to Hemple's?"

"All right. I'll tell my family."

She gave her diploma to Father. Uncle Mat had the sleeping Lucy in his arms. Jimmy was yawning. Aunt Lou nodded as she told where she was going. "Have a good time, honey. This is a big night for you. I'll leave the door unlocked."

She and Bill walked toward town, enjoying the fresh air after the stuffiness in the auditorium. They laughed over the "boners" in the program. Bill said next time he graduated from high school he would hold a stop watch, and any speaker who spoke longer than five minutes would be thrown out.

Other seniors had stopped at Hemple's, having Cokes, relaxing after the tiring graduation.

"Wouldn't you like a soda?" Bill asked.

"No." She didn't want Bill spending more than a nickel on her. He'd need his money for Northwestern.

It took a long time to walk home. Bill wanted to know about the vacation in Chicago, about her visits to college campuses in the area.

"You had better decide to go to Northwestern. It has a beautiful campus along Lake Michigan, close to Chicago too; you could go in and see those plays your aunt wants you to see and I could be with you every day."

Lizzie Lou was silent a long while. "I—I expect Northwestern is a fine place and I would like seeing you often, but mightn't it be better if I wasn't there and you went out with other girls? I wouldn't like to feel you were being nice to me just because you knew me in high school."

"I'll always want to be nice to you, Lizzie Lou."

"That's the way you feel now, but after you meet some of those Northwestern co-eds I've heard about, who knows what you'll feel. And you are the only boy I've ever dated," she confessed. "I expect

I should be getting to know some other fellows. It might be better if I went to the University of Chicago. We could see each other occasionally but would be making other friends too." These were the words she said, but in her heart she knew there would never be anyone but Bill.

"My goodness, you sound so wise and adult. Are you sure your diploma hasn't gone to your head?"

"Well, maybe it has, William Reginald, maybe it has."

They laughed and walked, hand in hand, along the dark quiet streets.

The double house loomed before them too soon, dark and waiting, waiting to take Lizzie Lou out of this magic spring night. Bill walked up on the porch with her. She put her hand on the doorknob and pushed the door open. She looked up at him in the dim light from the corner street lamp.

"Good night, Bill, I——"

Before she could go on, he kissed her. "Good night, Lizzie Lou. You are sweet, awfully sweet." And he was hurrying down the steps and was gone.

Inside she shut the door and with trembling fingers turned the key in the lock, stood a moment with her back against the door. She felt her burning face. Bill had kissed her! Kissed that plain Jones girl! Had she changed, was she beautiful and didn't know it? She had to see!

She made her way in the dark through the familiar rooms to the kitchen. She lit the light over the sink and stared at her flushed face in the mirror above.

Her eyes were shining, her cheeks were rosy. No. She was just the same, not exactly beautiful, but she must be beautiful enough, for he had kissed her. But, inside her, where her heart was pounding, pounding, inside, she felt as beautiful as spring!